GOOSE MUSIC

GOOSE MUSIC

— A NOVEL —

RICHARD HORAN

STEERFORTH PRESS
SOUTH ROYALTON, VERMONT

For information about permission to reproduce
selections from this book, write to:
Steerforth Press L.C., P.O. Box 70,
South Royalton, Vermont 05068

LIBRARY OF CONGRESS CATALOGING-IN-PUBLICATION DATA

Horan, Richard, 1957-
Goose music : a novel / Richard Horan.— 1st ed.
p.   cm.
ISBN 1-58642-017-8 (alk. paper)
1. Inheritance and succession—Fiction. 2. Children of the
rich—Fiction. 3. Brothers and sisters—Fiction. 4. Baraboo
(Wis.)—Fiction. 5. Mentally ill—Fiction. I. Title.
PS3558.O662 G66 2001
813'.54—dc21

00-012035

Printed and bound in Canada

FIRST EDITION

I think I have told you, but if I have not, you must have understood, that a man who has a vision is not able to use the power of it until after he has performed the vision on earth for the people to see.

— Black Elk, *Black Elk Speaks*

This book is dedicated to the Ho-Chunk Nation and to all the Native American peoples whose wisdom, harmony, and creativity give me hope for life on Earth.

When Jacob Siconski died of pancreatic cancer at age seventy-four, it was his only daughter, Mary, who made all the funeral arrangements — the pilgarlic's last wife had long since run off with one of the company's lawyers. And luck would have it that his estranged and youngest son, Leslie, had recently sent a letter to his sister from his newest residence on the island of Guam, where he had started a reef-touring business that catered to the Japanese and Korean tourists who vacationed there. She sent word of their father's passing and requested that he return home to Chicago immediately for the burial, and to be present for the reading of the last will and testament. He sent no reply. But on the day of the wake Mary looked across the dark, velvet-curtained interior of the funeral parlor and saw her younger brother standing there in the flesh. It was the first time she had laid eyes on him in almost twenty years. He cut an imposing figure, dressed in a gray flannel suit, tall, broad shouldered, and sunburned; his curly dark hair still stood straight up on his head like the biretta of a prelate. He walked defiantly up to the father's open casket with his hands clasped tightly in front of him. His dark, stony countenance, fixed on the cadaver, was unrepentant; so, too, was his body language. It was a powerful sight for Mary, and she rushed forward to embrace him tearfully. Colin Gallagher, her husband, looked on with ambivalence.

The reading of the last will and testament of Jacob Siconski was conducted at the "nationally registered historic" family home, uninhabited for years now, three days after the funeral. At the long walnut table consistent with the art deco style of the home's decorative motifs and perpendicular to the massive fieldstone hearth conceived as the ultimate expression of "warmth and protection" by the architect who'd built it, Frank Lloyd Wright, sat Mary, Leslie, Gallagher, two lawyers, and a longtime business associate. The affair was brief, cordial, professional — least of all "warm and protective." The associate got 50 percent of the doughnut magnate's franchise; all the rest of the estate — the stock portfolio, the house, the penthouse apartment, the condominium in the Cayman Islands, the Cadillac, the artwork, the furniture, all of it — went to Mary and, oddly, her older brother Charlie, whereabouts unknown. Total assets about twenty-seven million dollars. Nothing to sneeze at, considering most of the fortune had been siphoned off by numerous divorces through the years. Leslie didn't receive a penny, not even the big green number 40 Michigan State football jersey autographed by Don McAuliffe and the entire 1952 national championship team that had hung over his bed as a little boy — a gift for his fourth birthday from his father, an MSU alumnus. He'd been vindictively written out of the will.

Leslie's reaction was intriguing. After the lawyers read the final statement bequeathing the remainder of the estate to only two of the siblings, Leslie slammed his fist down hard on the table, rattling the glasses, tilted his head way back, and shouted with a grin in his voice, *"Trouvaille!"* — "sudden good fortune!" He gave no indication that he was upset, and he continued to laugh loudly for a long time as the lawyers packed up their papers. Later, holding the front door open for his sister and brother-in-law as they exited the abode he'd grown up in, he commented, "You gonna sell this rat trap?"

Leslie stayed with the Gallaghers. For five days he was a guest in their home. They felt increasingly uneasy the longer he stayed, because they didn't get much of a chance to interact with him — he was up very early in the morning and gone by the time either one of his hosts was out of bed. He usually returned around suppertime. At night he entertained them with humorous ditties on the piano. Around the dinner table he was quite the raconteur, dazzling them all with compelling reminiscences of exotic places he'd been and interesting people he'd known. He quoted poetry. But everything he said and did revealed little of the person who sat at the table with them. In fact, it seemed to them that all his histrionics were more an act of avoidance than revelation. There remained about him an impenetrable aloofness that made the Gallaghers uncomfortable. When they could, both Gallagher and Mary furtively studied the brother closely, hoping that hand gestures, facial expressions, articles of clothing would help them piece together this enigmatic wanderer who'd run away from home at age sixteen.

At night, before turning out the light, they spoke in low voices about their observations of the day — "Did you notice his occasional accent? It's kind of French," Mary said to her husband. "Just like my mother's. She had the same accent. But he couldn't have gotten that from her, he was only ten when she died. He must have gotten that from living in Canada with Uncle Pete and all over the world."

"How about the scars on his hands when he was playing the piano? Did you see those? Like knife wounds or handcuff burns," countered Gallagher.

Mary went on, "I couldn't get him to talk about Uncle Pete. You never met him. He was an interesting man. A bit of a rogue, my mother always said. It must have been hard on Leslie, losing him, too. Bad enough growing up without a mother . . . And the women my father brought home! He really got the brunt of it. That's why he ran away. I feel sorry for him. We should give him half our share of the inheritance. I wouldn't feel right if we didn't make that offer."

Gallagher shook his head. "We could, but he strikes me as the type of person who would never take a handout. Too much pride. No, too much . . . something. Don't you think?" She agreed reluctantly. She thought of the Cadillac, and after some discussion they decided to give it to him — the football jersey, too. They certainly didn't need them.

Leslie, they concluded, had probably led a hard life, because he looked much older than his thirty-five years. Certainly it was apparent that there was something broken, something disconnected inside. After the tragic death of his mother in a car accident, Leslie, she recalled, seemed to grow angrier at the world with each passing year. Emblazoned in her memory of her younger brother was an image of him, age twelve, eyes on fire, fists clenched, face ruby red with rage, screaming at her father from the top of the stairs — "I hate doughnuts, and I hate crullers, and I hate long johns, and I hate Mara [the third wife], and I hate you!" Finally, when the father sent him away to a military academy after he'd gotten into some trouble with the police, he up and ran away, never to return. He went to live with his Uncle Pete, the circus musician, up in Canada. But then he, too, was killed in a car accident. From then on, it was conjectured, Leslie had lived a picaresque life, unattached, alone, moving from place to place, country to country, continent to continent. Mary and Gallagher shook their heads sympathetically.

But certain of his mannerisms and physical characteristics — especially the way his eyebrows moved separately, and the high curly hair — reminded them so much of Charlie, the oldest of the three Siconski children. Charlie, too, had *taken wing* from the home. But his disappearance was altogether different. He was mentally ill, and considerably older. After surviving the car accident that killed his mother and almost killed him, Charlie suffered from severe panic attacks that left him all but paralyzed with anxiety. He managed to graduate from high school and college, but soon after he suffered a complete breakdown and became agoraphobic, living a reclusive existence in the museum-like family mansion for close to a decade. Then one day, about five years before the death of his father, he vanished without a trace. They didn't know if he ran away, or let someone into the house who murdered him, or jumped off a bridge. No clue to his whereabouts was ever found. Poor Mary certainly had experienced her fair share of family tragedy, and Gallagher always admired his wife's ability to overcome adversity. It was she, more than he, who remained undaunted through the trials they'd experienced trying to adopt a child. But they both noticed that Leslie seemed fixated on the eight-by-ten photograph of the lost older brother as a young boy that hung in their living room next to the kitchen door. In the photograph Charlie was holding a small pocket trumpet and standing next to his Uncle Pete, who had bought it for him on his eleventh birthday. In fact, Leslie was studying the photograph and eating a carrot noisily two nights after the reading of the will when the phone call came.

Gallagher answered. A steely voice on the other end requested to speak to a member of the Siconski family. That could be only one person now, and he passed the receiver to Leslie. With a heavy sigh, as if he'd been disturbed once too often that day, Leslie took hold of the receiver and barked, "Hello?" Suddenly, as if he had bitten into something unexpectedly bitter or unfamiliar, he flinched, then gasped. All eyes and ears were on him.

He spoke in cryptic statements and curious ejaculations, then hung up delicately, turned with a look of disbelief to his sister, walked softly across the plank floors, stopped for a moment in front of her, and, with a look of wonderment on his face, swept her up in his arms. With his hands locked around her shoulders and gushing with thanks and relief, he said, "They found him! Oh my God, they found Charlie!"

It took a few minutes for everyone to collect themselves and sit to listen to Leslie's explanation of what the man on the phone had told him. In brief, their lost brother Charlie's body had been found two months before frozen to death on top of an Indian effigy mound, up north in Wisconsin, outside the town of Baraboo. Apparently, after searching Charlie's possessions for clues to his identity, the sheriff's department there had finally been able to find a serial number etched into a little metal trumpet. Yes, the pocket trumpet! Mary and Gallagher remembered how among Charlie's few possessions, it alone had been missing from his room when they searched for clues to his whereabouts almost five years ago. From the serial number on the horn, the Sauk County Sheriff's Department was able to trace Charlie's remains back to the Gallaghers. Leslie told them how the man described their brother's dead body — badly beaten and scalped — yes, scalped like an Indian. They had no clues as to who might have beaten and disfigured him or why. Leslie declared that he would go the next morning to identify the remains and talk with the detective who had called to find out more. The body had been lying in an icebox for two months awaiting identification.

At dawn the next day, with only a gym bag, Leslie departed in the dark green 2000 Cadillac DeVille, headed north for Wisconsin. Before he left he gave the Gallaghers the name and telephone number of the Sauk County detective he'd spoken with. He added that he would call them as soon as he'd learned anything. Gallagher offered to go with him, but Leslie insisted that he wanted to go alone, urging his brother-in-law to stay where he was needed most — with his wife. Secretly, Gallagher was glad not to have to go. He had grown weary of the affairs of the Siconski family, even though he'd quite literally inherited a fortune. He longed to focus his attention back on his job and his wife and what he hoped was the imminent adoption of a child — their one great dream. With a dramatic inflection in his voice, Leslie told them that he felt there was some divine purpose to all of this happening while he was there. It was seven o'clock on a Monday morning in March.

"But you haven't eaten anything," his sister protested.

"No thanks, I'm too excited to eat." He jumped into the huge sedan and backed out of the driveway.

TWO NIGHTS PASSED and no word came to the Gallaghers. Leslie was not even on their minds, however, because the news for which they'd been waiting for so many years came to them two hours after Leslie's departure: There were two little Korean babies, sisters, twins, waiting for them at a Catholic hospital in Seoul, South Korea. Their adoption application had been approved. They were going to be parents. Mary was leaving the next day for Asia. She was going to bring their children home!

On the third morning, Leslie called. Mary answered the phone. She was quite distracted because she was running late preparing for her journey later that day. Leslie began a lengthy explanation. He told her excitedly that the body found was indeed Charlie's, but there were other more complicated matters to be thoroughly examined. He emphasized that he needed time to sort through them. He said it was very complicated. She didn't understand, but he went on anyway. He spoke of journals, poems, Ho-Chunk Indians, canoes, the circus, women and children. Poor Mary's head was swimming. She understood very little of what he said — it was like trying to grab a fistful of dry sand and mold it into form. He assured her that it would all make perfect sense soon, but for the time being he needed some money to keep the body where it was — he didn't have enough himself. She asked why he didn't just have Charlie's remains transferred back down to the local funeral home — they would pay for it — but Leslie adamantly rejected the idea. She asked him how much money he needed. He paused, then said, "Ten thousand dollars." She told him she'd send it right away. Then she told her brother her own wonderful news — the two Korean babies. She and Gallagher were going to be parents. When she finished, there was silence. For ten seconds no sound came from the receiver. "Hello?" Mary called, thinking they'd been cut off. There was a little cough, and then Leslie spoke in a low, comforting voice, beseeching her not to even think about the matter of Charlie's body, he would take care of everything. Not to worry.

IT WAS SIX weeks before Mary and Gallagher received what could be termed the final telephone call from Leslie. He explained that he had at last completed his research and composed a document that, he hoped, would describe for them in detail their long-lost brother's life after his disappearance. They were shocked and happy at the same time. After they'd read this document, he said, they would understand everything, and then they could "begin to finish Charlie's work" — that was how he put it. She was curious about that. He added that the document was on its way, and he would communicate with them after they'd had a chance to read it. She tried to get him to talk more about it, asking many questions, but he told her nothing more. She would have to wait for the document. He apologized for not delivering it himself, but he had promised a good friend he would babysit her boy while she was out of town. He would explain that also.

Three days later it arrived. That morning Mary had taken the two little girls to the pediatrician for more inoculations.

Gallagher was home alone and received the package from the mailman. It was wrapped in brown paper and firmly bound together with two leather laces. He brought it inside, untied it, tore back the paper, removed a manuscript from inside a plastic bag, and began to read.

PART I

Washchinggeka

ONE

Finding the Center

Ibecame aware of the drama inside myself on the ferry crossing the Wisconsin River at Merrimac. *There are no coincidences!* It was a cold, crisp, clear day in early March shortly after dawn. The steely light of the new day was touching the tops of the hills to the northwest, lighting up the muddy, ancient river with fierce exigency. I stood alone at the bow of the flat-bedded craft, the wind stinging my cheeks and singing in my ear. I was looking west across the wide river at the bulge of land in front of me, smelling the brew-odored water as it churned below my feet. Growing ever closer was a line of hills — demimountains. I had never thought of Wisconsin as a land of such grandeur, such majesty. The soft, distant hills seemed to call me to them. The world was very clear. There was something untoward happening, I could feel it. I felt I was entering the center of life.

Then, up above, a lone Canada goose, flying low, his sharply pointed wings winnowing the dank morning air, swooped down, like a swallow, turned his head, looked right at me, and honked. The note rattled inside my skull and shook something loose. There was no other sound in the world. I felt the air rush out of my lungs. There was a release; and at the same time a conception.

THE FERRY DOCKED gently on the bank at Merrimac, and I rolled down off the vessel, then drove along the river road up toward the hills. My heart was racing, my palms sweating. There was an excitement inside that I had never felt before. The sky directly above was an infinite blue, and the horizon was blushing in a thick orange haze. All around me the land gushed forth with verdure and glistened with dew. It was warmer than usual for that time of year — in fact, the ferry conductor had told me that they had opened almost a month earlier than normal. I turned right, following Route 113, a two-lane highway, up into the heart of the Baraboo Hills.

Everything looked familiar, old, welcoming. Something about the land was comforting to me, even vaguely recognizable. At the margins of this landscape were cornfields with black earth diced in clumps, and behind them thick hardwood forests. I'd lived in eleven different countries on five different continents over the past twenty-odd years, and yet just three hours from my place of birth I found a landscape that could put me under a spell.

I drove up through the hills, the windows open, breathing it all in. The road wound around, gently rising at first, through farms, then shooting straight up at a steep angle into the forest, into the Baraboo Hills themselves. To the left was the entrance to Devil's Lake. From the road I could see the high-rounded form of an ancient glacial cliff a mile away. Then like a curtain closing the trees of the forest canceled out the sight and poured their menacing shadows around the car. The thick foliage and the hill's steep ups and downs eventually dissipated, giving way to farmland again as the road continued to wind across the plain. In no time at all, it seemed, I entered the limits of the town of Baraboo.

The farms were the kind I'd expect to find in New England — two-story wooden houses with red barns behind, neat porches and gutters and dogs. Small-acreage places. I passed along a swollen, muddy river — the Baraboo. Then suddenly, coming around a corner, there appeared the candy-striped grounds of the

Circus World Museum. The detective who'd called me about Charlie had mentioned something about the museum, and as I passed the grounds I noticed how the river cut through the middle of them — like part of the act. Charlie had loved the circus. Uncle Pete had been his favorite relative. Pete had given Charlie the little pocket trumpet. I always thought Charlie sounded best when he played that little horn. Maybe all those years he'd simply wanted to be a circus musician like Uncle Pete. Maybe he ran away at age thirty-four to join the circus.

I almost came to a stop, marveling as I rolled slowly along the streets, looking at the historic buildings of the original Ringling Brothers Circus — brick structures, old barns, wooden-framed houses with small, rickety front porches painted white and sharp-angled rooflines. I had passed through a prehistoric landscape just moments before only to enter the 1890s. Mine was the only car on the road, and I half expected to see horse-drawn carriages, parasols, women in long dresses, and men wearing derbies.

The road turned to the right and inclined up a steep, twisting little hill to the center of town. Another road ran parallel to mine, and stacked up along the edges of both like uneven, multicolored dominoes were brick buildings with their dates — all 1880s — boldly displayed below the flat, ornate roof articulations. In the middle of the town was a square, raised three feet above the street level, and at its entrance stood a Civil War monument — a man in a Union uniform standing guard over the huge, gothic facade of the old gray-sandstone Sauk County Courthouse.

I parked at an angle in front of the Al Ringling Theatre, which was right across the street from the sheriff's department, in back of the courthouse. The old theater had a very low-hanging marquee that seemed to reach out like a hand and draw me in. I peeked inside the beveled-glass doors and noted the Gay Nineties interior of tile and red velvet. I was tempted to go in, but something about the detective's voice on the phone told me that arriving even five minutes late would not be acceptable. I locked the car, walked across the street, and entered the courthouse annex. The Sauk County Sheriff's Department was on the ground floor, first door on the left as I walked in.

The dispatch clerk told me to be seated, that the *detective* would be right out, correcting me on my use of the word *officer*. Sitting, I stared out the window and went over in my mind everything I'd been told about the circumstances surrounding the discovery of Charlie's body. The detective had been short on words — to the point. He told me that the body had been scalped, beaten pretty badly, and left in a field on an effigy mound; he called it the Man Mound. However, the medical examiner had listed the cause of death as hypothermia — apparently the injuries weren't severe enough to kill him, but the cold was. The detective said they were investigating but had no real leads as to who could have assaulted him. Poor Charlie. Who could possibly have wanted to harm him? He was such a passive, nonthreatening person. For a long time they hadn't been able to identify Charlie because they couldn't find any identification, which was no surprise. He had run away in order to live anonymously. That was his objective. Finally, the serial number on his little pocket trumpet led them back to Strasser's on Dearborn where Uncle Pete had purchased it twenty-eight years ago. Yes, I could see Charlie and that little trumpet, and forever jovial Uncle Pete. I remembered wistfully how as a boy Charlie would play it in the car with a mute, or while he watched television. The little pocket trumpet. I was nudged from this image by another — Charlie's feet. The detective had mentioned his size sixteen feet over the phone. It had to be Charlie. Nobody had size sixteen feet. But the detective also mentioned a couple of things that weren't like Charlie at all. Not the Charlie I remembered. First, the body was covered with tattoos. Not Charlie in a thousand years. Charlie was a nerd. And the other thing he told me was that a lot of people were quite anxious to claim the body, including the Circus World Museum. Apparently he had made friends, and that was not like Charlie either.

Detective McNutt charged out the door to the right of the dispatch station as if he were on an emergency call. I vaulted to my feet. My first knee-jerk impression of the man: Androgynous! The face was feminine, shrewish. In fact, had Detective Robert McNutt charged out of that room as Detective Roberta McNutt dressed in a schoolmarm outfit instead of the blindingly unfashionable slacks and cocoa-brown jacket with too-long sleeves, the effect would have been the same. It is perhaps safe to say that there was something amiss in the genetic makeup of the man. In his early thirties, he looked like a cross between the Michelin Man and the Pillsbury Doughboy. Short, boyish complexion to the extreme, fleshy around the neck area. In fact, he had virtually no chin, just one continuous flesh line from chest to head with a couple of wrinkles thrown in to suggest a chin. He had a huge rump like a pumpkin that didn't fit his body, bulging out at the sides and on the top and bottom — a size too big. His hair was blond and just beginning to fall out. He had glasses; large, sad gray eyes; thin little lips. It was these lips that bore his well-rehearsed flat affect — his make-believe indifference to all things lawful or unlawful. The lips lay in a long straight line, colorless, pulled in a tight, perfectly straight line against his placid countenance. The blank expression was indeed powerful, even threatening. It hung there like an icon — inscrutable, upsetting. This was no doubt something he'd worked on for a long time, perhaps his whole life. And there was something about his expression that communicated to one sensitive enough to interpret it that Detective McNutt had always been regarded by others as a little freak, and as a result cultivated a deep contempt and irrepressible suspicion of all people.

He introduced himself abruptly. "Robert McNutt."

"Leslie Siconski."

We shook hands. The detective's sad-dog, suspicious eyes did not meet mine; they wandered disinterestedly around the room. I was insulted by this lack of eye contact as I squeezed the diminutive, moist fist and looked at the man, who was a good head shorter than I am. Then, suddenly, his eyes beaded up and vaulted into mine. It took me by surprise. Those ugly peepers penetrated deeply. I felt violated. The eyes peered around inside me. He was looking to see if I was a suspect in my own brother's death. Satisfied, the eyes softened just a tad. McNutt was a fanatic. One hundred percent cop. It was all he'd ever wanted to be.

"Feel like riding with me in the cruiser?"

"That's fine."

"Let's go."

No wasted movement with Detective McNutt. We were out the door and into the March sunlight lickety-split. From behind I noticed that McNutt had a lot of moving parts as he walked — that huge butt swishing and sloshing along. The backside of his professional mien quite literally made an ass out of his front side. I inadvertently began to smile.

Outside in the fresh air the streets of Baraboo were alive. The cop cars were docked in a line in a receiving area hollowed out of the square just outside the station doors. McNutt hopped into the driver's seat of the cruiser closest to the street with a jingle and a jangle, and I followed his lead and jumped into the passenger side.

We were backing out of the lot almost before my door had closed all the way. The cruiser swung out into the road, the tires squealing slightly. The little maneuver said: *This is my town; my county.* He waited an instant or two at the light and, when it changed, shot up the road, engine roaring, heading toward West Baraboo. Neither of us spoke.

I didn't know what to say, maybe because I was certain it wasn't my place to talk first. This corpulent detective had found my brother dead, beaten, scalped, frozen, on top of some Indian mound and had called me. I felt it was his place to start the conversation. A long minute went by. McNutt said nothing. I grew more anxious with each passing second. I thought perhaps it was a detective thing not to talk, to wait for a suspect to start blathering. But I wasn't a suspect, which is perhaps why McNutt finally did start to speak.

"I don't remember if I told you, but we've got a portable morgue out by WalMart. That's where he is." His voice was nasal, girlishly high, cherubic. "Body's been out there almost nine weeks now. Had a lady last year we held six months. Never got an ID on her. Buried her as Jane Doe. Lot of people wanting to know if you're his brother." All this was said in one breath. This was how he did his business — made small talk, then inserted the important stuff right at the end when you least expected it. He never took a break from who he was.

"You said that over the phone. It just sounds strange. He was very shy, of course. He was ill that way," I offered.

"You said he was an agoraphobic. One of the Double Donut family."

"I didn't tell you that!"

"No, but I cross-checked his name under missing persons, read the original report."

"Well that has nothing to do with anything," I erupted. I've always been a bit defensive about people labeling me or associating me in any way with the company. Detective McNutt knew he'd struck a nerve and said nothing. I fought through my anger to return to the subject at hand. "Please fill me in now. A couple of things you said didn't sound like my brother. Maybe I should just wait to see the body. Maybe it's not him. But . . . but the size sixteen feet. That's got to be him."

"Measured them myself. If this is too difficult for you, I can just show you photographs, you know. We don't have to go out there to the body. Some people prefer it that way."

"No, I want to see him. I want to see the body."

"Okay."

He didn't slow a fig, nor did his facial expression reveal a twinge of remorse, as a squirrel raced in front of the car and went underneath the wheels, giving up the ghost with a little thud. It was an ominous sign. I couldn't believe it. I glared at the little-boy face in profile. McNutt made believe he hadn't seen or heard anything, driving on without the slightest discomfort.

Again, I fought through the distraction to get back to the matter that had brought me here. "You said there were lots of people waiting to claim the body? The Circus World Museum people?"

"Yeah. He was well-known down there. When he showed up four and a half years ago they tell me he started going to the circus every day. In fact, he became kind of a legend down there. All over town, really. We got an Indian out here, you'll see him when we get there, thinks your brother's some kind of god or something. Been sitting with the body ever since we brought it in. Every day, most nights, he's sitting out there just waiting. Lot of women, too. We've got three women want to claim the body. Say he's the father of their kids. They call every day just asking about him. I've seen some of them too. Pretty darn attractive."

"What!" My head shot back against the headrest. This was news. None of it had been mentioned over the phone. I hadn't even thought about the social aspect of Charlie's life up until this moment, let alone women. I had simply assumed that Charlie had been a recluse, like before, living in the woods; I figured his body was found only by chance. The circus angle made a little sense — he had always loved the circus. But women? Charlie siring progeny? No way.

I choked out, "I don't think this is him. Can't be."

McNutt didn't respond. The car sailed along, passing a small zoo to the left. There was silence for a few moments, then McNutt piped up again. "Lots of people knew Charlie around here. The museum people are serious about burying his body on their grounds. I've heard it said that they're ready to go to court for the right to bury him if he's not claimed. The three women, in fact, were beginning to mount some kind of a defense against the museum. The Indian, too. He's Ho-Chunk. They also want the body. They own the casino up the road, and they've got plenty of dough, probably more than the Circus World people. You're really going to clean up an ugly mess if you ID him, you know that?"

"Jesus. People fighting over my brother's body. He wasn't exactly what I'd call a people person."

"People liked him. You know, they've got an entire wall devoted to him down at the museum, in the entrance. They've got his bike, and we've loaned them the horn. It's in the big pavilion. You should go see it."

"A display? Why?"

"Like I said, he was a regular at the place. Went every day, they tell me. Paddled there in a canoe he made himself. When we go out there to his place, out east of town, you'll see it. It's right up alongside his house. One of the clowns down there I talked to, Judd Barkin, said he actually directed the circus band one summer. Played the trumpet. The same trumpet that led us to you. He was a real character."

"I don't think this could be him. Maybe we should just get there and identify him first before you tell me any more. It's very confusing." All this information was too strange. Nothing about it fit his personality.

"His name was Charlie, right?"

"Yes."

"That's definitely his little trumpet we got." We came to an intersection and McNutt pointed, saying, "He's over there."

THE PORTABLE MORGUE was a long trailer, like the kind pulled by semitrucks, set high up on steel legs and lying north to south. It was positioned at the south end of the huge WalMart parking lot. We pulled up alongside, parking perpendicular to it, and McNutt hobbled out, yanking insecurely on his unfashionable pants and extracting his ring of fifty-some keys in one tangled motion. I got out of the passenger side and walked slowly around the back end of the gold-colored cruiser. There were steps on the east side of the trailer, at its far end, and McNutt was already on them with the keys out, jingling and jangling as he pounded up the steps. I heard him mutter something under his breath about a "pain-in-the-ass Indian."

The sound of an engine turning over close by caught my attention. I turned back toward the street and saw a blue pickup truck about thirty yards away rolling toward me. There was a man inside, sitting quite straight. He was Asian looking with a brown shirt and graying hair. He had the window rolled down, and he was glaring at me with fierce, dark eyes. He must've been in his fifties or sixties, with dark skin wrinkled from exposure to the sun. We stared at one another, neither of us letting go of our optical grip, as the truck drew closer. Its motor sputtering, the pickup came to rest ten feet from where I stood. Our eyes were still locked onto one another's. He looked vaguely familiar. Then I recalled what McNutt had said about an Indian waiting with Charlie's body. I opened my mouth to speak, but nothing came out. The man's blazing eyes suddenly changed. Where they had been fierce, burning, severe, they suddenly became respectful, encouraging, avuncular. He said something to me over the sputtering engine. The word or words were unrecognizable. Then the truck began to roll away. The eyes were turned off, and the blue pickup crossed the parking lot, lurching with the shifting of gears. It slowed only at the stop sign, then slid out into traffic with a backfire. I stood and watched in quiet contemplation as the truck moved up the hill onto the two-lane highway and drifted from sight.

"We're all set for you, Mr. Siconski," McNutt called from the doorway, cupping his hands to be heard over the noise of the nearby traffic. He had already gone in and pulled Charlie's body out of the cooler. I glanced up at McNutt; from the platform he looked twice his actual size, even menacing. I moved slowly toward the stairs, aware of the cop's disrespectful impatience, but I didn't hurry. The world seemed to be slowing down.

It was freezing in there. There were four coolers stacked two by two along the back end of the trailer. One of the drawers, the lower right-hand one, was pulled out, and the edges of its stainless-steel door were white with frost. On it lay a dark green bag with a zipper; puffs of condensation coming out from inside the compartment swirled around it. It was a futuristic sight — like a body frozen cryogenically. A cold shiver slithered up my spine, and irrational fear quivered inside me. What if the body in the bag was not my brother, but someone else, someone ghoulish? What if it had all been some kind of sick joke in retaliation for my selfish life? I started to shake and held my breath, sure that I was going to pass out or lose control. I hadn't eaten a thing — just coffee.

"Again, if you feel uncomfortable about this, I can show you pictures and we can do it that way," McNutt said, glancing over at me and recognizing my anxiety. Still, his tone had just a hint of antagonism, like the bully on the block calling the little kid a scaredy-cat.

It was the Indian who gave me courage, who emboldened me. I saw those piercing eyes looking into mine, like the spots you see after looking directly at a lightbulb. He'd been there for months guarding the body. I was going to free him from that obligation now. My heart was racing. "No," I said. "I want to see with my own eyes."

McNutt was on one side of the body and I was on the other. All sensations seemed amplified as the whirring sound of the thick zipper echoed through the frigid box like the sound of a reel slowly giving out line to a fish. First the body, then the face appeared as through a mist of time, and I looked down with pounding heart. The head was elevated, resting on a block of wood. Though the eyes were closed, the silent face seemed to look up at me and smile sadly. The forehead was disfigured — the hair in the front was missing, along with a deep swath of scalp. The body was long, sallow around the edges, Christlike in its attitude. It was Charlie. It was him. No mistaking that distinctive nose and weak chin, the mouth, the elegant hands, the knees, the scars on the legs. I looked hard at the incongruous tattoos, strange in color and design, on the frozen torso. They glowed black-green, describing a shirt with a collar. They were fascinating. There was a bright goose tattoo right over his heart. Charlie's dark hair — what was left of it, in the back — was much longer than I'd ever seen it. And his smile spoke to me: *Death is a peaceful place, the dead do not feel tragedy; we feel sorry for the living who suffer from such misconceptions about the hereafter.* Poor Charlie. He'd always tried his best, always. The entire deck was stacked against him, yet he went on. Saw his own mother decapitated in the car seat right next to him. Almost died himself. Endured panic attacks that would have driven any normal person off a cliff. Worked for a father who was the most critical, miserable son of a bitch on the planet. Charlie! The one person in my life whom I trusted most of all. Dead. I let him down. I was a miserable coward in comparison to him. Poor Charlie. I began to cry. Everything clouded over. I heard the bag being zipped up, the tray with the body on it rumble back inside, and the door close with a thud. Charlie!

THE TRIP BACK to the station was an emotional roller-coaster ride. I fired questions at McNutt, asking him about leads, about clues, about suspects. "Who would want to kill my brother?" I demanded. McNutt didn't answer. He told me that they had a few possibilities but he didn't want to elaborate on them, he couldn't, not without "compromising the integrity of the investigation." But then McNutt lowered his tone and in a confidential manner admitted that they had one strong clue — a hair sample. Apparently, when they found the body Charlie was clutching a tuft of blond hair. They had it on file at some lab and were running tests on it. In fact, it was the same hair as that found on a blond scalp hanging on the wall of Charlie's "wigwam" — as McNutt referred to it. Then the diminutive detective said with some hubris, "There's a man out there walking around with part of his scalp missing. How hard can it be to find him? I'll get 'im. You can be sure I will."

But I could tell by the tone of his voice that the clues weren't yielding much. I could hear the emptiness behind the boast. He had nothing. He had a clump of hair and a dead body — finally an identified body, but nothing more. It was eating at him like a cancer.

BACK AT THE station we filled out paperwork. A form that had to be completed for the undertaker asked when the body would be transferred and where it would ultimately be buried. I had all those names and addresses still in my head from Dad's funeral — I could easily have put down the necessary information. But something told me to wait. Charlie's face said *wait;* so did that Indian's in the pickup truck. I rested the pen on the desk and told McNutt that I had to talk to my sister first. I asked if I could take the form with me, fill it out, then fax it back to him before the weekend. He grumbled, "Okay."

A half hour later McNutt seemed impatient about something, and it occurred to me that he was anxious to accompany me to Charlie's wigwam, perhaps thinking he would glean some new information from me. But I didn't want McNutt to come with me, and I told him so. His sad-dog eyes grew beady and his lips tightened and grew even thinner. The expression warned me that he didn't approve of this arrangement, not one bit, and by doing it this way I would be put back on his list of suspects. I didn't care.

"Look," I said with no embarrassment, "I'm sorry, but I really need to see how he lived out there by myself. If you think I might be able to give you some help in finding clues, I can't see how. Until today, I hadn't seen my brother in more than twenty years. I know nothing about his life here, and I barely know anything about it for the fifteen years before that. If he had enemies, I certainly don't know any. I just want to see how he lived. I hope you don't mind. It's my one opportunity to be alone with him. A little late now that he's dead, but better than nothing. If I do find something that seems out of place, I'll let you know. Now, if you could give me directions, I'd appreciate it."

"Sure, I can do that," McNutt pouted. He scribbled a little map, muttering a few comments about a bridge here, a bend in the road there. "It's a blue farmhouse. An old German lives there. In fact, Charlie worked for the old man. You can knock on his door and ask him about Charlie's house. Your brother's place is up on top of the ridge behind the house. He'll show you. Knock real loud 'cause he doesn't hear too good."

I took the directions, folded them neatly, and scurried out the door, happy to be done for a while with Detective McNutt.

TWO

Schniderwind

Iast of town, along County W, the countryside is like a picture postcard — neat little farms with hills covered in forests as a backdrop. It's beautiful.

The road dips as it crosses the Baraboo River, then rises to reveal an apple grove on the downslope of a wooded hillside to the left, dips again, curves right, then left, and rises once more; at the top of that rise is the blue farmhouse. What a view! In front of it, to the south, the demimountains climb to the horizon like a wall of green breakers and stretch in one unbroken line as far as the eye can see. To the north, behind the little house, is a cornfield, and beyond that, bulging three hundred feet from the ground, lies a hump of land like the raised backbone of a giant beast, covered with thick hardwood trees, a hundred acres across. In this area of the country such humps of land, formed by the last glacier that moved through, are called moraines.

I parked in the driveway and walked to the front door. Not a cloud in the sky as I glanced upward. I knocked loudly, as McNutt had instructed. A dog yapped inside. I waited. Nothing. I knocked again. The yapping redoubled. Suddenly a wrinkled face appeared in the window of the glass door. "Go 'round!" he instructed. The old man made a twisting motion with his hand, which I interpreted to mean the back of the house. So I wandered around to the back.

There the dog, a schnauzer, came hopping toward me, yapping angrily as if to say, *Who are you and why are you disturbing us?* The old man appeared in the small enclosed porch at the back, grumpily yelling at the dog — "Zigfried shtop, shtop barking!" He looked at me. "Who are you?" he asked, coming out and kicking lovingly at the dog.

I put out my hand, "I am Leslie Siconski, Charlie's younger brother."

"Ach du lieber Gott!" The old man's voice softened immediately. Siegfried was now carefully sniffing my leg. "Charlie's brozer." He shook my hand with great gusto. "Finally zey find you. I *told* zem he had family. He mentioned you to me. Coom in, coom in."

He was a ruddy-faced old German, still quite sturdy on his feet, even some red tint to his thin threads of hair, though it might have been dyed. He had on an old blue jumpsuit, a white T-shirt underneath, leather boots. He shuffled along with his head bent, thrust a bit forward from his stooped shoulders. He was not a big man, an inch or so under six feet, still somewhat sinewy, with monstrous hands that looked swollen and achy. He rattled his dentures in his mouth incessantly, but he had a noticeable gleam in his light blue eyes, an impish look that told me he had drunk of life and held no regrets.

He led me inside his home, which smelled of dog and wood wax. There were old pictures and patterned furniture from another era.

"Vould you like somezing drink? Somezing eat?" he asked politely.

"No thank you. I'd just like to go back and see where my brother lived. The detective downtown told me you'd be able to show me where he lived."

"Za leedle fat one? He's 'noxious. Ve call his kind *schweinhund.*

Yah, sure I show you. Just back zere, vhere za trees shtart. Far end of za field, at za top zere." He was pointing out the window, and I followed his crooked finger beyond the pane of glass. I couldn't see anything other than a blur of trees.

"You knew my brother?"

"Oh yah. Good boy, Charlie. He vorked for me every day. I miss him. Can't do za vork myself anymore. Hee hee hee, poor Charlie. He vas good boy, Charlie. Funny. Za animals here miss him, too. Ziggy misses his Charlie, don't you, Zigfried?" the old man said in a sad, childish voice to the dog at his feet. Siegfried wagged his stubby tail and shook his head, saliva flying across the room. He was an old dog, with rust colors mixed into the white-gray of his whiskers. "Ve miss Charlie. He die too young. Too cold for him to be outzide zat night. Too cold for Charlie. He did not take care of himself right. Never dressed warm."

"Someone beat him up pretty badly, too."

"*Nach!* He vas alvays falling down, he prob'ly do zat to himself, I zink. Alvays falling down, shtub his toe, bump his head. Those feet. Ach!" The old man laughed. "I tell you somezing funny — za first time I meet Charlie I remember vell because he coom early in za morning and he vas shtanding outside vhen I go out to milk za cow as if he vas vaiting for me. He vas funny-looking man, real tall man and big eyes, shtanding zere vis his long arms. Ziggy vas barking all 'round him, but he vas vagging his tail so I know he vas friendly man, vhich vas good sign to me because at first sight I zought maybe he vas coom shteal somezing. I shtop and he valk right over to me and say, 'Goot morning.' I ask him vhat he vants, and he says he just vants shleep on my land over back zere, up top of za hill. I ask him vhere he vants shleep. And he says up on za hill in za voods, look down on za river." Here the old man stopped and pointed at the great ridge of land beyond the window, and in his eyes was a look of enchantment. Old eyes that still glowed. He went on, "I shook my head and told him zat back zere vas za Indian grounds; za government protect zat place. He looks exzited vhen he hear zat and ask again, 'I just pitch tent,' he says to me. Now I shtart zink maybe my son zent to me Charlie, help out 'round za farm. He vas busy more zen vis his vife sick and vas not able coom by to help me vis za vork like before, so I zought he prob'ly send Charlie over to help. 'Fritzy send you over?' I ask him. He just shake his head up and down so I zink zat my son sent him to me to help out vis za farm work, you know, I'm eighty-six years old, but I shtill vork myself. 'You vork on za farm before?' I ask him, because he looks to me like a person who doesn't vork hard, he has vhite hands, shmooth and delicate. And again he shake his head up and down. I ask him, 'How long you vill shtay?' He shake his head, not knowing. 'Long time maybe,' he says. 'Vell zen, you shtart now,' I tell him and hand za bucket. 'You go in zere and milk Eva, zen you coom see me vhen you finish.' 'Zen I can shtay on za land?' he asks again, just like little boy. 'If you vant shtay back zere, pitch tent, you can do as you please,' I zay. 'If za government not kick you out, you can shtay zere.' So he take za bucket and into za barn he goes. I don't know how long — ten, fifteen minutes later I vas putting vheel into za tractor ven I hear shcreaming. '*Ooo ooo ooo!*' he vas shcreaming. I hurry go see vhat's matter and I coom inzide za barn and zere he is on za ground vis his foot, his great big foot, he is holding vis his hands. Za dog is barking 'round his shtrange behavior. 'She shtep on my foot,' he says to me vis tears in his eyes. I look and zere is no milk in za bucket. I'm vondering who is zis shtrange person my son send me not know how to milk a cow, great big foots. Ach! Zen he shtand up shtraight vis big eyes, very serious. 'I'm all right,' he says, and crawls back to za shtool and Eva's teat. 'She's dry,' he says to me, his face shtill vet vis his tears. 'Dry? You kid me, she about flooding over. You not know how to take za milk,' I say. I reach under and grab her teat. 'Like zis!' I say and show him how to do it. 'Pinch zen shqueeze. Pinch zen shqueeze. Like so.' He grab za teat and try it. He get just a little drop, shplash in za bottom of za bucket. 'Pull it down,' I tell him. He do as I say and he is milking za cow. 'You vill need boots if you vork 'round here, not za shneakers,' I tell him. Ach, vhat big foots he have." The old man finished his *shtory* with a look in his eyes as if he expected Charlie to come up and knock at the door. The eyes saddened when he realized that it could not be. But then he took a good look at me in front of him, assessing my face. "Charlie's little brozer. You coom to shtay, too?"

At that moment I felt a kind of certainty well up inside. "Yes," I said. And the old man nodded his approval.

WE SAT AT the old yellow Formica table, drinking tepid tea, Ziggy lying under my chair. I listened for a long time to the old man's heavily accented tales, looking occasionally out the window at the forested blur in the direction of where Charlie had lived. I yearned to go there, but stayed and patiently listened.

He was an interesting old man; perhaps it is acceptable to call him a great man. He had come to America and the Baraboo area from Germany during World War II as a prisoner of war. I never knew that the United States had sent its war prisoners back home to work the farms. He told one of the most touching stories I had ever heard. During his imprisonment he had worked in the fields just south of his camp, in the town of Lido. He fell in love with the land around, and the people, who seemed to care about him. The woman who was eventually to become his wife was a farmer's daughter from that town, of German lineage herself. One day, when he was working with the other prisoners out in a field, a young girl, maybe eighteen, beautiful, with blond hair that captured and reflected the sunlight, walked out to the prisoners with a tray full of sandwiches. The American prison guard ran up to her and told her to go away; the prisoners had already eaten. But she lit into the man, telling him that she had seen the sandwiches they'd eaten and noted that there wasn't a slice of meat in any of them. Her sandwiches were piled high with ham. She threatened him; said she'd not allow anyone to work her father's land without being properly fed. Said she'd be there every day with her tray of sandwiches until they were given meat. The next day the sandwiches at the prison camp had meat in them. She was a heroine among the German prisoners. When the war was over, he said he had but one thought in his head — to return to the wonderful land he had fallen in love with, find the girl he still worshiped, and marry her. And he did just that. His beautiful wife had died ten years before. He told stories about Charlie that made me laugh, but I pined to see my dead brother's home.

Finally, I could wait no longer and stood, thanked the old man, and walked outside. The temperature was almost like summer — in the sixties. It was about noon. A perfect day. Mr. Schniderwind followed me outside, motioned up at the sky, and, as if to apologize for having kept me so long, said, "Zis is vhy ve tell za shtories. Za sveet days." I smiled and waved, heading anxiously toward the hill. "Za field is muddy. You should vear za boots," the old man warned. I just shook my head and marched on. And as I walked I heard the wind whispering and the high wheezing giggle of the old farmer behind me.

THREE

Rightpath

I walked across the field. The dark soil under my feet was indeed moist and clung to my leather shoes just as the old farmer had warned. In a few moments I was carrying five extra pounds of loam with each step; it was as if I were walking with earthen flippers. But I trudged on. If the Wicked Witch of the West herself had been trying to thwart my advance on Charlie's homestead, she couldn't have stopped me. I felt that same uncanniness I had felt on the ferry earlier in the day, that same centeredness.

I hadn't been able to get a perspective on the size of the trees from the window of the farmhouse, but up close they were massive and old. Oaks and hickories, maples, walnuts, and ashes. The understory was amazingly clean, no cloying saplings or bushes of any kind; this gave it a fairy-tale quality, like the woods in Hansel and Gretel. I later learned that it was Charlie who had cleared the understory, using all the little saplings for his fire and to build his lodge.

At the edge of the woods and the bottom of the ridge, I smelled smoke. A pleasant, aromatic odor came from somewhere in the interior. Someone was up there building a fire. I peered into the diminishing umbrage and thought I could see something straight up, seventy yards away or more, through the trees, at the top of the hill to the south and west.

The leaves were crisp and dry, and I made a racket as I walked.

I thought of Indians treading silently through forests. Pictured them standing behind trees, feathers in their hair, clutching bows, choking with suppressed laughter at my clumsiness as I crashed along. It was serene under the trees, like an arboretum. All around the woods were joyously quiet, no birds sounding off. The air was sweet. It was a gentle upward grade.

Finally what appeared from afar to have been a cabin or house was revealed as two huge bur oaks close together. When I reached them, I was at the apex of the hill and in the center of the wood. Suddenly my heart skipped a beat — just below me about twenty yards away, where the southeastern side of the hill evened out to form a small terrace before dropping steeply down again, a round little hut sat magically with a triangular fieldstone chimney and smoke curling out of its spout. I hadn't expected it to look like this. There was a noticeable gap in the hardwood canopy around the wigwam, and the midday sun was pouring in, lighting the hut like an actor on a Broadway stage. I was stunned. I just stood and stared. It was as if I had come upon the home of Rumpelstiltskin. Then I heard a sound like a door, a light door, closing, and from around the front of the house a man appeared. It was the man I'd seen at the morgue. The Indian in the blue pickup. He had only one arm.

"How," he said with a smile, holding up his one hand in mockery of the stereotype. He looked younger in the dappled light of the wood than he had earlier in the day. Not his sixties; perhaps early to midfifties. The eyes seemed even bigger close up, and wider apart.

"Washchinggeka," he said. "Welcome. We've been waiting for you for some time. You came from the east. That's a good sign." He had a low, mellifluous voice and a sad yet comforting smile. It put me at ease immediately. His complexion was tawny, not as wrinkled as it had seemed earlier, and the right side of his face was disfigured with two jagged scars that zigzagged diagonally across his heavy cheekbone. They seemed to pull his flesh down. I had not seen this side of his face in the morgue parking lot. The nose was flat and less pronounced than most Native American noses — more Asian in quality; the huge black eyes were fierce, penetrating, omniscient. His lips were fat and almost awkward upon his face, bending down at the corners as if from gravity. His graying hair was pulled back in a ponytail. It reached to his shoulders. The sleeve of the missing arm was folded in half and tacked to his side. But his chest was broad, athletic. He was shorter than me by several inches, probably five foot eight or nine; solid at the stomach with no middle-aged bulge. He stepped toward me, still smiling. The legs underneath him were well balanced, bowed, and fluid. "You met our little friend, Detective McNutt. I'm surprised he didn't insist on coming with you," the Indian said laughingly.

"Actually, he did, but I told him I wanted to come here alone."

"Ha ha ha!" The sound exploded through the trees. The laugh was unabashed. "He won't go away too easily, Washchinggeka. We call his kind *wohinkcahirega*, you would say a laughingstock. He won't bother you if you always tell him the truth. His kind doesn't like the truth, because he doesn't like himself." Every culture, it seemed, had a name for a character like McNutt. "And you met the old German, Mr. Schniderwind?"

"Yes."

"Good. He likes to tell stories. He is full of good power."

"You're right."

"You're moving quickly, Washchinggeka. We've kept everything ready for you." He motioned back over his shoulder at the wigwam. "There's a lot to talk about."

It was all a little disconcerting at that moment to have a perfect stranger speaking to me like this, applauding my movements, telling me I'd been moving quickly and I'd been expected, calling

me by some strange name. And who was the *we* that he kept referring to? Next, he offered me his one hand in typical white fashion.
It was his right hand. "Oscar Rightpath," he said with a deep rumble. I stepped forward and gave him my name; we shook. The grip
was powerful. His huge, dark hand engulfed mine and he gave one
magnificent squeeze, very fast, bringing me to the point of gasp-
ing in anticipated pain. Then he let go. The handshake communicated in an instant that he had no handicap to be pitied; to the
contrary — this was someone with great power. Then he stood
back and motioned for me to look around, to take it all in, as if he
were a real estate agent and I a potential buyer.

The first item that came into view was Charlie's dugout canoe,
leaning against a nearby tree. It was just as McNutt had described.
At first it looked like any canoe, perhaps a little shorter and nar-
rower, but it became clear as I drew nearer that it wasn't.
Imperfect swirls of the chisel marks dimpled the entirety of the
craft. The hull curved evenly all the way around, and in the middle along the bottom, running the length of the vessel, a strip of
pointed, neatly carved wood acted as the keel. Its color was flesh-
like. I noted that Charlie must have coated it with shellac or some
kind of oil to keep the pulp so lustrous. "Made of cottonwood,"
Rightpath explained from behind. "Down there's the stump." His
one arm motioned toward the treeless, ten-yard-wide swath to
the riverbank. The stump of a tree sat up high on top of the bank,
directly below. Charlie sure had chosen a sublime spot to live.

"Did he clear this path through the trees?" I asked.

"No, it was done long ago. That's the direction . . ." — Rightpath
stopped as if the words were taboo — ". . . from which all enter
here."

"Why's that?"

But Rightpath did not respond, instead entering the hut, leaving me alone to continue my tour.

I walked over to the canoe and picked it up, feeling its weight. It was heavy but far lighter than it looked. Perhaps less than a hundred pounds. The interior of the craft was a continuation of the dimpled hull. Charlie had carved two seats into it, one on each end. The hull was thin all the way around — two inches thick, no more. To have crafted it by hand must have taken months and hundreds of hours of meticulous labor with a hammer and chisel. Incredible. And adding to the craftsmanship was a little engraving on the bow of a rabbit with large ears. I fingered it, then turned to study the house.

The great chimney was at the north end. I tried to picture Charlie laying stone on top of stone. The stonework stood a good three feet above the roof of the building, about twelve feet high at the apex. It tapered upward from about nine feet at its base to about three feet at the top. It was almost a yard thick, made of row upon row of round little blanched fieldstones, giving it the effect of human skulls stacked tightly.

Long oak beams, six inches in diameter, poked out the back of the chimney by about a foot. They had been built and cemented right into it to act like the horizontal cross beams of a ship's hull. Four rows ran the entire length of the structure, evenly distributed, with one on top that ran down the middle like a spine. They bowed out and sloped down from the chimney to the front, where the solidly footed frame of the one and only door held their ends. The tapering of the chimney was well formed to induce this bowing action of the walls. Ribs or studs were, of course, grated vertically into the beams for support, over which waterproof tarpaulins were tacked, some green, some camouflage colored. And on top of them, apparently to hold them more securely in place against the wind, and perhaps for simple decoration, the elastic saplings from the forest floor had been woven together tightly onto the frame. These intertwined branches gave the effect of a knitted home. And as I stood directly in front of it, ten feet from the storm-door entrance, it struck me that as a unit the lodge looked like a giant, cylindrical basket. It was the most amazing structure I'd ever laid eyes on.

"I have some coffee ready inside." Rightpath reappeared at the entrance.

He held open the windowed door for me, and upon entering I noticed a little webbed and pleached dream-catcher dangling down in the middle of the top window. A blue jay's feather hung from it. Charlie had made it, I was told. It was at eye level, inches from my face, and like a huge eye it seemed to stare back at me.

The windowed entrance was the only means to the outside, and it carved a broad aisle of sunlight right through the middle of the cavelike interior, ultimately disappearing into the fluttering flames of the fireplace. I stood in the very middle of the room, awestruck, my shadow casting an elongated image all around. I shook my head in disbelief and turned to Rightpath. "The fireplace is a masterpiece. Charlie made that by himself?"

"Used only two eighty-pound bags of cement. The stones are from Schniderwind's field."

"Wow." I couldn't get over all the details. Suddenly the fire crackled and popped, spitting out a little firebrand that landed inches from my foot. I watched it burn into the dirt and go out with a puff of smoke. It brought my attention to the floor. Dirt and deerskins. Half and half. Around furniture Charlie had placed deerskins, but in heavy-traffic spots the ground was left bare. The earth was hard, well beaten.

The inviting quality of the fireplace drew me toward it. It held half a dozen burning logs, and the fire was roaring. I took a step closer and the heat pressed against my face. A little snub-nosed coffeepot hung from a metal bar that spanned the interior of the opening, and after closer investigation, it was apparent that this bar had been cemented into place for that very purpose. The hearth-stone was made of four white flagstones, thick as a dictionary. It ran the full length of the chimney. The mantel above the wide opening of the fireplace was cemented into place and made of a peeled log, its top hewn flat and sanded smooth. The wood was darker and the grain lighter than the canoe's. Oak, I was informed. There were little trinkets resting on it — glasses, small baskets, pelts, candles. And there were five hardbound books: William Blake, J. Krishnamurti, Aldo Leopold, Black Elk, William C. Neal. The mantel, too, had been meticulously carved in bas-relief.

I walked up to investigate. The carving was a scene of a man in a canoe, on the river, paddle in hand, birds swirling overhead, trees, flowers, fish, and again the rabbit.

"What's with the rabbit?" I turned to Rightpath. "It was on the canoe, too."

"That's you, Washchinggeka."

"Me?"

"Yes. Little Hare. The third born. That's you."

The words didn't really sink in. I was too overwhelmed by it all to respond. But later the irony would explode inside me. Suddenly, I became aware of the bust of a buffalo looming over my head. It touched the ceiling at its highest point, perhaps nine feet off the ground, jutting out more than three feet from the chimney wall. It was prodigious, with tufts of fur hanging from its jowls. I took two steps back to get a better look. It had two long horns that emerged at wide angles from the top of its skull. I'd never looked at a buffalo's head before; I wasn't even aware that they had horns. The sad, black eyes seemed to look down knowingly at me, and the mouth was opened slightly as if it were about to speak, or bellow, or cry. Below it, and just above the mantel, was a bow and three arrows in a quiver. The bow was ancient and worm-eaten.

I looked back at Rightpath, who was nodding encouragingly at me, as if to say, *Continue.* Scanning the walls, I could see how the structure had been built. The vertical studs were tied in many spots as well as nailed into the cross beams. Pictures from magazines and posters, some in frames, hung on the skeletal walls more as coverings than as decorations. Most were of the circus. There was one large circus poster on the western wall — a menagerie of acrobats, elephants, horses, and contortionists. Very bright and colorful. Over the sleeping area were poems, xeroxed on white paper. Some were by William Blake; there was one strange one by e. e. cummings about Buffalo Bill; many others had no bylines, which, I learned, meant that they had been written by Charlie. An aphorism by William C. Neal held center stage in this little rhapsodic montage:

> I have no desire to "belong"; "belongingness" is no virtue
> in my eyes unless it be the cult of the fool. The cult of the
> fool is always the cult of those rich in life, the strong. I
> wish to belong to the Order of Holy Mischievousness.
> I'm happy as the devil when afloat.

Directly beneath this was a cartoon by Gary Larson of a young and "impressionable" Buffalo Bill being teased by three buffalo. The combination of meanings was indecipherable.

Next to the poems and cartoon, hanging down from the curving wall and almost touching the ground, was a magnificent, full-length raccoon coat. A dozen tails hung as a fringe from the bottom; its collar was fluffed high with tails as well. The fur was lustrous, puffy, healthy. I lifted it off its hook and examined it. The lining was soft denim, sewn firmly to the pelts. There were just two buttons on the inside of the coat — brass knobs and leather loops. Primitive, yet elegant. It must have weighed twenty-five pounds.

"Why wasn't he wearing this the night he froze to death?" I asked Rightpath.

"We don't know."

"Strange."

I turned again. By the door was a piece of cardboard with a musical score written on it in black marker. "Goose Music," it was titled. It was forty measures long with an incessant bass line.

"*This* was his masterpiece," Rightpath spoke, correcting my previous observation about the chimney. "I heard him play it on the trumpet once. Beautiful. Can you play?"

"A little. Charlie was the musician in the family. You know he had perfect pitch."

"They want to use this at the Circus World Museum. Maybe you can work out a deal with them."

"The song?"

Rightpath nodded.

There wasn't much furniture in the place. Half in the aisle of light streaming in from the door was a folding card table, brown, with three unmatched folding chairs pushed neatly under it. There was an ashtray in the middle of the table, a candle sticking up from a piece of wood that had been shaped into a candle-holder, and two cups with saucers that Rightpath had set. I thought it odd that there were saucers. An easy chair with thick, fluted arms, mauve in color, sat angled in front of the fireplace; next to it, coming up to the top of the right arm, was a round tree trunk two feet in diameter. It had a book on it — *Those Amazing Ringlings and Their Circus*. On the northeast side of the room, close to the hearth, lay a pile of fully opened sleeping bags, three stacked on top of each other, with two old blankets, one yellow, one maroon, on top of those. And a pillow. That was all.

Rightpath was pouring coffee. "Would you like cream?"

"Yes."

"This is real cream," he said.

"I'll bet it's from Mr. Schniderwind."

"Yep. Your brother was very close to the old man. He worked hard for him, and looked after him."

"Yes, he told me." Rightpath drank his coffee black. His eyes told me to sit. I did, then picked up the spoon he had set, stirred noisily, and took a sip. It was delicious.

Rightpath began to chant. I dropped my spoon, the sound was so startling. The words went on for a long time; they reminded me of the Buddhist monks I'd heard chanting in a temple in Thailand many years before. There was a twang to the nasalized vowels, and the inflections of the words rattled up and down. It lasted about a minute.

"This is sacred. Your coming here is a sacred event for our people. We must follow the ritual. We say *waikan*. Sacred. I can teach you much, but I will tell you truthfully now, you will have to learn most of it on your own. You are a keen observer, Washchinggeka, that's your gift." Rightpath delicately sipped at the edge of the cup. "I watched the way you drank in the sights here, like the coffee you are drinking now. Your eye is very keen. Very keen. And I can feel your mind now is full of questions. You want to ask me many things. We can answer some of them, but you must be patient. You will not believe me at first. I warn you. You must learn before you can believe. Listen to the words, yes, but don't expect the mind to understand."

Each word was spoken as if rehearsed, and as I drank more of the rich liquid, I became aware that when he spoke of *we*, Rightpath was speaking of his people, both past and present. His eyes seemed twice the size of a normal man's. The brown, black-rimmed pupils were round as dimes and pure, infinitely wise, with no trace of guile, and yet sad. He was right; the questions were pounding inside. I was bursting with them. I spit out — "Is it true what McNutt told me, that you believe my brother Charlie was the reincarnation of a god, a spirit?"

"Wakdjunkaga, firstborn of Earthmaker."

His answer was again direct, quick. The name, Wakdjunkaga, had a magical ring to it. It somehow fit Charlie. "Wak — how do you say it?"

"Wak-dee-zhun-kaga." His cheeks swelled and he laughed childishly at my attempts to pronounce it. "You'll learn."

"And what did you call me before? Washchingun? The little hare?"

"Wash-ching-geka."

"Was that the name you called me this morning at the morgue?"

"Yes."

"And I'm a god, too?"

"Washchinggeka. Little Hare. The third born."

"Who was the second?"

"Turtle."

"Where's he?"

"He was killed by your brother."

"So I'm Washchinggeka. And that means 'little hare'? It's funny because that's what my mother called me, only in French. *Petit lievre.* That's one of the only memories I have of her — the sound of her voice calling me by that name."

The Indian closed his eyes and a paternal smile lit his face. "She was a Decora, your mother."

That hit me like a heavy blow. He knew Mom's maiden name. It came right out of his mouth without the slightest hesitation. This changed everything. Suddenly I had the unsettling feeling that this man, this swarthy, one-armed, Oriental-looking man, knew everything about me and Charlie and everyone in my family. I was beginning to feel like I was under a spell.

"My brother must have told you that," I said with an accusatory tone. Rightpath did not respond; the eyes didn't budge. I noticed then a bluish area on the left side of his right eye, on the side of the face that was scarred. Cataracts. It flashed for a moment as he moved his head into the rays of light pouring in from the door. It gave him the appearance of a blind man, a mystic. "And where we're sitting now is on protected Indian ground?" It was like a game at this point. I felt I could have asked him any question at all and gotten a straight answer. Like talking to God.

"Yes."

"How old is it?"

"It goes back to a time when we were still afraid. Before we were able to hunt."

"How old is that?"

"Old," he nodded.

"Do you know who killed my brother?" I blurted out, using the technique I'd learned that morning from McNutt — like a fighter setting up his opponent for the knockout blow.

"Yes." Rightpath didn't blink.

"Who?"

"Buffalo Bill."

"*Plllp* — " A mouthful of coffee sprayed out and then dribbled down my chin. I vaulted to my feet, laughing, spitting coffee. I wiped my mouth and took a deep breath. "All right, what is this? What's this all about?" I was certain at this moment that I was the brunt of some masterful gag that Charlie had set up. I even felt exhilarated by the idea that Charlie was alive and well and able to think up such a scheme. I saw Charlie lying in that stupid trailer morgue . . . the epicene investigator . . . Buffalo Bill . . . what a great, great joke! My mind was quickly filling in all the blanks. Yes, I'd been a bastard to run away and never return. And since I'd never even seen Charlie as an agoraphobic, only heard about it, I was certain that it had all been made up for just this moment. My mind was working at blinding speed. But when I looked at Rightpath, whose face didn't flinch, the ideas fluttered and fell. No mortal could keep a straight face after a punch line like that. "What's the deal? Who are you?" I asked him again, this time without a trace of humor in my voice.

"Your transitioner."

"Transitioner to what, the biggest practical joke on earth?" I was angry now.

"That's what you have to learn."

I wanted to strangle him, one arm or no arms. "Where's my brother?"

Rightpath didn't answer. I stood now glowering at the man, but the kindly looking Indian just sat, his fat lips unfurled awkwardly on his face, his one arm perched on the card table. I still held on to a shred of hope that it was all a joke, but there was no joking in the face of the dark stranger in front of me. Then I asked straight out, "So does that mean that Detective McNutt is the Lone Ranger?"

We began to laugh. We lost ourselves in the laughter. The little hut was shaking with our laughter. Then it stopped abruptly.

"Sit down, Washchinggeka."

I obeyed.

FOUR

The Return of Wakdjunkaga

"Everything that Wakdjunkaga said and did was *waikan;* all the actions, antinomies, thoughts are bound into the mythic cycle. The sacred is an immediate condition of our experience. We do not attach labels of divinity to them; we do not consecrate them. We understand that all men are capable of extremes, of evil excesses, but we know also that each man is held accountable for those actions. There is no closet for him to go into and be magically absolved of his sins. He alone is responsible for those excesses that threaten the balance of nature. Earthmaker holds us all accountable. Wakdjunkaga returned to remind us of that. We can see clearer now. We know what we need to do as a result of his return.

"Wakdjunkaga had been trying to come back to the second realm for a long time — in fact, ever since the appearance of Buffalo Bill Cody and his Wild West shows, which is the reason for his failed appearance last time. I'm referring to George Wilkinson, a nineteenth-century man who claimed he was the reincarnation of Wakdjunkaga. But the transition was wrong; the body was not properly prepared, not well purged. Wakdjunkaga could see that the theatrical pogrom of our people by Cody and the Wild West shows was blasphemy and would introduce to the land a new level of evil excess. So he returned to the second realm in the body of your brother. Later Cody, like Wakdjunkaga, was reincarnated in order to defend his works. This is the yin and yang that the Easterners understand. The two forces are always in conflict. The struggle is forever manifest in the form of energy. The positive and the negative. Good versus evil. Cody knew Wakdjunkaga had returned to obliterate his work. The first world is forever involved in ours. His transitioner, whom you will meet, made it easy for him to return. In fact, Cody was not alone. He reified along with a partner, his creator, Ned Buntline, the man who wrote the dime-store novels about him, which eventually gave rise to his fame.

"But this makes little sense to you. Let me go back to your brother before he was Wakdjunkaga — back to the car accident twenty-five years ago, when your mother was killed. We know that the top of her head was severed. Horrible. I'm sorry to have to mention this. But she was a descendant of the Decora, the first white people who mixed with the Ho-Chunk. Great power was in her. The release of her dreams shook the first world. Our world, too, was in turmoil. Thunderstorms and tornadoes ripped through this area as a result of her death. The geese were full of music, singing the news, but confused. Many died that year. Dreams are the most powerful thing on Earth. They move continents, ocean waters, rivers, wind. In the seat next to your mother lay your brother, just a boy. He was bathed in the power of the dreams. You may remember that shortly afterward — perhaps you don't — your father brought your brother alone up here to the Baraboo Hills, to the circus, to convalesce. It was twenty-five years ago this month that your brother stood on the Man Mound, on the crotch of the mound — where he also died. Wakdjunkaga, waiting those many years, then entered into your brother. Yes, the symbol is right — he inseminated himself into your brother's body.

"The body was fully purged this time. You know how your

brother suffered. You call it agoraphobia, but this is how it had to be. He was closed off from the outside world for ten years. Yes, you nod your head, you know. That was the great purge needed to prepare for his work here. He had to be completely desocialized, to break all ties with man and society, to remove himself completely from the excesses of the world around him in order to prepare himself for his work here. The cleansing was long and difficult, but it had to be so. He would suffer great waves of guilt and anxiety, fearing the evil excesses of mankind around him. Most would have died from such suffering. But the power of your mother's dreams sustained him. When the time finally came, he heeded the call, following the music of the geese north and west, finally coming to rest here, right here, where we sit now. Fantastic, yes, but it is the way.

"Now you, Washchinggeka, Little Hare — Siconski, our Assiniboin brothers call you — you've come as the cycle requires."

"Siconski? Our last name?" I was confused. "An Indian name? I don't think so! My father's family were Ukranian Jews."

"We are all far more closely connected than your white society knows. The anthropologists are just now beginning to figure that out. We know that the white man was here on this continent long before Columbus. Our ancestors tell of fighting red-haired giants. The Vikings. We have swords from the eighth century buried in our mounds. Copper from our mines can be found all over Europe, yet no one knows how it got there. You, Washchinggeka, are the third, the fixer, the repairer. Wakdjunkaga is the first, strong and powerful, charismatic but foolish. He leaves behind many problems, many mistakes. You must fix them. You will see that you have much work to do. You will see, Washchinggeka."

"But why the circus? What's the connection there?" I had been anxious to ask this question all day. "He apparently made quite an impression down there. McNutt says that the Circus World

Museum wants his body buried on the grounds. They have an entire display devoted to him. I need to go down there to see it. To talk to them."

"Yes, that is a good question, and an easy one to answer," Rightpath encouraged. "I will give you books to read so that you can learn more about this. The clown, you see, is the most powerful of all beings. That is why many children are afraid of clowns. They feel that awesome power. Most people believe the clown is just for fun. But this is not so. A clown possesses the power of the first world. The actions, the buffoonery of the clown are not so much to induce laughter as to symbolize the knowledge of the first world — a shapeless, noncorporeal world of pure energy. The ridiculous actions of the clown not only subliminally suggest the actions of the first world, but also actually open people up to it. I believe it was Black Elk, the famed medicine man, who said, 'People are made to laugh and feel jolly so that it may be easier for the power to come to them.' As a clown, Wakdjunkaga was imbued with the most power he could attain. And that is why he came to us as a clown."

"My brother was a clown? But as a kid he was deathly afraid of clowns."

"You will learn."

"When did my brother first appear? When were you first aware that Charlie was here?"

"The return of Wakdjunkaga to our people is *waikan*, not *worak*. It is a sacred story, not simply a narrative. Your brother Charlie was Wakdjunkaga. Because it is *waikan*, I must ask permission from the ancient counselors to tell the story to you." He began to chant again, this time for a full two minutes. His eyes were closed; the one arm would occasionally rise into the air as if describing images to itself. The notes were full of weird sibilants and nasalized vowels, and they were repeated at least four times that I could make out. Finished, he opened his eyes and looked across the table at me.

"Wakdjunkaga, the Tricky One, came back to our people on October thirty-first, nineteen ninety-seven. We had known ever since the release of the dream spirits of the granddaughter Decora twenty years before that Wakdjunkaga was trying to return. My grandfather, Joseph Rightpath, born ninety-three winters before Wakdjunkaga's return, son of the chief counselor of the Ho-Chunk people, had been appointed the transitioner of Wakdjunkaga from the very first. And I, as historian for my people, had been chosen to be the witness.

"My mother had called me from my work in Madison, fearing that my grandfather would not live through the week. He had lain ill for weeks, bedridden. At this stage of his illness he drifted in and out of consciousness. The doctors gave him little hope of recovery — his lungs were racked irreparably with emphysema. Then the day came; he knew it in his heart. Miraculously, he got out of his bed, put on his ceremonial robe, walked into the living room, and sat down and waited, chanting to himself softly. All day he sat as if expecting someone to come, chanting quietly, using the sacred words of the ancients in between painful gasps for air. It was close to suppertime when there was heard the barking of dogs and then the ringing of a bell far off in the distance. It was the tinny clang of a small bell — the kind found on the handlebars of young people's bicycles. Bells signify a coming, an appearing. The dogs of the neighborhood responded almost immediately, in unison, to the sound of the bell. Dogs are the sentinels of the earth. Throughout the neighborhood there grew such a commotion of dogs barking that it was almost impossible to hear the bell. But my grandfather heard it. He began to shake all over, and his chanting grew louder and louder. Then, as the commotion of barking dogs drew nearer to our home, he stood up and said in the language of my people, 'He has arrived!'

"And with the pronouncement of these words, there was heard from outside the ominous crash of a man on a bicycle falling into a cluster of garbage cans next to our home. I ran to the front door, opened it wide, and there was Wakdjunkaga, Charlie, the Tricky One, dogs barking all around him, lying under his bicycle and underneath a galvanized garbage can. He was bleeding on his face and hand. My mother, too, ran to the door, and together we dug him out. 'It is him!' my grandfather exclaimed. Amazingly, he had walked to the door and was looking down from there as we sat Wakdjunkaga up. 'Look at the left hand, it is badly cut. It is the sign of the Tricky One,' he said.

"Wakdjunkaga was dazed and incoherent, unable to sit up without assistance. He smelled of the dank water of the Baraboo, which is the name of our people, given to us by our enemies — Winnebago means 'people of the stinking water.' We now prefer to call ourselves Ho-Chunk, 'people of the big voice,' for obvious reasons. My grandfather, with a wild look in his eyes, climbed down the steps of our house, a herculean feat for a man so debilitated, and approached the Tricky One. Putting his hands in the air, he said again in the language of our people, 'Welcome. We have been expecting you. And why have you come?'

"Wakdjunkaga responded, with perfect diction of the sacred tongue, 'To cohabitate with the women.' Many thousands of years ago, Wakdjunkaga, as the chief of his village, was going on the warpath, and in accordance with the rites and customs his first order of business was to sleep with the women of the village before he took the war bundle and made war. But as my people know, Wakdjunkaga never made war, he just slept with women and did foolish things. He tried to distract his people so that they wouldn't go to war. So for Wakdjunkaga to say that he had come to cohabitate with women proved he was truly Wakdjunkaga: That is what the Tricky One did best and most often. He had indeed returned.

"We helped both him and my grandfather into the house and sat them down together on my mother's couch. My grandfather was smiling. Wakdjunkaga was still dazed. My mother prepared a wet cloth, wiped his bleeding brow, and wrapped gauze around his hand. It was while she was doing this that Wakdjunkaga spoke again. 'Are you Joseph Rightpath?'

"'Yes, Wakdjunkaga, you have found me.' My grandfather laughed proudly like a young boy.

"'I forget why I wanted to talk to you,' the Tricky One said, holding the cold compress my mother had given him to his forehead, frowning deeply.

"My grandfather continued to laugh. 'I know why you have come,' he chuckled. 'You have come to ask about the women.'

"'Women?' Wakdjunkaga pretended to be surprised.

"This made my grandfather laugh louder. 'Yes, the women. And how do you like them? Do you like them with long legs and well muscled?'

"'Well, I guess I do,' responded Wakdjunkaga.

"'And with great big breasts, you like that too?' asked my grandfather.

"'Who doesn't?'

"'And daring in bed, you most certainly crave that type of woman?'

"'Daring?'

"My grandfather kept laughing at the responses of Wakdjunkaga. And at that moment he looked like a man half his age. He pushed himself from his seat and stood, beaming, in a different world, looking at my mother and me but not seeing us. He shouted in our native language, 'Prepare the sweat tent. We must welcome the Tricky One properly.'

"The sweat tent is the place where the men of the village meet to exculpate their sins, to speak truths, to admit their shortcomings; of course it is used for healing, too. Since there were only six members of our tribe in the neighborhood, we had only my grandfather and I, our cousin, Richard Proudheart, an auto mechanic, and his son, just seventeen years old, take a sweat with Wakdjunkaga. The rocks were heated well with choice, dried oakwood. The ceremonial skins were laid on the outside to keep in the heat. Inside the sweat lodge, the men circled the steaming rocks. My grandfather, though weak, was still miraculously strong enough to say the ancient litanies and pour the water on the rocks at the appointed phrases. Then the *man-ka*, the medicine balls, were passed around. *Man-ka* is peyote, and it wasn't normally used in sweats, nor was it traditionally used by our people until early in the twentieth century, and even then by only a handful. But with Wakdjunkaga there, it was necessary in order to understand completely his words and actions. *Man-ka* induces powerful understanding and focus. Without it, many of the cryptic comments and actions of Wakdjunkaga would not have been interpreted correctly. Prayers were said so that the thoughts would be focused not on the self but on the purpose of the gathering. And since this was a special gathering, the focus was on Wakdjunkaga.

"The *man-ka* balls were passed around and each of us took one to eat. They went around several times, and as they were passed, more prayers were offered up to Earthmaker for the return of Wakdjunkaga. Sitting on the ground with us, the Tricky One continued to act as if dazed. He ate the balls, but each time he did so he would repeat to us that he couldn't remember why he had come. My grandfather chuckled, knowing well what Wakdjunkaga was all about.

"The men began to come loose with their confessions, and

often my grandfather as the elder would offer advice and counsel, but as the peyote took effect, much of the heartfelt confession evolved into talk of women and lovemaking. All became carefree and open, laughing as each told of a recent exploit with the opposite sex. Wakdjunkaga was the most reticent in the sweat tent, but as time passed he began laughing more and more. Finally beside himself with laughter, he stood up and held his penis in his hands, as all the men in a sweat lodge are naked, and began to talk to it. It talked back, saying the most absurd things imaginable, sounding as one would who spoke out of the side of his mouth. And he began to laugh and dance, staggering seemingly out of control around the scalded rocks, in between the legs and feet of the men, laughing wildly and clapping his hands, moving his legs at blinding speed, yet never falling as he went faster and faster around the lodge. It was an enthralling dance, acrobatic, circular, hypnotizing. All of a sudden with his huge feet he stepped awkwardly on the leg of our cousin's young son and spilled backward into the hot rocks, burning his anus. His laughter turned to shrieks of pain and we all yanked him from his predicament. He rested as a dog, on all four appendages, retching violently. Then out popped his intestines, which he immediately gathered back up and swallowed again. My grandfather howled with glee, for he had witnessed in person the story he had heard as a little boy, told to him by his elders around the same sacred fires, of how Wakdjunkaga had burned his anus and eaten his own intestines.

"When the Tricky One had lapped up his viscera, he ran naked, screaming, from the sweat hut and did not return until the next day. He appeared at our door late in the morning, naked. My mother invited him in but he declined, asking only for his clothes and for my grandfather. We left him outside, retrieved his clothes, and brought my grandfather from the bed out to the front step to talk with him.

"'Sir,' said the Tricky One as he buttoned his shirt, 'I remember now why I came to see you yesterday.'

"'Yes?'

"'Your headdress, like the one you wore in the picture with Buffalo Bill's Wild West show. Do you have one like that? I would like to buy it from you.'

"'Of course,' responded my grandfather. 'The war bundle, I almost forgot. Daughter, the skins and the headdress, bring them to us.' My grandfather motioned to my mother. She knew just where they were, where they had been stored for many, many years wrapped in an old woolen blanket. She carried them to my grandfather, who took them from her and held them high, saying the words of our ancestors: 'Take them, brother, they are yours.'

"Wakdjunkaga climbed the steps and, with a look of rapture, took them from my grandfather, bowing. He said nothing but walked back to his bicycle, still lying in the cluster of garbage cans close to our stoop. There he turned and said to my grandfather, 'I would like to come back and talk to you about the Wild West shows sometime. I have many questions.'

"'Of course,' nodded my grandfather.

"With a kick or two from his giant feet, the cans tumbled out of the way, and he lifted the bike upright, mounted it, and rode off, the dogs of the neighborhood chasing after him. That is the story of the return of Wakdjunkaga to the Ho-Chunk.

"My grandfather died two days later. But he died happy, knowing that he had served his purpose — knowing that a new and hopeful future was in place for his people now that Wakdjunkaga had come back. I know it must be difficult for you to assimilate this — that your brother Charlie was a deity. Of course that makes no sense to you. But you will see. You will learn and then you will believe.

"But now we have to prepare you for your opus."

Rightpath removed a small, round, painted wooden box from a leather pouch that hung on the back of the folding chair. He placed it on the table unopened and fumbled with his one hand inside his pocket. He finally managed to find what he was looking for and brought it forth, holding it ceremoniously — a small stone pipe. I sat across the table from him watching with great interest. The one hand and arm prepared the two offerings. He placed a mixture in the stone pipe, then opened the painted box and delicately removed what looked like little round cookies or dough balls made from dark wheat and dried hard. He placed some of them on the white china saucer in front of me and an equal amount on the saucer in front of himself. The balls were about an inch and a half in diameter. There were twenty in all — I counted them — ten on each plate. Rightpath lit the weed, breathed in deeply, then passed the pipe to me. I took a small drag of the bitter smoke, held it for a moment in my lungs, and exhaled. It was tobacco, but very harsh; I had to fight the urge to cough. The pipe went back and forth between us for some time until the bowl was spent. Neither of us spoke a word. Next, Rightpath delicately picked up one of the balls and popped it in his mouth. He motioned for me to do the same.

"No thanks." I waved my hand over the offering. As I said this, the wind outside began to blow fiercely, and the door, which had not been shut tight, flew open and bashed against the outside of the hut. I ran to close it; when I returned to my seat the little *man-ka* balls were there waiting for me. I was sweating now as the flames in the fireplace pitched to and fro, reflecting a liquid movement across the side of Rightpath's scarred face. The world seemed to be moving or flowing like water, swaying and pulling, like a subtle tide.

"You will need help understanding, Washchinggeka, otherwise it will all be too abstruse. *Man-ka* is the last step in the ritual cycle. I believe we have prepared you well by providing the proper beginning. Now you must start to interpret it all; to act. The cycle moves very quickly once engaged. Eat them, Washchinggeka; chew slowly. It will make things clearer. It will set you on the right path. You have much to do. Now is the time."

The wind outside was really picking up. The little round lodge squeaked and creaked eerily, and the sun that had been streaming in through the front door was extinguished by a monstrous cumulus cloud that had drifted in from the east. The world was changing. I felt a powerful sense of urgency all around me. I looked down at the little balls before me. They looked innocent, like marshmallows. I mentally reviewed what little I knew about peyote's power. I had read something about it once. It was a hallucinogen. Still I sat musing, unsure. What a day it had been for me. Nothing I'd ever done in my life had prepared me for this day. I needed help deciding. I looked across the table at the Indian, staring deeply into his dark eyes. They did not look away. They invited me to investigate deeper. Then, like a siren, the honk of a lone goose directly overhead shattered the moment. The same sensation I had had on the ferry that morning came surging back. The goose call sang to me, telling me, *Take them and eat them now!* I gently plucked one of the balls from the table and placed it in my mouth. It was terribly bitter. Indescribable. I heaved.

"Chew it slowly," Rightpath instructed. "The bad taste will go away. Take more."

I chewed slowly. Done, I took two more; chewed slowly. They were very dry. I wanted water but, seeing none, figured water was not part of the ritual. In fifteen minutes' time I had eaten all ten. Rightpath, too, had eaten his.

"What is my work?" I asked him, barely able to talk from the odd feeling in my mouth. "You said that I have come back to clean up all the messes, but everything seems in order. This house. The old German. What's there to do?"

Rightpath laughed, but his eyes were wide with thought. "You will see. But you must work very hard. You are in danger now from the same evil spirits that threatened your brother. You must be very careful not to be killed yourself. Do not trust anyone, no matter how generous or kind they may seem. Remember, the little hare is always being chased. You are not a hunter but the hunted. You must be wary. Rely on your speed and cunning. That is what you do best. Observe; you are good at that. Follow your instincts."

The next thing I knew Rightpath's face changed form. The peyote was obviously taking effect. Across the table was a long-bearded white man from the end of the nineteenth century. He was dressed in a gray suit with a high-collared white shirt and a black tie; he was balding. He looked like one of the Ringling brothers I had seen in a photograph earlier in the day. Then, just as suddenly, he transformed again, this time into a black man, an African shaman with bones woven into his hair, no shirt, his skin beaded with sweat, a zebra skin slung from one shoulder across his chest, and his earlobes stretched grotesquely to hold coins. He became an Oriental woman in colored silk with a demure look. Then he was a coyote, dusty brown but beautiful, with bright white teeth and a bold black nose. He hopped down from his chair and scampered to the door. He was saying something to me, but his voice was elongated, high-pitched, as if he were speaking through a tube. I was almost sick with fright. But I stood up and followed the canine, trying to decipher his words. His voice grew more distant, receding, fading, and he was growing smaller, like an image seen through the wrong end of a telescope.

"You've been sent to teach people to live a better life, Washchinggeka. That's why you've roamed all over the world. You must do away with all the hindrances. You have learned much in your travels; now you must exploit your knowledge." He trotted out the door.

"Wait!" I cried, and ran after him. The wind was screaming outside. There were strange sounds against the walls of the lodge, as if people were outside laughing and scratching to be let in. I could see him, like a tiny portrait in a locket, standing in line with the wind, in profile. He was a lustrous, brown canine in the diminishing light, his tail held high and proud.

"Watch out, Washchinggeka. Don't eat for four days. Keep your ears flat when hiding. Don't eat . . ." After this the words were too far away and the wind too loud. The tail dropped suddenly and he was out of sight in the blink of an eye.

"Wait!" I yelled, but he was gone. I walked back inside and turned to look out through the glass. The door swung closed in my face, the spring hinge making a comic *boing* sound, like a sound effect in a cartoon. The little dream-catcher vaulted out from the door, bounced once, then twice, and began to spin like a coin as I turned to study it. It twirled and twirled, faster and faster in front of my split nose and whiskers . . .

FIVE

Washchinggeka Vanquishes Buffalo Bill

Washchinggeka was jumping on the dream-catcher in the middle of the room as if it were a trampoline. It was huge; or rather he was small; or both. Up and down he went, higher and higher. Outside the wind was whirling and spinning. The trees were doubled over with laughter.

Little Hare jumped higher and higher and suddenly he was outside, high above the lodge. The clouds were angry looking, marching hurriedly across the sky. He was carried along by the wind. Below, the land watched. Occasionally lively clumps of green grass waved to him. Little Hare could hear them giggling as he tumbled through the sky, head over heels, his ears beating higgledy-piggledy against his back. The marching clouds looked down in disapproval.

A rocky bluff pierced the sky, too low, and Little Hare fell into it. He was caught by the branch of a tamarack tree. With little trouble, he swung from the branch and landed on the ground on all four feet, facing east. His legs, his hind legs, were springy. He jumped twice to feel the extent of his hop. It was as if he had wings on his feet.

Little Hare was on the shelf of a rocky cliff. Below, the water of a great lake was blue. The trees around him

looked more like flowers than woody plants. The clouds were gone. Off in the distance Hare heard the baying of mules or herd animals. A crow swooped down, cawing —
"There is Little Hare! There he is!"

Instinct told him to run. Hare ran like the wind. He sought shelter in a thicket, but he was immediately discovered again by the crow. "Little Hare has run into the thicket!" So he scampered out, ran to an old log, and hid under it. "Now he's hiding under the log," cawed the crow. Again he ran off, this time hiding in a hole in the ground. But it was no use — "He's in that hole!" Little Hare was scared, and he ran out of the hole into the hollow of a tree. "I saw him go into the hollow of that tree," sang the crow. Hare had had enough. He raced through the woods fast as lightning until he came to a lodge, where a voice from within spoke to him.

"Come in, Grandson."

Hare entered. Inside he found a man with his head wrapped in bandages. The man was white with yellow hair and a beard, and he dressed in frayed buckskin.

"I sent the crow to find you. I aimed to talk to you. I need yer help. You must be hungry. Would you like some grub?"

"No, I can't eat," said Little Hare.

"Kettle, git off 'n there and git Little Hare some grub."

The kettle hopped from the fire, saluted the man, and began to ladle out a portion of its contents into a bowl. Hare watched in wonder. "How does it do that?" he asked.

"Do you like that? Watch this: Kettle, git yerself some more water and then hang back in the fire." The kettle did just as it was told — moving about the lodge, pouring water into itself, then jumping back up onto its hook.

"*Now, plate,*" the blond man said to the dishes on the shelf, "*put some corn in the kettle and some buffalo ribs, too.*" As instructed, one of the plates jumped off the shelf and got to work. Little Hare was amazed. "*Now, plate, serve up the food on yerself and give it to Little Hare.*"

"*Grandfather, I do not want to eat.*"

"*But you must be hungry, Grandson.*"

"*I am not.*" Actually, Little Hare was quite hungry, but something inside him told him not to eat the food, to beware.

"*Put the food back, clean yerself, and return to yer spot on the shelf,*" said the man to the plate. In a jiffy the plate did as it was told. "*Grandson, I have called you here because I want you to do something fer me. You see how I look. My head's bandaged. That's because yer brother stole my scalp. Now the womanish man with the pumpkin rump who drives the rubber-wheeled vehicle has taken it away somewhere. I have tried to git it back but have failed. I would like you to try to git it fer me. Yer a very clever fellow, and fast, too. If'n you git it fer me I'll give you the power to order things around the way I was doin' before. How'dja like that, huh?*"

"*Grandfather, I will try my best to get it back for you,*" Little Hare responded, thinking greedily of the things he would do with such powers.

"*Ahh, Grandson, that makes me happy. You can sleep here and start in the morning.*"

"*Actually, I would prefer to start right now,*" retorted Hare.

"*Now? But you need yer sleep for such a long and difficult journey.*"

"*No. I will leave now.*" And Little Hare got up, but he

realized that all the exits had been closed off by plates and pots. This had all been a trap. The yellow-haired man wanted Hare for his fur, because it matched his own scalp. Suddenly a fat white man with a huge head appeared from under a bearskin rug and shot at Hare, missing. Little Hare spied an opening and ran out.

"Git 'im!" he heard the big-headed man say.

Hare ran fast through the forest. He heard his pursuers stumbling and crashing far behind him. But the dishes and plates that the man commanded were full of power, and they were able to keep pace with him. The plates ran strangely, wobbling the way they do after they've been spun. Every once in a while a dish or a pan would say, "There he is, catch him! Catch him!"

Finally Little Hare was so tired that he ran and hid inside a tree. The two men and all the dishes and pans arrived, circling the tree and talking among themselves. The big-headed man said, "Let's gnaw the tree down." So they began to eat the tree trunk. While they did, Hare jumped out a hole in the side and ran away again.

"There he is! He's escaped again! Chase him!"

They chased him until he got tired and ran and hid inside another tree. Again they began to gnaw it down, and again Little Hare escaped.

Little Hare was very fast, but the plates and pots were able to stay close. He ran in a tree for the third time and just like before they gnawed at it; once again he escaped. The fourth time this happened, the blond-haired man stopped gnawing and said, "It's too dang bitter. Stop gnawing. We'll just wait till he comes down." And they began spitting out the wood pulp. They waited, and poor Little Hare was very tired and worried that he could not *escape this time. But he had an idea. He began to sing a song, a very pleasant song that had a somnolent effect on his pursuers.*

> *Goose music! Goose music!*
> *The sound is so bright and so free.*
> *Goose music! Goose music!*
> *The sound is so bright and so free.*
> *Overhead, in the sky above,*
> *The sweet sweet song you'll be dreaming of.*
> *Led by the drake that knows the way,*
> *Five hundred miles they'll fly in one day.*
> *A gaggle of honkers, maybe a score,*
> *Shaped like an arrow they're set for their chore.*
> *Necks outstretched like snakes on a vine*
> *With paintbrush wings that winnow and whine,*
> *They sing a song that fills the air,*
> *Listen to me now, listen to Hare:*
> *Goose music! Goose music!*
> *The sound is so bright and so free!*
> *Goose music! Goose music!*
> *The sound is so bright and so free!*

After he had sung the song four times, they all fell asleep. Then he snuck down quietly, but as he reached the ground he made a noise. The big-headed man woke up and shouted, "There he is!" They gave chase again, shooting their guns over Little Hare's outstretched ears.

Hare ran like the wind, never turning around, thinking only of escape. Finally he was safe, and instead of running, he hopped lazily along, full of self-satisfaction for having outsmarted his pursuers. He came upon a prairie where a herd of bison trotted quickly toward the sun. He ran out to inquire about them.

"Grandfather, why are you hurrying away?" he asked the first bull he came upon.

"We are afraid, Grandson. There are human beings shooting us for our tongues."

"Why do they want your tongues, Grandfather?"

"Because they think that by stealing our tongues they will acquire our gentle ways and be able to stop their wars."

"Where will you go?"

"To join our bro — "

But the bison was not able to finish his sentence, for a shot rang out that struck him in the head and he fell to the ground, dead. The herd stampeded. Little Hare was in danger of being trampled under the feet of the great beasts, and he had to run as fast as he was able, zigzagging in and out of the pounding hooves.

Finally he got clear of the herd and raced up a nearby knoll, where he sat on a log to catch his breath, his ears flat against his back. He became aware of voices nearby, grow-ing closer. It was his pursuers — the yellow-haired man with the bandages on his head and the big-headed man. They walked right by him, not seeing him, then hunkered down and crawled to the edge of the knoll on hands and knees. They lay on their bellies looking over the grassy ridge at the stampeding bison.

"That was a hell of a shot, Cody, right off the hip. Hit 'im where it hurts."

"Yeah. Look at 'em, Bunt. Perty an' delicious lookin', just like Belgium chocolates."

"You hungry, too?"

"Watch now, I'll shoot two wif one bullit."

"Git out, you ain't no Davey Crockett."

"Crockett. Tagh! What kinder name is that? Sound like a frog takin' a crap. Now, you could wallpaper ev'ry dagnabbled house in this country wif the buffalo I shoot."

"You still ain't no Crockett."

"Don't git me all-fired mad now. Shut up and watch me shoot. And you stank, you know that."

"Betcha cayn't."

"Agh, stop breathin' on me, you yeller-livered Dutchman, you smell worser than a Chinaman's pisspot."

He raised his gun barrel and began to aim. Suddenly the old log on which Little Hare sat, his ears tucked tightly against his back, gave way beneath his feet. He gave a little squeal.

A shot was fired, then immediately he heard *"freckin-hareheis!"* all in one word. He ran with all his might. A bullet broke a branch right next to his ears.

He ran until he came to a river. It was a mighty river, wide and fast flowing. He backed up a good distance, then raced toward the water. At its edge he gave a mighty push with his hind legs and sailed over the river like a kite, landing safely on the other side.

Then his pursuers came to the same place where Little Hare had jumped, and they stopped.

"You see that! He jumped clear across the river. It's a big river," said the portly, big-headed man.

"Let's jump, too," encouraged the yellow-haired man.

"We won't make it!"

"Agh, yer yeller."

"I ain't!" barked the fathead. *"It's just that I ain't got the right shoes on."*

"Agh!" The yellow-haired man backed up and the big-headed man followed him, and together the two men raced down to the water's edge and jumped, but they failed to reach the other side, and they both fell into the river and were drowned.

Little Hare returned to his big brother's lodge, pulled the blankets over himself, and fell asleep immediately, quite tired from his adventure.

SIX

A Note from Rightpath

I awoke in Charlie's bed in the lodge. I looked at my watch but it was gone. I had no idea what time it was. My head was spinning, my throat felt like someone had paved a road down through it, my feet were sore, both hamstrings ached, and my buttocks were two hard knots. There was only a thin light in the room, more like a red glow, from the embers in the fire. Looking toward the glass door, I could just make out a hint of pink in the dark void beyond. For some reason the dream-catcher was the first thing that came to my mind. It was not there in the window.

I struggled to extract myself from under the blankets, groaning as I got to my feet. The interior of the lodge was chilly. I could see my breath. I took a step toward the fireplace, intent on stoking up the hot coals, when I stepped on something. I looked down. It was the dream-catcher, sitting in the middle of the floor. My head ached and I rubbed at my forehead. I stood swaying, more from my thoughts than from the weakness of my muscles. In my mind I saw a little hare running like the wind . . .

GATHERING MY WITS about me, I tended the fire, trying hard to wash the jumbled images from my brain. Lazily, I stirred up the coals and added logs. In ten minutes' time my thoughts had calmed a bit, and the lodge was filled with heat. Feeling a bit better, I poured myself a tall glass of water and took a seat in Charlie's big-armed chair in front of the fire. "Ahh, that's more like it." I comforted myself with spoken words. Then I recalled the coffee from the day before. A cup of that coffee was just the thing I needed. My eyes wandered over to the black kettle to the left of the hearth, next to which sat the coffeepot. It was right where I thought it would be. But an envelope was taped to it. Written in bold print was the name WASHCHINGGEKA. I walked over to the pot and opened the envelope.

Washchinggeka —

We heard the sounds of a great battle last night. The children were afraid. They heard the whistling of the wind and the frightening cries of the evil spirits that ran through the forest and tried to kill you. All night we kept the fires ablaze, praying for your victory over the evil forces. This morning, shortly after sunrise, the geese came to us and told us that you had vanquished your brother's killers. They are drowned in the wide Wisconsin. I hurried over to see if you were hurt, but you were sleeping very deeply under the blankets. So I sat down to write this note.

I will put it on the coffeepot because I know that you will be hungry; you will want something in your stomach when you wake up. But you must resist. You must not eat for four days. Otherwise you will lose power, and the knowledge will not come easily to you. Drink the water. It is good water from the well of the old German.

I am leaving you three important bits of information:

Number one, the two Radin books on the card table will tell you the basics of the myths and cycles that are now manifest in you. Read them, read Radin's notations — most are accurate — but don't try to connect your observations and thoughts with them right away. That will take time. Learning about the myth cycles will give you great knowledge about the reasons why, which is all you need.

Second, the names and addresses on the paper herewith are the allies and enemies of your brother. They hold key information about his life and his work, and you must meet with them and get to know them intimately in order to learn all that you can about Wakdjunkaga. Allies and enemies are the determinants of our fate. You will find out from the very start that the first man on the list, Jasper Miles, the Buffalo Bill historian, was your brother's nemesis. And in fact, he was the transitioner for the reification of Buffalo Bill and Buffalo Bill's creator, Edward Zane Carol Judson, aka Ned Buntline, through two Denver drunks, indirect descendants of the two aforementioned. Their original names are not known to me. No doubt our Detective McNutt will soon find the two drowned bodies and connect the hair samples. But that should take a few days, maybe more. However, the reason I list Professor Miles first is because in order to know a man, it is imperative to know his enemies best. By listening to and closely observing Professor Miles, you will quickly divine the cause of Wakdjunkaga's counteractions and beliefs. All the rest of the people on the list had intimate contact with your brother as well, especially the young women who bore his children, and they will be able to provide valuable clues. This, of course, will take time. But it will also take an incredible amount of energy and concentration. Use the fasting period for reading and restoring energy. You will be able to read a lot while fasting.

Finally, the journals. This may come as quite a shock to you — not that you aren't already overwhelmed by the events in your life at present — but Wakdjunkaga, your brother Charlie, kept a complete inventory of his life from the moment he left his suburban home to the night before he died. Twenty-six journals in all; five thousand handwritten pages. This document is *waikan,* and we were able to save it all from exposure before the body was found. Yes, we knew Wakdjunkaga had died. The geese told us he had. We let him lie as he was on top of the Man Mound. The body had to be returned to the white world for a while; it was only fair. We would have it in the end. We knew that. But we secured the journals. (They are hidden inside the buffalo head.) In his old life Wakdjunkaga as Charlie was a follower of J. Krishnamurti, a very wise philosopher and healer from the East. He believed what Krishnamurti offered as advice — that in order to stop the bad thoughts of the mind, one had to bring closure to those same thoughts each day. By recording his bad thoughts at the end of every day, Charlie felt he could, in fact, bring closure to them. This was the reasoning behind his journals.

You must learn before you can believe much of what I am saying. The mythic cycles, though already told, continue to live in us. We relive them through our dreams. Every dream is a myth. And every myth is a dream. They are universal. One must look closely for them, but they can be found in all people throughout the world through the ages. I believe the writer Joseph Campbell exposes this. For example, your own counterpart, Aristeas, was the wanderer in Greek tradition. He was a poet who alternately appeared and disappeared over a period of some four hundred years. He appeared first as Homer's teacher, and thereafter in utterly different places and characters. He was considered by Heroditus to be a magician whose soul could leave and reenter its body at will. The phonemic similarity between the English word *hare* and the Greek *aris* can be easily deduced. The myths come alive in those souls aware enough to understand them, Washchinggeka. You are living proof of this. All that you do now is an expansion of the myths that you will read about in the Radin books. Life is cyclical, but ever changing as well. All who live wisely know this.

As for your brother's body, I know you have not called to make arrangements for its burial. Sometime soon you may want to call Detective McNutt and tell him you are having some problems securing an undertaker. Stall for time. The body is well protected; don't worry about it. But in the end, it must be delivered to its rightful place.

I will check in with you in a few days.

Pleasant dreams.

O. R.

P.S. Burn this letter after you read it. And remove and read just one journal at a time. We don't want them to get into the wrong hands.

I tossed the letter into the fire, watching it wither and then ignite in a gust. Remaining inside the envelope, on another piece of unlined paper, was a list of names, addresses, and brief descriptions. I took it out, unfolded it, and began to read.

ALLIES AND ENEMIES

1. Jasper Miles, PH.D., Buffalo Bill historian, Parkinson Library on grounds of Circus World Museum. (There only the first Monday through Wednesday of every month. He divides his time among the various B. B. museums.) Please be careful!
2. Rolf Schniderwind, farmer. You met him. He will supply you with food and water when you are ready. He was the first ally to meet your brother.
3. Charlotte Klabunde and Lorraine Hotz (twin sisters), co-owners of Stetson's General Store in Baraboo — 16 Main Street. They are volunteers down at the circus and knew your brother from his time spent there. They were the second people to welcome him.
4. Ms. Jane Reardon, MLS, head librarian of the Baraboo Public Library. She was the first woman to have sexual relations with your brother and the second to bear him a child. She has much power and knowledge.
5. Judd Barkin, aka Squeaky the Clown, Circus World Museum. He lives in the second-to-the-last trailer on the left side in the staff trailer park next to the big top. He was the first to befriend your brother at Circus World.
6. Daniel "Chappy" Lewis-Clark, city dump attendant. The dump is located off Route 113 on Manchester Road south of town. Of all the allies, he spent the most time with your brother. He has much to tell.
7. Gino Crivello, tattoo artist, 101 Main Street, Baraboo. He fished with your brother. He also gave him the spectacular tattoos.

8. Karina Romanoff, aerial performance artist, Circus World Museum. She lives directly across from Judd Barkin's trailer on the right side of the trailer park. She was the third woman, and the only ally other than myself to enter Wakdjunkaga's lodge. She was the first to bear his child.

9. Willam "Billy" Czerniejewski, band director, Circus World Museum. He lives in the first trailer on the right. He was there the first night Wakdjunkaga joined our people in celebration.

10. Susan Green, ph.d., resident botanist at the Leopold Shack, 671 State Street, Madison, Wisconsin. She was the last woman to meet your brother and ultimately bear his child. She inspired him with music.

What a list. The names, the professions. I tried to picture what these people looked like. *Czerniejewski* — how was it even pronounced? Women. Lovers. Children. How could it have been true? I sat mulling over all of this, and then, with a start, I remembered the journals.

The buffalo head above the fireplace was eying me, wondering why I was taking so long. I grabbed one of the folding chairs from the card table, placed it on the hearth, put a foot up on one of the chimney stones, and hefted down the bust. It was easily fifty pounds. Charlie must have cemented two iron hooks into the chimney just to hold the head, because screwed into its thick leather neck were two large eye hooks.

Indeed there were twenty-six Penway composition notebooks held in the cavity — like buried treasure. Each had the same speckled black-and-white cover with NAME, SCHOOL, and GRADE written on it. Next to NAME Charlie had filled in the dates that the journals had recorded. Each book represented about two months' worth of entries. Beside SCHOOL he had numbered the journals. I took them out and thumbed through. They were all filled with writing. Charlie's neat, cursive script, small and tight, filled up every page in every book except the last one.

With trembling hands I laid them all out on top of the card table, stacked in two high columns, and stood back to look at them, shaking all over. It was an impressive sight. One person had filled up all those volumes with words! Seeing them stacked there, it hit me full force — Charlie's flight had not been a desperate, suicidal impulse as everyone had perceived it to be, but rather an Olympian pilgrimage. The journals proclaimed this. Then Rightpath's warning to read just one book at a time lest the journals be discovered by the wrong people rang a bell in my skull — McNutt. Quickly, I replaced all but the first book in the buffalo and remounted that beastly head with much effort. I stoked the fire, poured myself a tall glass of water, settled into the comfortable chair, and began to read.

SEVEN

The Journals

Tears streamed down my cheeks with each passage I read. Written in a strange, second-person voice, the journals sang a song of self-discovery, self-doubt, self-love. And the song grew, progressing in wisdom, from that of a frightened child at the onset — lost, unsure, confused — to that of a man infinitely wise, boldly defiant, harmoniously focused. I was consumed with the words and images. The tears began with the second half of the very first entry, dated September 24, 1997 — the day Charlie had disappeared almost five years before.

> One step from horror, two steps from happiness. You keep on walking even though your mind is falling through an abyss. It disorients you. You feel you will go insane, lose control, never find . . . never find . . . what is it you're looking for? What are you looking for? Is it solid ground? Some back pasture of your mind where there is peace, where there is security, where there is a reality that makes sense? You separate yourself from your own mind, don't you? How can you be real and it not? Nothing is real, yet how can you deny it's not? You try. That keeps you sane, the trying. But then it catches up with you and you panic and you swirl inside your mind, growing more hysterical as you spin. You want to scream. You want to

die. But you live. You come close to losing control of your mind, but you regain control, or a semblance of it. Then again, like Sisyphus, you repeat and repeat the same mania over and over again, up the hill and back down. This thought brings more anguish. The repetition. The thought of having to face it again and again and again . . . You know that the mind is an abyss that can't be escaped, a mountain that can't be surmounted. But you try. Panic attacks! Panic attacks for the rest of your life. The horror!

So you run away. Why do you run away? Do you think you can walk it off like a drunk? What about your Xanax pills? Do you truly believe you will find that back pasture? What if you meet a crowd of people? What if you are forced to be around an audience, and then you panic? You're worried about that. So worried your stomach aches. But now you feel that the truth, deep down, is that you have run away in order to spare your fellow man the sight of a person scaring himself to death. You'll die soon, you're thinking. Writing now in your book like Krishnamurti, it is as if you need a way to prove to yourself that you are sane, that you are real, that you are separate from your fears, that you are in control. By chronicling every thought, every action, you think you will be able to negate the disorder antistrophically. "To be aware without introspection." Thought is the enemy. Ha ha ha! But you're always thinking about it. Always thinking about panicking. Except before when you had that thought about Prokofiev's opus 67, "Peter and the Wolf," the instrumentation, how your life right now sounds like that. You could hear it and see it:

The bird is a flute
The duck is an oboe
The cat is a clarinet
Grandfather is a bassoon
The wolf is three French horns
The hunters are kettledrums and a bass drum
And Peter is the strings

But instead of the wolf, your mind is the three French horns, and Peter isn't Peter, but you; and he's not three strings but one lone cello. The horror is that there are no hunters. And there's no bird or duck or cat or grandfather either. The only thing you've got is your pen and your book and your pocket trumpet against the hysterical drone of your own mind aka the wolf — like Peter's pop gun. Ha ha ha. Good luck, soldier! Yes, the night is very dark. But you've got to stop writing. Better to keep on walking; write it all down later. Good thing you brought lots of changes of underwear.

The inner voice that spoke in the journals was like a resident antagonist of the mind, an in-your-face psychologist, constantly pointing out his fears, repeating his thoughts, and reflecting on his emotions. I came to see as I read that this second-person technique had the right effect. It was working. Something was happening to the entries as a result of the voice. Fewer fears were being pointed out as the days and weeks went by. More activities, more creative ideas were developing. The new life with its infinite variety of sights and experiences and personalities was forcing out of the mind all the fear, all the sickness. In no time at all Charlie's world was full, romantic, heroic. And as I read, the list of characters provided by Rightpath serendipitously traipsed into his life, one right after the other, like characters in a play. They were the bird, the duck, the cat, the grandfather, and the hunters absent that first night. In no time the sound of his lone cello blossomed into a magnificent symphony, while the panic atrophied to an occasional tweet. But I'm getting ahead of myself.

Charlie walked to his new life. He followed Route 12 from Illinois all the way to the Wisconsin River, almost nonstop, not eating a thing for four days. He walked a hundred miles. Upon reaching that river, he turned east for some reason onto Route 188 until he came upon the ferry at Merrimac, the same one I had taken the day before. Charlie crossed the river there and wound around the hills, walking first east, and then back west again toward Baraboo, as if he were being called back by some force or voice. He managed to find himself on County W, which is where he came upon the ridge and the ancient Indian grounds and, ineluctably, his home. It was on the fourth day that he finally came to rest. It was on the fourth day that Charlie had his epiphany.

SEPTEMBER 27, 1997

Why are there two realities — the dreaming state and the conscious state? Why would God do that? What's the point? The two realities encourage division within the self, creating separate entities — which is the whole problem. You thought about this for a long time as you walked. You looked in the Krishnamurti book and you couldn't find the part about dreaming. Dreaming is half of life, yet it is not pondered or considered nearly enough. Then you began to think about your dreams. The thought of your dreams filled you with confidence. You realized that you are never afraid in your dreams; you don't suffer panic attacks while dreaming.

You'd been walking and thinking a long time without

noticing anything. When you looked up, you saw the field full of geese. You were drawn to them. There must have been fifty or more. They looked almost like cattle with their swollen bodies out there in that field. And the way the rays of the sun streamed down on them through a break in the clouds was wondrous. That's when that song came into your head. It was like the Prokofiev's opus 67 from the previous night, but it was happier; clownish even. Of course you hadn't had a bite to eat in four days. So weak. You'd walked through the night with no sleep. But you took out your pocket trumpet and played it. You had the notes right there under your fingers, which would indicate you'd played it before. But you still can't place it. Key of C. A kid's song. Two measures repeated, then an octave change. What is it? Where is it from? The geese never moved even though you aimed the bell right at them and gave them a lungful.

Then your eye settled on that tree-covered ridge and what looked like an embankment with soft grass at the base of it, where the trees met the field. The sun was shining on it, too. The spot looked so inviting. It was perhaps two hundred yards away, and you trudged through the muddy soil, past an old farmhouse, until you reached it. You must have had five pounds of mud on the bottom of each shoe by the time you got there. And though you came within a couple of dozen yards of those fat honkers, they never moved. In fact, they watched you, studied your movements as you walked abreast of them, like a gaggle of women in a town square.

You lay on the grassy embankment in the sun. It was soft and warm on that spot. You fell asleep almost immediately and in the process had that dream, the very kind of dream you had been thinking about for hours as you walked:

You were an Indian, covered with tattoos, dressed in a breechcloth. You were lying in the sun exactly where you were sleeping, only you weren't sleeping, you were wide awake, looking at the great expanse of sky above with your arms winged out under your head. You could even feel the heat of your hands radiating through your hair into your scalp. Then, suddenly, from below you, came a scattering of honks. A few at first, then a roar, a deafening cacophony. In the dream you jumped to your feet looking down at the geese, hands on hips, nodding at them as if in approval, as if they were your own flock. The geese looked up at you, and a thunderous chorus of honking ensued as if to acknowledge your preeminence. You became aroused. The honking grew louder. You began to laugh, and your penis grew like Pinocchio's nose. You threw your head back and great guffaws came rolling out.

That's when you woke up. You were laughing when you awoke. You've never done that before in your life, woke up laughing, and with an erection to boot. Up above you, darkening the sky, the geese in flight — their white, swollen underbellies undulating; their long necks like penises; their streamlined, paintbrush wings outstretched as they flew overhead. You felt like you could have reached up and touched them. You felt them pulling you upward. Their wings made a whistling sound, like tiny birds chirping, between the honks. The world was filled with their ululations and chirps and clouded over with their bulbous bodies and tubular necks. It literally took your breath away. You lost yourself in their flight.

There was immortality in it all, like wind, like ocean, like a child being born.

Then suddenly you were alone on the spot, lying on the ground looking up at where they had been. That's when the thought came back to you about the two consciousnesses. You felt something new, something very positive, light, free, and, yes, even hopeful. You kept trying to dispense with it, but it wouldn't go away. Hope. You weren't sure if you could define it, exactly, but then after thinking about it for a long while, you could. You understood that there is a moment between waking and dreaming — a transition point between dreaming and waking — where both realities meet. It's just an instant, no more. But you felt it. You still heard it in your head. An instant where dream meets consciousness, and consciousness concedes to dream that it would rather continue to dream even though it knows it can't. That's where the hope lies, in that brief instant, that quick discussion between the two — dream and waking — where dream asks waking what he would do if his conscious reality could remain a dream. That is the moment, the point, the one great question of hope. Because you heard the answer. You heard them agree upon an idea. Your conscious mind said it would rather be up there with the geese in flight, honking and playing your trumpet as you flew. Half goose, half man. Then you looked around at the place where you were lying and realized you had never seen such a beautiful spot in all your life. And you resolved right then to build a hut in the woods above you and live right there, between dream and waking, for the rest of your life.

EIGHT

McNutt Returns

I read the first journal that night, cover to cover. And following the directions given by Rightpath, I dutifully replaced it, when I was finished, back in the buffalo head. As luck would have it, it was a damn good thing I did.

Who knows what time it was — I'd lost track of the world. I was starving, too. I nervously kept stoking the fire and drinking glasses of water. Every hour or so I had to go outside to relieve myself. The wind was making the trees dance. The noises in the night were unnerving. But the air smelled so fresh. I walked around the place studying things. I tried on the raccoon coat. It fit well; a little long on me. What an outfit. I pictured Charlie wearing it. I read the Blake poem three times, and the e. e. cummings poem about Buffalo Bill. Charlie must have felt that the entire world was talking directly to him. Perhaps when the world is completely in focus, it is.

Rightpath's books were on the card table. A red one called *The Trickster* with a three-headed animal on the cover — one of the heads was a rabbit — struck my eye. I took it back to the big chair by the fire and again began to read. Amazingly, I had been reading the journal for hours and hours, and now here I was reaching for another book without the slightest sense of fatigue. Rightpath was right; all you need to do is fast for a few days to get some good reading done.

Peyote is a hard drug, and its effects are not easily distanced from the mind and body. The book that I was reading had something to do with it as well, and before too long I slipped off into a dream world. I remember the last dream I had, just before I was rudely awakened.

Little Hare found himself in bed with a beautiful woman. Or many women. They kept changing. One after another, their faces changing while he made love to them. He was staring into the dark eyes of the last of his paramours, who was lying on a bed of white feathers. The eyes were sparkling and changing like a kaleidoscope. Hypnotizing. Suddenly there was a stirring, then a shaking, then a roaring. Little Hare became distracted, but still he stared at the eyes. The eyes began to grow dull, then gray, sad, flat. The woman's face transformed from beautiful to brutish . . .

Standing in front of me, staring down at me with his deadpan eyes, was Detective McNutt.

"Detective McNutt, I, ah . . ." I rose from the chair, *The Trickster* falling to the floor. It was disquieting, to say the least, to think that McNutt had been there without my knowing it, trying to insinuate himself between me and my dreams. I stood blinking down at him. He said nothing, but his expression told me I was a suspect again. The silence was very uncomfortable, but I fought through it. Not being the first to speak was the McNutt game, and I could play as well as he could now.

"You never called about the body. I was wondering where you were and what was going on," he said phlegmatically, disappointed he'd lost our little contest.

"Oh, uh, yeah." Like a schoolkid, my first impulse was to make up an excuse. But then Rightpath's words came flooding in. "Can you believe it? I totally forgot to call you."

He gave me a look. "What *have* you been doing, Mr. Siconski?" I was being interrogated.

"Reading."

"Reading?" McNutt took a dramatic look around, a glaring, suspicious look. He walked over to the card table. The other Radin book was there, as was the list of names, spread out and bent up like a paper boat. He slowly picked it up and began to read. I felt violated and angry. I thought of the journals and how astute Rightpath had been in advising me to put them away — for this very reason. "Where did you get these names?"

"Mr. Rightpath."

"That Indian was here?"

"Yes."

"Inside the house?"

"Yes."

"Damn it! He's not supposed to be. This hut is off limits to everyone. It's evidence," he growled. "Reading . . . for two days, huh?" Now the words were quite accusatory. He put the list back on the tabletop and walked closer to me. "I talked to Mr. Schniderwind this morning. He told me you left your car in his driveway on Monday about noon, two days ago, and haven't been back to it since. What's going on, Mr. Siconski?"

"I don't understand your question."

"What are you doing here?"

"What do you think I'm doing here?"

The eyes grew noticeably beady. I knew deaf people who would have taken this facial assault the same way a hearing person would react to a punch in the mouth. McNutt stood for a long while, glowering, then he suddenly looked away, walked over to the dream-catcher that still lay on the floor, picked it up, and turned it around in his hand. It was a symbolic act. It said, *I own this place, and for the time being, I own you.* He put the dream-catcher down on the table, then his eyes leaped up and dove into mine like succubi. I held my ground and stared back. It seemed like an infinity before he spoke. "I want you out of here today. This hut is supposed to be closed off. It's evidence in a murder case. You can't stay here."

"Yes he can!" From the door came the low, familiar rumble of Oscar Rightpath, who marched in, eyes on fire.

"I've told you to stay out of here," McNutt snapped. He turned and walked to block the Indian's way.

"No sir, it is I who advised *you* to stay out of here." Rightpath didn't slow his stride, and in two steps he was within inches of McNutt's porcine countenance. He came to a stop like a gymnast sticking a landing, half a head taller than the puffy little white man. "Now, I've said this once before to you, sir, and I'll say it for the last time — until you provide me with a document from your government, a very official document, giving you bullying rights over our land, you can't come in here. And if you do, I'll contact our lawyer, and you know how he likes to do things fast, just the way you white people do things." The two men stood eye to eye and toe to toe. It was a powerful image: the lily-white poppin' fresh doughboy and the one-armed mystic. The yin and the yang. There was a long moment of tingly anticipation. No one moved; each man stood his ground. The burning black eyes versus the well-practiced flat affect. Once again, red versus white. But what a difference a genocide makes! The normally incontestable edifice of police blue wavered unsteadily in the body of McNutt, then stepped back and away from the sacred Native American. Rightpath had won the round. The inviolable rights of the Native Americans loomed too high for even the long arm of the law to reach around.

McNutt began to storm out of the room, but when he got to

the door he spun back around to face us. He opened his mouth, raised the index finger of his right hand, and pointed at me menacingly: "You better come and get your brother's body. We've kept him on ice long enough." The eyes gloated. He was not leaving without a little piece of victory. "Do it tomorrow or we'll dump him in the street." Then the eyes flashed, recalling again the ignominious defeat he had just suffered. There was great rage in them. There was something pitiful yet desperate about him. The arm fell limp to his side, and with a disrespectful push, he went out the door and walked off.

"The truth, Washchinggeka, he doesn't like it." Then Rightpath pointed at the Gary Larson cartoon of the young Buffalo Bill being teased by three buffalo. "That was him as a kid. The cartoonist was right: Violence is the end result of teasing."

I walked to the door, then out and around the lodge to see if McNutt was still there, sneaking around to listen in. No, he was marching down the slope toward the river, that big butt moving in all directions at once. It was a gray day outside, wet and chilling. I went back in and asked Rightpath about the two bodies he had mentioned the day before. "Have they found them yet?"

"Yes, this morning. It will take a few days for them to make the connection."

"Does McNutt suspect — "

"Not yet. Here is a phone." He withdrew a cell phone from his pocket. It didn't seem right that he would be carrying around that kind of technology. My look must have communicated my impression, because Rightpath said, "We do not reject all inventions. Call your sister. Tell her what's happened. Tell her the truth."

"About what? Buffalo Bill?"

"No. About what you want done with the body. You know that much by now. If you don't get that body out of there by tomorrow, that man will dump your brother in the street, there's no question. Do you have some money? Money will make anything possible."

"Not enough, unless I sell the car."

"Call your sister."

That's when I called.

(I tried to explain everything. It was confusing, I know. But I did manage to convince you that I needed a little more time to figure it all out and, of course, some money to keep the body fresh. You consented. Then you told me about the girls. It was my turn to be confused, nonplussed.)

I hung up and returned the phone to Rightpath.

"You will have to pay them to keep the body there," he admonished.

"Yes, I know. I will. She's sending money."

"Things are moving very fast, Washchinggeka. You must be on your guard and be very careful, but you must move fast as well. Miles, your brother's nemesis, is leaving later today to return to Denver. His name is at the top of the list. You must go talk to him. He holds the most vital information for you. Your brother's primary mission involved eliminating the glorification of the shows — the Wild West shows. You'll see. He is at the Parkinson Library behind the museum. Go talk to him. Hear it from him firsthand. But don't eat."

"I've got to go to the police station. What if they don't allow me to keep him there another day?"

"Money allows for many things."

"But how long can we keep the body there? We'll have to move it eventually."

"You'll know soon. I have to go to Black River Falls for a religious gathering. I will be gone until Sunday. My cousin will take my place. He knows to come here if there is any trouble."

"Do you expect any trouble?" He didn't answer. "But what if

they come here asking about those two bodies? What do I say? I can't tell the truth — that they were chasing me around in a dream and I was a rabbit and they tried to follow me and drowned."

He laughed. "No, you can't say that. You will figure it out when the time comes, Washchinggeka. Remember, don't eat for another two days."

"Doughnut?"

"I don't understand?"

"Sounded like you said *doughnut.*"

NINE

Pinch, Zen Shqueeze, Like So!

fter Rightpath left, I jogged down to old man Schniderwind's house. I knocked loudly on the back door, and almost immediately his wizened old face appeared in the window, sporting a warm smile.

"Coom in," he said.

I was happy to see that smile. After what McNutt had said I was afraid that I might have angered him for being so inconsiderate with the car. "Just came to apologize for keeping my car in your driveway. I got so engrossed in my brother's things up there, I kind of forgot about the rest of the world for a couple of days."

"Nach, no problem. Zat leedle fat one find you?"

"Yeah."

"You vant eat somezing?"

"No thank you. I . . . I was wondering if it would be all right to park the car here for a couple more days. I . . . I want to finish with my brother's things, and it will take some doing."

"Sure, sure. No problem. You keep it parked as long as you vant. Vhat you eat up zere?"

He was really pressing me about the food. My stomach was growling like a junkyard dog. "Oh, there were some cans of tuna and stuff, I'm fine."

"Vhat? Charlie don't eat zings from za can. He had no cans tuna zere."

"No no, I brought them just in case." I made up one little white lie and it ricocheted back and hit me hard. *The truth!* Rightpath's words mocked me.

"Hmm, you look very pale. Let me get you some soup."

"No no, really."

"You vant milk? Bring back up zere to za vigvam? You can milk za cow? I have to vait for my son coom to milk her. I can't bend down to do zat now. Poor Eva she sits and vaits too long."

"I can do that," I offered.

"You sure? No, it's ask too much."

"Really, it's no problem. I'd like to, as a matter of fact."

"Za bucket is out zere in za barn hanging next to her. You sure you know how milk za cow?"

"Yes, I think so."

"Vatch your feet, don't be like your brozer."

"Yeah, pinch, then squeeze, right?"

"Zat's right." He laughed. "You know."

My stomach growling, my bloodshot eyes blinking in the brightness of the sky-blue day, I walked out to the barn laughing to myself. I had simply reiterated the old man's words. I'd heard the story from him, and the night before I'd read about it in the journal. It was the fifth entry, in fact.

> You decided to walk up to the house first thing in the morning and inquire about the land, and if need be propose a rental price. You were prepared to offer all the money you had.
>
> . . . He's an old German, about eighty, maybe older. Mr. Schniderwind. What a terrific accent! "Pinch, zen shqueeze, like so." He lives alone in that farmhouse with his little dog Ziggy, a schnauzer. He was standing outside in the back by the barn as if he'd been waiting for you all

morning. Five days you hadn't eaten and he fed you breakfast just like that. He took one look at you and could see right away that you were hungry. He knew. Tears rolled down your cheeks as you bit into that crusty old roll with butter and then slopped up the eggs with it. "Vhy you cry?" he asked. "Allergies," you lied. Food! Glorious food! Oliver was right.

. . . He needs help around the farm, he told you. In fact, he thought his son had sent you over to help around the place. He said he'd pay you four dollars an hour. You agreed you'd do it, but only if you could sleep up on top of the ridge, in the woods. That was your one condition. He said the land wasn't his, it was Indian ground, protected by the government. He supposed you could pitch a tent up there and nobody would complain. He said he never saw anyone go up there. He offered you a room in his own house. You didn't want that.

Then he gave you a bucket to milk the cow. The cow's name is Eva. What a pretty cow she is. Eyes like a woman. She smells so exotic, so raw. Manure is like a salve that washes away panic. You like it. You tried to milk her but you didn't know how. Then she stepped on your foot. Ouch! *Sacre bleu* it hurt. He saw you there on the ground holding your foot in your hands. He seemed really annoyed by that, and for a moment you thought he might rescind his offer. Then he showed you how — "Pinch, zen shqueeze, like so." What a terrific accent. "Take za teat, see, zen pinch, zen shqueeze, like so." The words are musical. All day long now you heard the words, "Pinch, zen shqeeze, like so." They, too, wash away the bad thoughts. You wrote a poem:

Pinch, zen shqueeze, like so!
That's all you need to know
To milk a cow
To forget the now
Pinch, zen shqueeze, like so!

SO I, TOO, milked the cow, Eva. And the old man was very pleased when I came back with a bucketful of milk.

"You take zat now, for yourself."

"I have to go into town. I'll come back for it later, if that's okay?"

"Sure sure. You come back later and ve eat dinner togezer."

"No, I have dinner plans. But maybe tomorrow . . . no, Thursday," I did the math in my head — two plus one is four . . . no, two plus two is four.

"Okay. You be careful." I turned to go, then did a double-take. Why had Mr. Schniderwind said that? I opened my mouth to ask, but something told me to eat the thought. There was probably nothing to his remark. Still, as I walked out to my car, I wondered if the old German knew about all the Buffalo Bill stuff, too. Or was he just saying that to be nice?

TEN

Professor Miles

It was nine o'clock when I arrived at the Parkinson Library on the grounds of the Circus World Museum. There was just one car parked out in front of the place, a white Cadillac El Dorado, about a 1998, with a hood ornament — a bucking bronco. I parked directly behind it.

The library building was made of cream-colored brick, with rounded walls at the entrance decorated with opaque block glass in art deco style. An ample building for a one-subject library. Inside it was not at all what I had expected. Where were the ten-by-ten-foot circus posters? the artifacts? the clown costumes hanging from the walls? It wasn't circusy in the least. Instead it was angular, brightly lit, with nothing on the walls but a few promotional flyers tacked to a little bulletin board in a corner. All of the books fit neatly in four seven-foot-high by ten-foot-long shelves on the south wall. The reading area, in the very middle of the room, was composed of four dark brown, veneered rectangular tables. The rest was a motley assemblage of file cabinets, a turntable, and a stack of old record albums, with a reel-to-reel magnetic tape player next to it, all lined up against the walls. The vast majority of the interior of the library wasn't about books and tables at all but rather offices and desks, separated from the reading area by a long countertop. The countertop separator was wide, more than an arm's length across, and it cut the room in half, from wall to glass partition. The glassed-in area on the north side took up about one full quarter of the interior, the same amount as the reading area. It housed the private offices.

Two women sat at desks behind the long counter, working busily.

I strolled in with a knowing look, pretending to be focused on a particular volume, trying hard not to look too conspicuous. There was a section on just about anything circus related — clowns, animals, contortionists, fire eaters, aerial artists, freaks, Annie Oakley, the Ringlings, Barnum and Bailey, Buffalo Bill. I stopped there to thumb through a book or two. I studied a picture of the man mounted on a white horse. It was called *Grande Finale* — a black-and-white photograph of COLONEL WILLIAM FREDERICK CODY, AKA BUFFALO BILL, SHORTLY BEFORE HIS DEATH. Little mounds of gooseflesh appeared on my arms — it was the same man I had seen in my dream as the Hare. I stared for a long time and began to feel faint, confused, physically drained. How could this be? I took a deep breath, replaced the volume, then went over to investigate the wide file cabinets.

They were picture files. Interesting stuff. I read the title of one drawer — SIDE SHOWS. Inside were photographs of all manner of beings *sui generis* — the Ubangis (the people with the plate-lips), Sausage Man, bearded women, fat women, rubber men, giants, and more.

Out of the corner of my eye I saw him. He came bounding out of one of the back rooms and walked down the small hall right toward me, behind the plate glass, not fifteen feet away. He was short and swollen, a perfectly round little man, with puffed red-apple cheeks, jet-black hair slicked back, a balding pate, and a shiny forehead reflecting a round globe of light. He wore a light brown, western-style three-piece suit with a thin black bolo tie knotted with a silver medallion. He looked oily, as if he had a difficult time keeping his body from secreting grease. My first impression of him was that he resembled an old-time mountebank getting ready to sell snake oil from the back of a covered wagon. And the way he walked — leaning way back on his heels, his legs far out in front of the rest of him — was almost cartoonish. I watched him approach the women at their desks and speak loudly to them in a rather theatrical manner. The voice was stentorian, pompous — Mr. Micawber, but with a twang.

"Just wanted y'all to know that I got a call from the sheriff's department. Apparently two men were found dead, drowned in the Wisconsin River, and one of them had a ticket stub from the Cody Museum in his pocket. I'm goin' down there to find out what it's all about."

Something told me that now was the time to strike. I strode up to the counter. "Are you Professor Miles?"

The little round man turned and looked at me with a squint, trying to place my face. He had a porcine nose that wiggled as he spoke. "Yes?"

"My name is Leslie Siconski. You knew my brother Charlie. I was wondering if you had a few minutes to talk to me about him."

The sharp, beady little eyes grew larger; the snout twisted. He had known Charlie all right. For all his attempts to feign ignorance of the name, his antipathy toward it was too strong to hide. I had taken the little butterball by surprise. There was almost a growl in his voice when he spoke. "Charlie? You mean Crazy Charlie? The one they found dead a couple of months back?" His tone was condescending, disrespectful.

"Yes sir."

"Why do you want to talk to me?" His manner suggested that Charlie wasn't important enough to waste his time on.

"Because I was told you knew him."

"Who told you that?"

I paused. I couldn't think of what to say until I heard Rightpath's voice once again — *Tell the truth!* "Gentleman named Oscar Rightpath."

Miles wrinkled up his brow, indicating that he did not recognize the name. "Many people knew Charlie." His accent seemed to flatten out. Perhaps it was affected. "Barbara here knew him, too. And Jenny as well." He was nodding at the women behind him. He was a real charmer. "I'm sorry, I'm just a little distracted. Just got a strange phone call. I need to go down to the sheriff's department in town. Perhaps we can talk after that."

"As a matter of fact, I have to go to the station myself," I pushed.

"Is that right? Here in town?"

"Yes sir. Believe it or not, my brother's body is still at the morgue. We have some family controversy about the plot and, uh, we need the body to remain there another week. But if you like, we can go down there together in my car, and I can ask you a couple of questions on the way."

"Better yet, why not I take you? I just hope they'll be quick about it, and I won't have to keep you waitin'."

"Oh, I'm in no hurry today, sir. That would be fine."

"Fine. Then let me just grab a few things."

He waddled back behind the glass. After just a moment he came back out holding a cowboy hat and joined me in the public area.

WE LEFT THE library and got into his white, two-door deluxe El Dorado with the bronco on the hood and the plush red-leather interior.

"That yer stallion behind mine?" he asked, giving the 2000 DeVille the eye.

"Yeah. Inherited it from my father."

"He's got good taste. Nothing like a Cadillac out on the road."

He slid into the front seat with an *umpf,* removing his Stetson at the last possible second. I got in on the passenger side. "Crazy Charlie's brother. You ain't crazy, too?" He laughed as he started up the car. It was a nervous, jerking laugh. It struck me as a mechanism he used, defensive but at the same time quite offensive.

His seat was lifted to its fullest height and jammed in close to the wheel so that his short legs could reach the pedals. He pulled out onto the road with a roar of horsepower and then drove leisurely along. In no time his southern drawl, much too twangy, began to grate on me. "Younger, older? No, look at you, yer a good deal younger. Yer just a b — kid." For a second there I thought for sure he was going to call me a boy.

"Younger by five years. I'm thirty-five."

"Well, let me tell you, goddamn it, we had some fun with yer brother. Yes sir, he was a pain in the ass, no doubt about that, and not playin' with a full fifty-two, but we sure did have some fun with him around here. He sure did liven up the place. Rest in peace."

"What do you mean, had some fun?" Miles's face lost its felicity at that question — as if someone had kicked him in the shin.

"Well, hell, with all due respect, he wasn't all there, yer brother. He was psycho. But you know that. He'd come in there with them tattoos all over himself and them feet o' his. What size you packin'?" He looked down at my feet. "Not the same as his."

"No. I'm only a twelve."

"Shit, what was his size, eighteen?"

"Sixteen."

"Magnanimous! That Charlie, he'd say he was gonna get us throwed out of the circus business. Said we didn't have no rights bein' attached to the circus. Said the Colonel himself wasn't nothin' more than a cowboy Nazi — 'a comic-book Eichmann' was his very words. He could sure get it goin', yer brother Charlie."

"Why do you think he felt that way?"

"Know egg-zactly why he felt that way. I'll tell you why right now. You listenin'? When yer brother wanted to play, he went all out, yes sir he did. He had his toys all lined up in row — tattoos and deerskins, canoes and little trumpets. Yep, he wanted to play cowboys and Indians with me in the worst kinder way. He was the Indian, and I was the cowboy. But I just wasn't gonna oblige him, you know what I mean? That's what really got his goat. That's what got him goin'. I didn't wanna play." I could tell by the tone of his voice that he had given this explanation a few times before, and each time he repeated it he believed the words more.

"But don't you believe he was hostile to the Wild West shows because he didn't think they belonged with the circus?" In his first journal he had spoken about the Wild West shows being, for all intents and purposes, totally unconnected to the circus.

"Exhibits."

"Exhibits? What do you mean?"

"The Colonel didn't like to call them Wild West *shows*, he called them *exhibits*."

"Oh. I see. Sorry."

"Well, I'll tell you, Jerry —"

"Leslie."

"— I was there one day he came in. The girls tell me he was nosin' around the Wild West books fer hours. Readin', studyin', even listenin' to some of the old records. He had that musical penchant. 'Course, you know. Then he came up to the counter and started askin' about the Wild West. He'd seen some pictures in the files there. Wanted to know specifically about the Indians in it — Was they real? Where'd they all come from? What was they doin' in the exhibits? I happened to be out front and he started askin' me, and I told 'im they was real Lakota Sioux. Some of 'em fought Custer at the Little Big Horn, and some even fought at the battle of Wounded Knee. Told him about the nineteen braves the Colonel sprung from Fort Sheridan, Illinois, who'd been locked up after the Knee. But he couldn't understand how the Colonel got the Indians to reenact it — their own losin' battle and all that. 'The Colonel was that great,' I told him. 'He was a great friend of the Native American, paid 'em handsomely, too. Like an older brother. Hell, the exhibits preserved the culture and values of the clans just at the time when the bureau was outlawin' the Sun Dance, cuttin' their hair, puttin 'em in knickers, and then sendin' 'em off to boardin' schools.' Yer brother didn't want to hear none o' that. He said he thought they was all massacred there at the Knee. No, I told him that it was a real, honest to goodness battle. Then he started askin' ignorant questions about how they worked it out. How they put on a circus with the Wild West going at the same time. He was confused on that point. Didn't understand how it was at all. 'Did they have different arenas set up?' he wanted to know. That's when I had to set him straight. The circus and the Wild West wasn't attached, wasn't the same enterprise. He didn't know that. They was two separate entities most of their lives. Oh, at the end there, Sells Floto joined the show, or I should say the Wild West joined the circus, in 'aught-seven, but that was toward the end when things was gettin' tight. It wasn't really the same, anyway. But that's the information that got him all riled up. Since the Wild West wasn't related to the circus, he couldn't understand why we was here at Circus World, why the Wild West had an exhibit at the circus. See, I looked at Charlie as a purist. I could understand that about him, God rest his soul. I like that kinder enthusiasm in a man. All or nothin'. That's the kinder person I am, too. But he was just a tad bit too zealous, you know what I mean?"

We were almost at the county courthouse, and I still had many more questions. One in particular I couldn't help but ask: "Wounded Knee? I thought that *was* a massacre and not a battle?"

He laughed. "See you been readin' the same books as yer brother. No, that was an honest to goodness battle." The snout on him twisted strangely, and the beady eyes shot out a thin beam of light.

"Did Charlie ever say what he was going to do, exactly, about the Wild West sh — exhibits?"

"Sure did. Nary every time I was there, said he'd come back one day and buy the whole exhibit up, every lock, stock, and barrel, put it in a pile, an' burn it up. Oh, he'd get it goin', I'll tell you. He'd get it goin' an' we'd about split a side pretendin' we was worried. He was somethin' else, yer brother. I'll tell you. But get this right, he was a good circus man. He had that quality. You ask 'em down there at the trailers, every one of 'em will tell you he had it. He had the circus gift. Crazy as a coot, but he had the circus gift in 'im."

Miles pulled in right in front of the Al Ringling Theatre, in almost the exact same spot where I'd parked a few days before. He snorted, rocked once, twice, then struggled out of the car, his pudgy face turning brilliant red. He flipped his coat together, buttoned it, looked up at the marquee, placed his Stetson on his head, and stood for a moment as if posing for *Life* magazine. "You want to see a movie theater, now, you want to pop yer head in there. That's what I call regal. That's the kinder place where the crowned heads of Europe take in a show."

"I haven't seen it yet. When they open later today, I'll take a look. Apparently my brother liked to go there. He mentioned it —" the words about the journals almost snuck out, but I caught them just in time — "or rather one of the people who hung out with my brother mentioned that he liked to go there."

"I see." Miles could tell there was something off center in my answer, and he gave a little cough.

We crossed the street and entered that imposing edifice. The professor was indeed a charlatan — the style, the voice, his whole presentation. Always talking, always in control of the conversation. He walked up to the dispatch window, not even waiting for the woman to finish what she was doing. "I'm Dr. Miles here to see Detective McNutt. He called me this morning, something about a body with a ticket stub and a man who looks like Buffalo Bill. I'll tell you, I'll be all-fired mad if that turns out to be the Colonel himself, because I'll have been spreadin' rumors about his bein' dead all these years. Hya hya hya. This young gentleman behind me here has come to make arrangements for his brother's corpse."

I walked up to the window.

"Detective McNutt will be out in a minute, gentlemen," she said, not letting me speak.

We drifted away from the window and looked out across the street at the theater. "How did yer brother die ag'in?" Miles asked, his arms behind his back, rocking on the balls of his feet. I noticed that his stubby little hands each held a ring on the pinkie. I wanted to ask about them but thought better of it, knowing full well the answer would be long and probably not worth the effort.

"They found him dead, frozen to death, on top of the Man Mound, the Indian effigy mound, east of town. Someone had beaten him up pretty badly."

"Is that a fact?" I could tell that Miles knew damn well how Charlie had died.

"He'd been scalped."

"No kiddin'?" Miles's tone was soft, distracted, and insincere.

"Now, don't take this wrong, sir, I'm just asking because all of this is very curious to me. But could there be anyone associated with the Buffalo Bill show who —"

"Exhibit."

"I'm sorry, exhibit. Could there be anyone associated with the Wild West exhibit who would have, perhaps, disliked Charlie enough to want him dead?"

"Don't see who. Detective McNutt asked the same question a few months back. Just me and the girls the only people takin' care of business on this end, and the girls only work for me when I'm in town. Charlie could get us hoppin' mad, rise up our blood pressure, but we knew he wasn't . . . well, knew he wasn't compos mentis, you know what I mean? There just ain't no one else he bothered."

"I —" Before I could get the words out, McNutt burst out of the back in his typical impatient manner. The sad eyes grew wide seeing me there next to Miles.

"How did you find out about this?" he growled.

"I was up talking with Professor Miles."

"Well, I think we might have found your brother's attackers." There was a note of victory in his voice. The tone said, *You might have bumped my fender, but I still own the road.* "We've got a preliminary match on hair samples."

"Really?" I feigned excitement.

"Is that a fact?" Miles broke in. "Now, what's this about a Cody Museum ticket stub?"

McNutt turned to the portly rodomont. His eyes softened immediately. I could tell that McNutt liked Miles, even admired him. The two had obviously struck up a friendship through all this. "You'll be interested to see these two gentlemen, Professor Miles. Like I said, they look like something right out of the Wild West exhibits." Miles must have indoctrinated him, too, about *exhibits.* "If they had a Buffalo Bill impersonator's contest, the blond-haired man we found would get my vote. If you wouldn't mind, I'd like to take you out to the morgue and have you take a look. Like I said, we found just one ticket stub in the man's pocket — no ID, just the ticket from the museum. You're out there in Cody more than you're here. Maybe you'll recognize these guys. They might even have worked for you. Do you have interpreters out at the Cody Museum, people who make believe they're living in the Wild West?"

"Well, sure we do, Detective. Take a gander here! The Colonel and his ilk won the West so's folks like us could walk around and dress up like we do." Laughing, he put his thumbs in his lapel, gave a tug, and dusted off the top of his hat.

"It's a good thing you didn't take that body. We want to run some more tests. There's a bite mark on your brother's arm that we'd like to measure to see if it matches the teeth of one of the two men. It'll take a few days." McNutt was talking to me but looking at Miles.

"Sure, that's fine. In fact, I just came down to make arrangements for the body to stay at the morgue for another week."

"Oh?" McNutt was forever suspicious.

"We've had some family controversy about the burial plot, and I just thought, well, if it's okay . . . I mean, we'd be willing to pay whatever it costs to keep the body there until we clear things up."

"We'll have to talk about that." McNutt turned his eyes on me and studied me carefully, looking for signs of guilt. Finding nothing, he turned back to Miles. "Professor, would you mind driving with me out to the morgue?"

"Actually, I'd prefer to drive myself; you know that about me, Detective. Brigham takes me everywhere I need to go, whether it's down to the corner or up to Lookout Mountain. Besides, my partner here came along with me. We was talkin' about his brother. He's doin' his own investigatin'."

"Really?" McNutt gave me a little scowl as if to say, *What could this idiot possibly know about investigating?*

"He might come see the bodies as well. If they was the ones who killed his brother, he should have a look, too. Maybe he'll recognize 'em. Charlie might've had some enemies from home before he drug himself up to these parts." Miles fancied that he had life completely figured out.

"That would be fine. Mr. Siconski, would you like to come to the morgue with us to view the bodies?" McNutt had to make it official by asking me himself.

I consented. McNutt then held his arms out, motioning for us to file out the door.

WE WALKED ACROSS the street to the wide white El Dorado — Brigham, as he called it. I kept a step behind them, pretending to defer to their authority. From my angle, the two men in front of me were buffoonish. Miles was only an inch or two taller than McNutt, and both were almost a head shorter than me. Side by side, they were a study in obesity. One had flesh on top of flesh — dropsical, grabbable flab; the other swelled like an imitation of stuffed sausage left out at high noon on a summer's day. McNutt with that womanish behind, Miles next to him walking way back on his heels — now *they* were circus.

Miles opened his door and I squeezed into the back, not for a moment considering sitting up front. With a grunt and a *humpf,* the two pudgeballs sat. And off we went.

"Well, can't say as I've had the experience of viewin' a drowned body. Seen many a shot-up body back in graduate school. 'Course, most of what I seen was all skeletons, bones and such, nothin' with flesh still on it. Now, how did these two gentlemen drown, Detective?" He turned slightly to McNutt on his right.

"We don't know. No boat has been found, so we can't say they simply fell overboard. They weren't wearing life jackets. The bodies show no signs of a struggle. But there was a high alcohol content in their bloodstream. Both of them. Just no boat."

"No boat, huh. Well, they wasn't swimmin', was they?"

"No. Water's forty-seven degrees."

Miles guffawed. "Story goes, you know, when the Colonel took the Wild West over to England the first time, they hit some nasty weather out there crossin' the Atlantic. It looked for a while like the boat was gonna go down. All the Indians was gathered in a circle up on deck, makin' a racket, singing the death song to the Great Spirit. They wouldn't put on any life vests. They was like that. Said it was a good day to die, you know, typical Indian fashion. They sat there with the waves crashin' over the sides, singin' the death song. The Colonel come along, he's of course undaunted by such a prospect, stands there for a minute listenin', arms folded across his chest, then he turns to one of the scouts, Parker Doyle, one of his assistants, and says, 'You know, I don't mind them singin', but if they's gonna sing, I wish they'd sing in venison.' Hya hya hya ha. Wish they'd sing in venison." McNutt let loose some horrible wheezing sounds that were his rare laugh. I didn't make a peep. I was convinced that Miles was *miles* deep in apocrypha.

AT THE MORGUE I was amazed to see Rightpath's pickup truck parked in the same spot. But Rightpath wasn't in it; some other man was. I couldn't see who. I was struck by the vigilance of the Ho-Chunk. They were really looking after the body, day and night, and for that reason I resolved to get it buried soon — it wasn't right to have these people standing watch all the time.

The two roly-polies went inside the morgue without even glancing at me. While they huffed and puffed up the stairs, I was trying to see who was in the cab of the truck. I couldn't make out the face; he was too far away, and in the shade of a tree. With growing uneasiness I climbed the steps of the trailer and stood on the threshold of that godforsaken place again, looking in. They were there, side by side, scurrying around excitedly, muttering to one another, opening up two coolers. It struck me as funny: They looked like obese rodents, making strange noises, excited about the possibility of food. I went in.

"Would you look at that!" barked the professor upon unzipping one of the two bags. It was the cooler next to Charlie's. I craned my neck to see. They had the man laid out in full view. "By God, he does look just like the Colonel. Yes indeed sir, I have seen this man, yes I have. Many years ago. His hair wasn't as long. No, he didn't have the goatee and the mustache. He worked at the Lookout Mountain museum in Denver. Haven't seen him in years, come to think of it. Dead ringer for the Colonel. We used him that way back then. Had the dipsomania bad. Difficult to work with, as I recall. What do you suppose he was doin' out here in Wisconsin?"

"We don't know. How about this other man?" McNutt unzipped the bag on top. It was at eye level for those two stubs.

Miles gave a long look, then shook his head. "Nope. He kinder looks familiar, but I can't say as I recognize the face. That big head. Can't place him. Sorry."

McNutt wormed his finger at me. He was like an elementary school teacher calling a student over in the hall. "You recognize this man?"

"Nope." I looked closely, my heart pounding. It was the big-headed man from my Hare vision the other night. My stomach gave a growl. The sight of that bloated, white-gray, dead face suddenly forced the lower part of my stomach up toward my throat. For some reason, the fat fingers and the black fingernails brought back the fear, the anxiety of the chase. I gagged. The room started to spin. I doubled over.

The room moved all around him. Little Hare was spinning fast. He heard echoing voices, faces, explosions going off. He looked up through blurry eyes and saw a big rat and a crooked-toothed 'possum sniffing next to his head. Their whiskers were tickling his nose. He vomited, then hopped away from the two. He felt very ill and crawled

into a ball and lay against the wall. They came back, sniff-
ing and tickling. He ran for the light . . .

The next thing I knew there were three of them there, looking
down at me. The sky was an explosion of geese; a hundred
honkers lit up the day. My head was filled with the sound. The
third man was unfamiliar. It was the man in the pickup truck. It
had to be. He smiled and nodded and talked in a soothing manner over the cacophony of goose music. He had big brown eyes.
"Better now?" he said, rubbing the back of my neck. Then the
voice went Indian. At first I didn't understand it, but then there
came a kind of ringing or clicking noise and the words began to
make sense. "You've got to watch out, Washchinggeka. Don't let
them get that close . . ." was one of his phrases. "Keep them back
. . ." And the last phrase — "Don't eat!" He gave a little pat and
rub to my neck like a corner man sending his boxer back out into
the fray. I shook my head and rubbed my eyes, then looked up.
The man was gone. So was the goose music.

WE WERE BACK in the El Dorado, red leather all around,
driving toward town at an even pace. I had a towel in my lap. The
two up front were discussing the bodies at the morgue, and Miles
was growling about his suit getting soiled. The world outside the
window was moving too fast. I felt very weak and vulnerable.

"Don't you worry, Detective, I'll call my girls in Denver; they'll
have that man's name and we'll have it all in at the kill for you
before the day's over. But not until after we eat." Two beady eyes
glowed in the rearview mirror at me. I felt them even before I saw
them. "Looks like he's been eatin' a green 'simmon. What he needs
is a steak, dagnabbit. Let's take him over to the Village Cafe. They
got a nice buttery steak sandwich there makes me think you folks
here in Wisconsin know a little somethin' 'bout beef."

"Ever eat bison, Professor?" McNutt asked out of the blue.

"Damn right. I prefer it. Leaner, redder than cattle. You can smell the difference even before you sink yer teeth in, it's a richer flavor. Not as greasy, but meatier, grittier. It holds the heat better, more H_2O in it, sizzles loud on the griddle. Mmm, oh yeah, Detective, you got to try it. Yes sir, you ready for a nice steak back there?"

I was hungrier than I ever remember being. Yes I wanted a steak. Damn, I wanted it in the worst way. And I could have eaten it, too. I wasn't hooked on the whole vision quest notion, with the four-day fast and all that stuff. But there was no denying that the world was a different place for me now. Something was happening to me, I could feel it. The journals had something to do with it; so did Rightpath, and so did the two clowns in the front seat. Charlie's life in Baraboo had changed my way of thinking. There was something powerful, something heroic about life that I had never noticed before. Something was beginning to open up inside me, and this opening up was revealing a truth about my own emptiness, my own potential. Oh, all the other stuff about the Hare vision and fasting and Buffalo Bill and all that Oscar Rightpath had told me . . . I wasn't sure of any of it. I didn't disbelieve it, but I didn't exactly believe it either. I was more inclined at this point to think that the peyote I had eaten a couple of days before was responsible for many of my strange experiences. But things were happening so fast that all I could do was sit back and go along for the ride. As Rightpath said, I had to rely on my instincts. "Don't eat!" I'd heard that said three times in a day. My instincts told me to trust what was being said. I certainly didn't trust McNutt or Miles. Not as far as I could throw either one of them. What was most convincing at that moment was the fact that they were very, *very* insistent on buying me a meal, yet I knew that they both disliked me.

"If you wouldn't mind, just take me back to my car. I need to get some rest. I haven't slept well in a couple of days. That's the problem."

"Do I hear right? You turnin' down a steak dinner? The professor's buying." Predictably he referred to himself in the third person.

"Yeah, thanks, but food's not going to do it. That'll make me sicker. Thank you anyway. I think I ate something last night that made me sick."

"Where are you going to sleep? Not back in the wooden tunnel, I hope?" jabbed McNutt.

"Yeah. It's comfortable there. It's not that bad."

"Where are you gettin' food?"

I was tempted to say something snippy, but I held my tongue. "Mr. Schniderwind. He's been very nice."

"They got good fried onion rings over where we're goin', as I remember," went on Miles. My stomach gave a long, loud growl. I made some noise to cover it up. "Don't they have a banana cream pie there, too, Detective? Chocolate on the bottom, nice and crispy? And a big helpin' they give you, too, like you was kin to the man in the kitchen."

"I believe so," answered the detective.

"Think I'll have some of that."

"Me too," said the corpulent cop.

FINALLY WE WERE back at the library. I walked weakly toward my car, and McNutt hollered to me, "What you need to do is come by the station tomorrow and we'll talk about what we're going to do with your brother's body. Come in the afternoon. The tests will take a while." There was a *do-as-I-say* tone to his voice. I nodded in agreement and jumped behind the wheel. I started up the car and looked to my left just in time to see two rodent heads whiz by the driver's side window.

ELEVEN

The Apotheosis

I parked the car a little farther away from old man Schniderwind's house and walked across the field to the lodge. I thought for sure the old German would come out and accost me, so I walked extra quickly, expecting to hear a call from behind. It never came. I was glad of that. The last thing I needed right then was someone else insisting that I eat *somezing*. It was early afternoon, maybe one o'clock.

Back at the lodge I got right to work. I stoked up the fire. Then, with that empty stomach singing like a chorus, I put some water in the pot and boiled it. Fasting is a strange exercise. The mind, full of energy, works twice as fast as normal and all the senses are so open, so sharp, yet the muscles don't work the same. Reaching for a glass is just a little different. The sense of smell is extraordinary. It occurred to me that perhaps the reason animals have such good noses is that they're always hungry. I could smell food cooking from across the county. Hell, I could smell McNutt's and Miles's steak sandwiches.

I had a chill, and hot water helped break that. I drank three cups of steaming water with a little lemon I found in a box on the floor. Next, I got down two journals from the buffalo head. This was what I needed to spend time on — I needed to understand more of what was happening. I was confident McNutt wasn't going to come barging in, not for a while anyway. I sat in the big chair in front of a roaring fire and read.

Many of Miles's words echoed through my frontal lobes — all his swaggering talk about the Wild West *exhibits*, Buffalo Bill, the Indians. The faces of those two drowned men lying on the cooler trays kept reappearing, giving me a vague sense of nausea. It didn't quite fit together — like a puzzle with pieces of a similar size and color on one side, and different-colored and larger pieces on the other. What, exactly, was Charlie doing here? The circus, the Indians, the goose music, the Wild West *shows*? Why was it that he didn't want the Wild West on display? The journals offered answers. I turned to the October 30 entry I'd read the previous night and read it again.

OCTOBER 30, 1997

Wow, you never realized that Buffalo Bill's Wild West show was *not* part of the Ringling Brothers and Barnum and Bailey Circus. And yet they have all that Buffalo Bill memorabilia down there at Circus World. You'd thought the two shows were one and the same thing, but they were completely unconnected. You met the man who runs the Wild West component. A little butterball of a man. Bombastic. He seemed to be the very personification of western expansionism; one who still, perhaps, holds on to the notion that the only good Indian is a dead one. He kept saying, "How the West was *won.*" Kept saying that. Kept talking about the honorable Buffalo Bill. Colonel William F. Cody. The Colonel. Then you started to read the book about him. The Colonel, the honorable Buffalo Bill, admitted to killing 4,280 buffalo. He was discovered sleeping under a wagon by a man named Edward Zane Carol Judson, aka Ned Buntline. Buntline was a swollen drunk of a man; a parttime actor, gambler, Union soldier, accused murderer, head of a political organization called the Know-Nothing party, and dime-store novelist. There's even an eponym, *Buntlinism*, meaning "a rowdy, jingoistic, political doctrine." But the latter profession, dime-store novelist, is what created the American icon Buffalo Bill. You read how Buntline went out West looking for a character to write about. He asked, I think Wild Bill Hickok, if he wouldn't mind being used as the hero of his books, but Hickok shook him off and jokingly pointed to a young blond man sleeping off a bender underneath a wagon. It was William Cody. Buntline gave him the name Buffalo Bill, and the rest became spurious history. He wrote more than four hundred books about Buffalo Bill. Later Buffalo Bill went to Broadway and played himself — badly — on stage. And *that* was how the West was won.

Incredibly, if any one man could be held responsible for the extinction of the buffalo and ultimately the pogrom of the Plains Indians in North America, plus a thousand other concomitant calamities, Buffalo Bill is that person. His job was to kill the buffalo in order to feed the workers on the Transcontinental Railroad. Later, he ran buffalo-hunting expeditions for rich, thrill-seeking easterners called dudes. That was basically the end of the buffalo right there, because it put the idea into everyone's head that going out West and killing buffalo was *très chic*. For thirty years the country was crazy with killing buffalo. Until, of course, there were none left.

But then this Professor Miles said something that rattled against your skull like an iron pipe. He said that the Indians employed by the Wild West shows were real

Indians, and some had even fought at Wounded Knee.
You asked him how that could be. He said that Buffalo
Bill was a great friend of the Indian. He asked and they
came. The Colonel had even sprung some Indians out of
prison after the Wounded Knee battle. But you corrected
him and said you thought it was a massacre, not a battle.
He laughed that off. Laughed!

You talked to the women behind the counter and
asked them about the Indians. You wanted to know if
there were any still alive you could talk to. They told you
about a man, a Ho-Chunk, who lived right in town.
They said his name and address were in the phone book.
They had a picture of him on file. They showed you the
picture. He was a young man, a boy really, when it had
been taken back in 1915. He was dressed in full Indian
regalia. You stared at the photograph for a long time. You
resolved to find his address and pay him a visit.
Rightpath is his name.

Then you went back to the Buffalo Bill book and read
more. A fact struck you. Custer's Last Stand occurred
after Buntline had created the Buffalo Bill character in
his books and the character had become a Broadway hit.
Custer was jealous of all the attention Buffalo Bill was
getting, so he went out to the Little Big Horn with the
hope of eclipsing the fame of the ersatz hero! He suc-
ceeded all right, but not exactly as planned.

The Wild West shows did have a band. And you listened for a long time to the music. Hollywood kept coming to mind. You realized that the Wild West shows are
the father of Hollywood! The blockbusters, the shoot-
'em-up, beat-'em-up mentality . . . it all started with the
Wild West shows. And you read on about Annie Oakley.

She had some dandy udders on her, didn't she!

A poem came over you:

? Bill

Buffalo Bill, your name's all wrong!
You killed buffalo, you didn't just string along.
You should be called Unbuffalo Bill
Or Debuffalo Bill
Or just Kill-the-Buffalo Bill.
But definitely not *Buffalo* Bill!

This journal entry marked the beginning of Charlie's mission — to completely divorce Buffalo Bill's Wild West shows from the circus. After reading this, I understood. Charlie was convinced that the Wild West shows represented a turning point in American history, and perhaps in the world. In these shows, violence became a form of entertainment; the good wholesome fun found by young and old alike at the circus was no longer of interest to people. He called it a kickback to the days of the gladiators and the Colosseum — "the reappearance of that prurient chimera in the human psyche," he wrote some months later. He believed this fascination with violence had far-reaching ramifications, all of them destructive. And Buffalo Bill, or the creation of this character by Buntline and later the *shows* themselves, was representative of this "galloping consumption" (a phrase Charlie used often, borrowed from the obscure moral psychologist William C. Neal) that he saw as the dominant feature of American society. He felt strongly that the Wild West shows had no right to be honored and glorified along with the circus at the Circus World Museum. It became his preoccupation. Toward the end of his life, his passion grew fervid. Skipping all the way to the last journal, I found a passage that described the degree of Charlie's antipathy for Buffalo Bill and his Wild West. Three months before his death he wrote:

> The West wasn't won. It wasn't heroic or splendid, an epic of valiant men and women vanquishing the land and wild heathens in an attempt to further the cause of Christianity or civilization. To the contrary. The West was a race to see which ignoramus could rape, pillage, torture, sodomize, and murder the fastest. And the Transcontinental Railroad couldn't be a better metaphor for that all-nasty penile insertion! . . .

Charlie's feelings about Buffalo Bill and his Wild West shows had reached their full evolution. It was in the last journal that I came upon my favorite Buffalo Bill passage of all. It was a brief one, written a few days after the above. It reminded me of that Gary Larson cartoon, but it was vintage Charlie.

> Do you suppose that B. B. — I mean when he was young, starry eyed, and just starting out his long, bloody, and illustrious career — was ever forced to take a temporary position as, say, hide counter for a leather outfit?

Four days before his death Charlie wrote:

> The show must certainly *not* go on for the Wild West. It must be eradicated in order for the world to heal. Glorifying the genocide of the most harmonious race of mankind is, perhaps, what has made you and everyone else ill. It is the linchpin that holds the wheel of violence and fear in place.

I read and I read, all through the night, skipping months and years. I read three entire journals, and I became intimate with the people on the list — the women, the men, what they did together, how they interacted with Charlie, their likes, their dislikes, their motivations. By the end of the night, I knew that in order to complete Charlie's work, I would have to make the journals, the lifestyle, the thoughts, all of it available to others by publishing it, documenting the entire account in a narrative. My work would be to edit, to expurgate. Just reading the journals wasn't going to be enough for the world to understand. Reading them would be too grueling, too exhausting; readers would miss the message. Rightpath was right: I was the Hare, Washchinggeka, who tidied up after Wakdjunkaga. I had a hell of a lot of work to do.

I REMAINED AWAKE all night reading and thinking, trying to reassure my stomach that all would be okay. Finally, morning came calling me out of the lodge as a blush of pink to the east drifted in from the outside like a bashful neighbor tapping amicably at the door. I had no idea of the time. I recalled a vague promise I had made to old man Schniderwind, grabbed my coat, glanced around the lodge to make sure all was secure, and went down the hill to the barn.

By the time I got there the new day was almost in view. Stratified clouds were stacked like a wrinkled brow on the horizon, reflecting a mounting sun of crimson and gold — a half circle and rising. The world seemed on the verge of blooming, or purging; I couldn't decide which. I filled my lungs with sweet air.

There were no lights on in the old farmhouse as I entered the barn. Eva was there with her big Bambi eyes. She seemed to smile at me and nod her head as if to say, *Yes, finally.* I milked her dry. The way my hand fit around her teats, the way the milk filled and then drained from the veiny udders, the texture of the soft fur around the pink flesh, all the many charms about her dazzled me. I understood why Charlie had fallen in love with milking a cow.

When I was done, I took the bucket over to the house. There were still no lights on. I found a towel, draped it over the top of the bucket, and left it there on the porch so that Mr. Schniderwind could find it. I peeked in the window and saw no movement at all. But the clock on the Formica table read five forty-five. Time had slowed down.

The mud didn't stick to my shoes quite as much as it had a few days before as I trudged back to the lair. What a comfortable, homey place it was. From Charlie's bed I studied the angles of the hut, the feel of it around me, the colors, the warmth. It was like living in the torso of a giant. Truly "organic" architecture. Which made me think of the house that Charlie and I had grown up in. Absurd. Ridiculous! The flat roofline, towering ceilings, "the guiding shapes and forms," blah blah blah. What did Frank Lloyd Wright know about organic architecture? There was Charlie, holed up in that godforsaken museum piece all those years, alone, afraid of the world. No wonder he was afraid. That house! Finally he escaped from it and built himself a truly magnificent structure that flew in the face of all Wright's decorative motifs, his "relations of masses to voids." This was beyond all of that. *This* was a home! *This* was organic!

I read and I read until I could read no more. Toward nightfall I wandered over to the pile of sleeping bags and blankets and lay down. I slept the sleep of the just, and I dreamed a thousand dreams.

Little Hare was in the lodge with his mother. She was very old with gray hair and wrinkles on her face. Her head was bandaged. But she was active, pleasant, caring. She kept scolding him for all that he had done. Together the two tended the fire. Then there was a voice, a loud voice out-side. It was talking to Little Hare.

"Hey you, in there with the old lady, I'm gonna eat you," it said.

"Let's hide under the sleeping bags and blankets," Little Hare suggested to his mother.

Like a loudspeaker, the voice spoke up immediately: "If you hide between the blankets I'll find you and eat you."

Hare was scared. He told his mother that they had to hide in the corner, behind the chair.

The voice again spoke in a tinny tone: "You, inside with the old lady, if you hide behind the chair I'll find you and eat you."

Hare was beside himself with fear. He told his mother that they should somehow get into the fire, hide in the fire, sit under the hot embers.

But again the voice responded: "If you hide in the fire, under the embers, I'll find you and eat you."

Little Hare no longer was afraid. He was furious. He decided to confront the beast. He rushed outside with a shovel but could find nothing, nothing at all. He went back inside and asked his mother if she knew where the thing was. She pointed. "Over there," she said. He went back out and looked in the direction she had pointed and found only a frog.

"So it's you, then?" Little Hare demanded. "What's the big idea scarin' me like that?"

The stupid frog shrugged.

"You talk too much!" Little Hare yelled, and he smashed the frog with the shovel. He wondered how something so small could talk so loud. When he opened its mouth, he saw that it had long teeth like a cat. Little Hare knocked out the

*teeth, took the smashed body back inside, threw it into the
fire, and watched it burn. His mother smiled. She pointed
at his ears. They were long and straight.*
"They are full of blood," she said.

I had many dreams like this during the night. I remember this
particular one because I awoke just after it, thinking there was
someone outside with a megaphone calling my name. I lay awake
for a long time, listening. It was silent. I was certain that there
was someone outside, like the frog, calling my name. I even got
up and went to look. It was a dark night. The sky was full of stars
twinkling happily overhead. All was quiet, expectant. The moon
was a white saucer, round and bright, directly above. The earth
felt canny.

The next morning I awoke at dawn feeling light and new. I
went directly down to the barn and milked Eva. Old man
Schniderwind came in just as I was done. Together we walked
back to the house and into the kitchen. His smile was better than
sunshine. He made boiled eggs and English muffins with jam. I
cried, like Charlie had cried, as I bit into the food. I, too, lied and
said I had an allergy — "a hereditary condition."

AFTER BREAKFAST I used the old farmer's phone and made
arrangements to meet with the people from the journals — the
"allies," as Rightpath called them. Over a period of several days I
met them all and recorded every word they said. It was the sum
total of their stories, combined with the journals, that together
added up to the life Charlie lived in Baraboo, and to the return of
Wakdjunkaga.

PART 2

Wakdjunkaga and the Allies

TWELVE

The Twins

The sisters who ran Stetson's General Store were duplicates of one another — not only did they look alike, but they talked and moved alike. If I had closed my eyes during the interview I would have been lost as to who was who. Both women were in amazing physical condition for their age — agile, solid on their feet, on the short side. Little dynamos! They wore the same color of auburn hair, obviously dyed. Best of all, their loud, wide-open blue-gray eyes glowed with love and sympathy for their fellow man.

They had a plate of relishes, pickles, and crackers for me to nosh as I listened.

Charlotte:
Let me tell you about your brother.

Lorraine:
Yes, you go ahead and tell him, Charlotte.

Charlotte:
The first time we met Charlie, ha ha ha, we couldn't forget that, ha ha ha.

Lorraine:
No, we couldn't forget that, ha ha ha.

Charlotte:
How many times do you have a customer who comes into the store who's so tall and wants to buy a size sixteen boot? Ha ha ha. He was quite a character all right, but such a sweet man. Very polite and thorough, yes *thorough* is the word, because he wanted to know all about the boots and how they were made and where they were made and how long they would last and all about the store and the town and just everything.

Lorraine:
Very thorough person, and always very polite. He would say "Yes ma'am" and "No ma'am," and you don't get that from kids anymore.

Charlotte:
No, you certainly don't get that from kids anymore these days. He wasn't a kid, of course; he was a man.

Lorraine:
No, he wasn't a kid. He was a little nervous, though.

Charlotte:
Yes, he had that nervousness about him. Always looking behind himself like someone was watching him. But he was young and healthy. Oh yes, we hit it off right away. He was looking for boots that first time we met him.

Lorraine:
I'll never forget him, because of that hair.

Charlotte:
Hair? You mean the feet! Why, he came into the store and I noticed him right away. Like I said, he was very tall and different in so many ways. Very . . .

Lorraine:

. . . unusual looking.

Charlotte:

Yes, unusual looking. He was looking all around with that long neck of his and the big round eyes, you know how he is or was, and he says, "Do you have boots?" and I says to him, "Sure we have boots. Back this way, just follow me."

Lorraine:

I was waiting on a customer at the time.

Charlotte:

So I lead him back to the shoe section. "We of course don't have the biggest shoe selection in town," I says to him. "If you want the best selection, you have to go out there on Route Thirty-Three to Kohls or WalMart, even Boegler's has a bigger selection than we have," I says. But he don't want all that, he just wants boots, he says. So I says, "What kind of boots are you looking for, we have three different kinds." And he says, "A work boot." "Oh, then you'll want the Timberland boot," I says. Then we both look down at his feet. Ha ha ha, he smiled and I all but burst out laughing, but I dasn't, of course, for fear of insulting him.

Lorraine:

Size sixteen. You dasn't laugh.

Charlotte:

Size sixteen. "Why," I says, "why, I'm not sure if we have anything in your size, we might have to special-order those. What size are you?" I ask and he says,

"Sixteen." I says, "Sixteen! You won't need skis with feet like that." So I go in the back room and you know what, there's this old pair of size sixteen Timberlands, probably been sitting there for five years. We keep a few odd-size pairs of shoes and boots around for that very purpose, you never know when someone like Charlie is going to walk in and want a pair of boots. Actually, we had them in the window for a few years just as a kind of showpiece. Now we were going to actually sell them as boots. Ha ha ha, can you imagine?

Lorraine:
We had a man come in once had a size eighteen foot. And not so tall as Charlie.

Charlotte:
No, not nearly so tall. But very broad. A Negro man from the circus. So I bring them out to him, your brother, and I says, "You won't believe it but we've got a pair of size sixteen Timberlands."

Lorraine:
He smiled so brightly.

Charlotte:
That's right. He had a wonderful smile. So he sits down in the chair and takes off his sneakers. "Ouch!" he says when I go to put the boots on. "Cow stepped on my foot yesterday morning." "Oh, that must've hurt. You sure you haven't broken anything? That's a lot of weight, and your foot is a delicate thing," I says.

Lorraine:

More bones in your foot than in any other part of your body.

Charlotte:

That's right. But he shook his head and said, "No, I think it's okay." We put the boots on and they fit. "They're good," he says. I told him I would give him a discount because the boots were so old, and like I said, we used them out in our window for display.

Lorraine:

And we don't give discounts to everybody.

Charlotte:

No, just people we know. It's a well-kept secret.

Lorraine:

He was new in town and just so nice. Working out at Mr. Schniderwind's farm, he said. We know the family.

Charlotte:

Yes, we liked him the minute we saw him. Then he sees the Indian moccasins we get from Minnetonka up north and he wants to know all about them.

Lorraine:

Came right up to me and asked if they were real leather. I had finished with my customer and I came to see how things were going.

Charlotte:

"Now, there's a shoe I have got in your size," I says, because we have the only selection of the Minnetonkas in the area and we stock a lot of them. He says he wants a pair of them and I go back to get him some.

Lorraine:

No no no, get the story right. I went back and got them.

Charlotte:

Oh right, yes, you went back and got them. Anyway, Lorraine finds a pair and brings them out. He smiles real big and wants to try them on. Just like an excited child he was. So I help him put them on, and the whole time he is asking me —

Lorraine:

Not you, me!

Charlotte:

— asking Lorraine all about the moccasins and the Indian mounds, but he was also askin' all sorts of questions about the store and all of that. Told him how the store is in its fourth generation. My great-grandfather started the store in eighteen seventy-two. His brother was killed at the Little Big Horn, you know. Oh, he wanted to know all about that. And he wanted to know all about the Circus World Museum.

Lorraine:

No, he didn't want to *know* about it, because he didn't know about it. You're getting the story all wrong. He said he wondered if there was a circus in town because he had suddenly recalled coming to the circus here in Baraboo when he was a boy.

Charlotte:

Oh, that's right. He asked if we had a circus in town because he had seen some posters.

Lorraine:

That's when we told him about the Circus World Museum. He didn't know about that. See, we're volunteers there.

Charlotte:

We volunteer down there a couple of times a week in the summer. Oh, he was real interested in that. Oh yes, real interested in that.

Lorraine:

'Course later he was a regular down there. Came every day. Everybody knew him. The children loved him.

Charlotte:

So did the adults. But let me finish, because that's another story. I put those moccasins on and he smiles very pleasantly. They fit just right. He liked them.

Lorraine:

His whole face lit right up. Remember?

Charlotte:

Like a Christmas tree. They fit just right. You could tell he was real comfortable and pleased.

Lorraine:

He walked around and around with them, trying them out. Oh, you should have seen the smile on his face. Like a little boy.

Charlotte:

Just like a little boy. And like I said, he was real interested in everything and he just kept asking questions and I dasn't act rude just because he was so curious about everything. Besides, I like talking, so we just stood there and talked for the longest time, right there in the shoe section, and we had customers in the store but we didn't even care.

Lorraine:

Didn't even care at all.

Charlotte:

Then I says to him, "You should go to the town library, they have plenty of information if you want to know all about those Indian mounds and the Ringlings." He was talking about the Indians and the Indian mounds and the circus, all of it at once. "There's even a library out back of the museum. Biggest circus library in the world. You can't go wrong at the library. The shoes always fit there," I says. He smiled real wide at that.

Lorraine:

Real wide.

Charlotte:

He paid cash for the shoes, both pairs, a hundred and sixty-three dollars. Oh, he was a wonderful person.

Lorraine:

A wonderful person. We miss him a lot.

Charlotte:

A real lot.

CHARLIE DIDN'T RECORD much about his meeting with
the twins in his journal, mentioning it only briefly. What he did
write about was his first encounter with the circus. The words
practically jump for joy right off the page. Immediately upon
departure from Stetson's General Store, he walked down the hill
to Ringlingsville, where the Circus World Museum was located.
And then he saw it!

OCTOBER 1, 1997

Le cirque! You came here as a kid. You spent three days
here with your dad when you were fifteen years old.
Twenty years ago. You remember it all now. The memory
came flooding in from somewhere back there, in the
locked forgetery of your mind. It was just after the accident. You can see it clearly. It was fall, the same time of
year. The trees were full of bright colors, like the circus
itself. You can't believe it, can you? You must have been
headed here subconsciously the whole time. It had to be!
The twin sisters at the general store told you about it.
They told you how they volunteer down at the circus and
you got this funny feeling, kind of déjà vu. So you left the
store, and as you walked down the hill and got closer to
the Circus World Museum, it all started to come back
like a dream.

Then there it was! It was exactly as you remembered
it. The muddy river that runs through the middle of the
grounds. It could be the same river that's near your spot.
It meanders slowly along, bisecting the grounds in a sort
of bold, cursive handwriting. You could see the carp fins
poking out of the water, suggestive of poisonous serpents
in a medieval moat. The big top is there at the end of the
facility like a man-made mountain of blue canvas full of

happy stars and bright red fringe, and there's a flag at the top of the centermost pole waving excitedly. Waving at you! You could see the camels and giraffes eating hay in their outdoor pens from your spot on the riverbank. The sky above was so blue. It was a smorgasbord of smells — hot dogs, candy, big-animal manure mixed with hay, and popcorn and cut grass and people . . .

There was a little parade with elephants going on when you arrived. The big workhorses were in the lead, pulling the famous circus wagons, and there were clowns riding on donkeys, and people and kids all dressed in bright colors, and music, and that fresco-blue sky up above. It was like a mirage — too beautiful to describe. One clown had a pocket trumpet, too, and was playing "Put Another Nickel in the Nickelodeon." His tuning was really bad on that thing, much worse than yours, but he had real easy fingering and good time. You had an urge to take out your own pocket trumpet and echo him, but you thought it wouldn't be appropriate. The people would all look your way. Then for a second there you thought you heard a connection between the texture of that circus tune and those two measures you keep hearing over and over in your head . . .

You thought about the library the twins had mentioned. You made a mental note to visit it. Then you wanted to go inside. You walked over to the ticket booth, but you'd spent almost all of the cash you had in your wallet on the two pairs of new shoes. You couldn't pay the entrance fee. Tomorrow you'll go. You'll eat hot dogs and cotton candy and watch the show and shake a clown's hand and not be afraid. There are shows every day at ten and three o'clock. *Le cirque!* If only Uncle

Pete could be here. You just can't believe it, can you? Baraboo, Wisconsin! You'll have to tell Mr. Schniderwind tomorrow that you can do chores for him only until lunchtime every day until the end of the month when they close for the season; that way you'll have lots of time to spend there . . .

Later you were followed by a chipmunk as you walked along the river, back to your home. You thought he was a bird at first by the sound he made. He kept chirping and playing peekaboo, hiding in the hollow of a dead oak, then popping his head up out of a hole to look at you. It struck you. A poem:

The Chip

The chip needs a clip
Of his name to fame.
The skunk is the monk.
It's his stink I think.

THE NEXT DAY Charlie went right back into town to visit the two libraries. He was beginning to build his lodge, and he needed information about how to build one Indian-style. Afterward, he went to the Robert L. Parkinson Library in search of the music in his head. He met Squeaky the Clown instead.

THIRTEEN

Jane Reardon,
MLS, Head Librarian

Ms. Jane Reardon, MLS, head librarian, could perhaps be described as two parts Circe and one part Lucille Ball. Attractive, yet comedic. Eager to please, and yet pompous. With her baby-soft skin, black button eyes, silken black hair, tremendous breasts, and double-wide hips that swayed from side to side like a Grand Canyon burro, Ms. Jane Reardon, MLS, head librarian, was a seductress in the "librarian-next-door" sense. She was very tall, verging on six feet, with a slender, yogurt-smooth neck, long sloping arms, and hauntingly beautiful and graceful legs. Her features were an amalgam of northern European, southern European, and — the pièce de résistance — Native American. She sat on the edge of her seat as if on the verge of getting up to attend to some other business.

"THE FUNNIEST THING was the day he came into the library for the first time. I'll never forget. He tripped over the book display I had just finished setting up! Ta ha ha. Can you believe it? Oh, he made me realize immediately that I had set the display up much too close to the entrance stiles, for he took two steps into the library and crash, there were books and limbs strewn all about the place, and there he lay, prostrate. But what was most unusual about his entrance wasn't so much the tripping; it was what occurred subsequently. Instead of climbing instantly back to his feet once the shock of his mishap had been assimilated, he simply lay there on the floor, looking at one of the display books. Ta ha ha. I remember distinctly it was the Lorant book, *Indians of the New World,* a beautiful volume of some of the earliest engravings of Native Americans and the indigenous flora and fauna by Theodore De Bry. Nonetheless, he lay there on the floor, not in the least concerned about how he got there, but more overwhelmed with the contents of the volume. By the time I got to him, he was leafing insouciantly through the pages, still lying there on the floor. I noticed he was a bit disheveled, not so much from the fall, but as if he had been hiking a long distance and hadn't had the opportunity to wash properly. I used to love to bathe him. Oh my. Anyway, he had on his new boots. 'I'm terribly sorry,' I said, 'that was my fault, I shouldn't have put the display table so close.' 'Oh no, it was my fault,' he insisted. 'I just bought new boots and I haven't gotten used to them yet,' he offered as his excuse. 'I should have worn my moccasins,' he went on. Then I looked at the feet. Oh my, what feet. So large. So *very* large. I felt a deep tickle inside looking at those feet. Yes, that was prescient, wasn't it, that deep tickle?

"'May I help you get up?' I asked him. 'Oh yes, I guess I should get up, shouldn't I?' he said. I offered my hand and he took it ever so gently, holding it but not resting any of his weight on it in order not to pose any undue onus to me. When our eyes met, of course, it was love at first sight. He gathered his feet under himself and we both stood there spellbound. So pure and innocent we were. With the volume in hand, I led him over to the oak table by the reference books and sat him down. 'You're interested in the

Native American collection?' I asked. 'Yes,' he responded distractedly. 'And the circus,' he added. 'The circus, too? Well, with the circus you'd be better off going to the source. They have the Robert L. Parkinson, no relationship to the disease Parkinson, Library and Research Center. That's the best circus library of its kind in the world.' 'Oh, is it?' he responded. Then he blushed. He must have had some amorous thought at that moment, for his face grew feverishly flushed, and out of respect for him I withdrew, realizing his attraction to me was causing him some discomfort down below.

"An hour or so later, before he left, he came to find me and from his pocket he pulled forth a little purple-flecked ball. It was a gall. He wanted to know about it because he'd found it in the woods. He'd never seen one before and thought it was a turtle egg. How adorable he was. A gall! Can you picture it? I explained to him what galls were, having studied some forest biology in college. He was quite interested in the little fellow and gingerly put it back in his pocket. Then he asked how he could find the Parkinson Library. I gave him instructions and he thanked me profusely. When I went to offer him my hand he paused, and for the briefest moment I thought he was going to press his lips to it, but instead he ever so tenderly took my hand and squeezed it just once, a little hard, almost too hard, like a pulse it was, erotic, oh most definitely, like one might use to squeeze the teat of a cow's udder, yet in that squeeze I understood everything — his desire for me, his manly needs, his passion."

OCTOBER 2, 1997
You thought it was a turtle egg and you were thinking of eating it. But it wasn't a turtle egg at all. You showed it to that big-uddered librarian in town, who explained to

you that it was a gall and she told you what was inside. So you wrote a poem about it:

A Gall

A gall's a small,
Little puff of a ball.
It's green with some red
And unusually speckléd.
Inside you will discover
A larva undercover.
He fell off the oak
Unwanted folk.

. . . It was the librarian's fault that you tripped. She had set the book display table too close to the turnstiles. One of the legs was sticking out, and you tripped coming in. If she had meant to do it, it would have been the perfect trap. But you knocked over that Indian book and it was all right there, the pictures of the lodge, the tattoos, everything. You started looking at the book and she ran up to you with her huge breasts dangling within inches of your nose. Those huge udders of hers were right there in front of your hands, you had the impulse to squeeze one of them like Eva's teat, but fortunately she moved back just as you started to reach for them.

. . . She told you about the other library in town, the one the twins told you about yesterday called the Parkinson Library, the largest circus library in the world. So you headed over there.

FOURTEEN

Squeaky the Clown

They say a criminal can spot a cop in a crowd of people no matter how he's dressed. It's his mien, his whole manner of motion and being. The same holds true for clowns. It wouldn't take a criminal to finger a clown, just the child inside all of us.

Even in civilian clothes, Judd Barkin, aka Squeaky the Clown, had the unmistakable look and manner of a clown. He was in his late fifties, I would guess, and stood a gritty five feet three inches, with his bald pate and big, sad, watery eyes. Originally from Bridgeport, Connecticut, he had a kind of tough-sounding accent. Brooklynese, but not so hard. Most distinctive about his voice was its squeaky, cartoonish quality. If you closed your eyes you would have thought you were watching the Loony Tunes channel just listening to him.

The interview was conducted at his place, in his trailer out behind the big top on the grounds of the Circus World Museum. It was nine-thirty in the morning. Of course it was a small place — all trailers are — but fairly neat, with lots of photographs on the fake wood paneling. He was in every one of the photos, standing next to famous people. It was like a little Hall of Fame for himself. He was drinking a Bloody Mary and smoking a long cigar. His little feet rested cavalierly on the cocktail table most of the time — socks, no shoes. Next to him on the couch was an old squeezable horn that he would use occasionally when he let slip a joke. It became apparent to me that for him, squeezing that rubber bulb was an uncontrollable tic. He told me the story of his first meeting with Charlie.

"CHARLIE WAS A unique guy. A classic. Wonderful. Great wit' the kids, and great for the museum, too. Yeah, he was a little weird, you know, a little different, he liked dressin' up like a Indian, rowin' a canoe around and all that shit, but hey, who am I to call someone different, you know? I'd be callin' the kettle black. They was lucky to have him around. Never asked for nothin'. Never took a dime for all that playin' he done back in 'ninety-eight. How many people you find like that these days, huh? Help you out any way he could. Give you the shirt off his back . . . if he ever wore one — *Honk! Honk!* [He tooted his horn.]

"First time I seen him, I remember that. That was funny. He came into the Parkinson Library when I just happened to be up there. Back then, five years ago, I was spendin' a little more time there helpin' them wit' resources when they get stuff sent from private collections, you know, helpin' them figure out where the stuff goes or whether we just trash the crap, sometimes it's just junk. I been in the circus business forty-eight years, so I know what's what wit' the old business, stuff before 'fifty-nine when they stopped the tour and moved it all here permanent. I might not look it, but I'm sixty-seven. Knew Mike Marshall, Merle Evans, Jimmie Whalen, all the legends. Anyways, I was there at the library out of uniform, you know, off-duty clown, but, hey, we still carry our heaters — *Honk! Honk!* Huh? Gotcha!

"So there's this goofy-looking guy walks in. We got some real lunatics come in the library from time to time. Some sickos that like lookin' at the pictures of the side shows, get their jollies that way. Friggin' psychotics, you know what I mean? Anyways . . . Jesus he had some flippers on him, huh? He was a clown, he wouldn't need the stretch, you follow? He comes in gawkin', just overcome by the place like he was a kid seein' a elephant for the first time. He just walks around studyin' the place, lookin' at everythin' real close, you know. I got a table full of pictures all spread out in the front area there, the readin' area, and I got my file journal out, see, and I'm tryin' to figure out if the pictures we got in is new stuff we don't have or whether it's more friggin' food for the trash can. He comes over to the table and watches me.

"I figure like most people he's gonna watch a couple seconds then go about his business. Not him, nope. Charlie don't do nothin' halfway. He stands there for ten friggin' minutes watchin' every move I make wit' those big peepers of his like I'm teachin' a elephant to dance. Finally I get to feelin' a little funny about him there so I stop what I'm doin' and I ask him if I can help him wit' somethin', you know, not angry or nothin', just askin'. 'That Merle Evans?' he asks me, starin' at one of the pictures. 'Yeah,' I says, 'Merle Evans. You know Merle Evans, do you?' I says. 'Not personally, no,' he says, kind of dignified soundin' for a guy who looked the way he did at the time, which was actually the most presentable he ever looked to me now that I remember what he looked like after that. Anyways, he's starin' at the picture of Merle Evans and he asks, 'I betcha he could play some trumpet?' 'Sure,' I say. 'And wit' one hand most of the time, too. Actually, he played a cornet,' I add. 'Played a King cornet, nineteen thirty, silver, wit' a one-C mouthpiece — they've got it over in the case at the exhibit barns,' he responds. 'Would it be possible,' he suddenly asks, 'to listen to a recording of Merle Evans playing?' 'Yeah, sure, they got all that stuff over there on the shelves,' I tell him, pointin' at 'em. 'Go over to the desk and they'll fix you up,' I tell him. He thanks me and walks away.

"Now, this particular project I was workin' on was involved because the old lady that sent the pictures was an old-timer and she had some real good stuff, had a real good collection of photographs and a lot of it was rare pictures we ain't never seen, so I'm kinda lost into the work for hours. Then Barb, one of the librarian assistants there, comes over and asks me if I want to stay late 'cause it's time to close up shop and she's goin' home. I tell her, 'Yeah, I'll lock it up, I got just another half hour's work or so,' I tell her. She walks over to your brother, who's been sittin' for hours wit' the earphones on listenin' to Merle, beatin' his feet, shakin' the whole friggin' room. Anyways, the next thing I know she's yellin' loud, 'Sir! *Sir!* The library's closing!' Well, he must of heard her the second time around and pulled the earplug outa the tape machine instead of turnin' down the volume 'cause the next second Merle Evans's horn is screamin 'Roses of Memory.' Jesus H. Christ! Then there's this big crash and the music stops abruptly. Barb screams. I run over there and there's this goofy guy, pardon the description, lyin' on the ground, got his big pods coiled in the tape player cord, which is completely busted on the floor, and he's holdin' his head. 'Are you all right, sir?' Barb is askin', 'cause he seems a little dazed lyin' there holding his head. He suddenly kinda comes to and jumps up, the tape machine flyin' around his legs, smackin' against the tile floor a couple more times — *Crash! Bang!* — he's still got it all twisted around him. 'Oh, I'm so sorry, I'm sorry, I just got these new shoes and I can't seem to get used to them,' he says. Well, I can't help it and I start to laugh. I give old Squeaky here a couple o' pops — *Honk! Honk! Honk! Honk!* And then he starts to laugh. And Barb, she's all freaked out, and she just scurries away, don't want no part of it. 'Did you get a chance to hear what you was lookin' for?' I ask him. I said this jokin', you know, he must of been there for three hours. 'Oh yeah, yeah!' he smiled. He followed me home here. He sat right where you're sittin' now. Told him all about the clown's life. Yeah, what a trip that guy was, pun intended — *Honk! Honk!*"

CHARLIE WROTE ABOUT the encounter with Judd Barkin. In fact, he wrote a poem about him.

OCTOBER 2, 1997

A Clown

[written in the shape of a clown's face]

He wobbles all around the ring
His pockets stuffed with silly things.
His hair is pink and his nose is red,
His floppy shoes seem made of lead.
He kicks his pal who trips and falls
He walks on hands and juggles balls.
So what's so funny about a clown?
Why do we fuss when he's in town?
Is it his painted face? His silly hair?
Or any of that comedic stuff he wears?
What makes a clown a laughingstock?
His foolish stunts? The way he mocks?
No, it's who he is that makes us smirk —
A man in drag paid to do that work.

There are three types of clowns, you learned today. Auguste (pronounced oh-goost), white faced, and character. An auguste clown is one who doesn't paint his face all white; he just paints on heavy eyebrows and a big white mouth, then puts a cherry on his nose. He's the one with the big feet who's usually the butt of all the jokes. You used to be afraid of clowns.

Squeaky is a white-faced clown. The head clown. He's been a clown for more than forty years. He knew Emmit Kelley. Emmit Kelley was a character clown. Squeaky said you would make a great clown because you wouldn't need to wear extra-large shoes. Then he honked the horn that he always carries like a sheriff with his six-shooter. It's a C$\sharp$. You met him at the Parkinson Library. You were looking for those two measures in your head. You still couldn't find them.

FIFTEEN

Chappy

Mr. Daniel "Chappy" Lewis-Clark was sitting out in the sun on a beach chair, watching the clouds pass overhead as a large pile of yard waste burned behind him.

Chappy was a corpsman in the Korean War, and ever since then he'd been cleaning up the messes; sorting through the refuse of humanity, animate and inanimate, organizing it, fostering it, and selecting its final resting place. Just one look into his dark, jaundiced eyes and immediately you were aware of a rare wisdom. Like an Eastern seer. There was a blinding quality to one as black as Chappy — he was all eyes and darkness around. And when he spoke, his huge, white-palmed hands flashed in gesticulation. Of average height and weight, his sinewy body, though seventy-five years old, moved with grace and ease.

"FIRS' TIME I seen him walk through that gate I says to myself, 'Chappy, here come sompfin' now.' Jus' Plain Chaz. He didn' have no las' name 'roun' here. I axe him one time, I says, 'Chaz, what be yo' las' name?' And he jus' smile at me and say, 'I don' have no las' name, Chappy, it jus' Plain Chaz.' 'Course you says he gots a las' name soun' like the helicopter, Sikorski, sompfin'. Yeah. Don' soun' right, he jus' always Plain Chaz 'roun' here. But what's a name gonna tell you 'bout a person 'cept maybe if he a man o' a woman, an' sometime it don' even tell you that.

Like my name, for instan'. They cawed me Dan'l when I was a pup. Don' like be cawed Dan'l. My pappy didn' like the name Dan'l neither, it was his father-in-law name, so he go 'roun' cawin' me Chappy. It stuck that way. 'Course our las' name confusin'. My pappy related to one o' the famous explorers, one o' they descendan's. But the history gots all mix' up over the years an' by the time my family come along they ain' sure which one it is we all related to, so they cawed theyselves by both they names jus' to make sure." He took a long pause, got up out of his chair and stirred the fire. It took him a while. He was in no hurry about anything he did.

"Now, firs' time I seen the Chaz Man walk in, like I says, I says to myself, 'Here come sompfin' now, Chappy, don't know what it is, but it sompfin'.' This before he gots the tattoos all over hisself; before he gots the buckskins. But he still tall then, too, and that hair, not so long yet, but still crazy wil'. Ooo-weee he sompfin'. He come marchin' in here, hot day, too. We gets col' up here, but we don' get much hot. I don' recall when it was, but it was hot. I'm pushin' the cart 'roun' the recyclables here, sweatin', movin' a load o' aluminum an' up he come wit' his big feet, up that dir' road behin' you there, kickin' up a cloud o' dus' give hisself almos' a holy aura, you follow? He gots that curly dark hair all sweatin' down his ears an' them big ole eyes open wide takin' it all in, see. Jus' like you was a secon' ago. 'Wha'chu need, Mister?' I axe him. 'Not sure,' he say. 'Comin' in to browse aroun'?' I axe him. 'Nothin' wrong wit' it, people does it all the time,' I says. Knowed a guy who'd come here to the dump wit' a load in his truck, but by the time he gots done browsin', he done had mo'n his truck than when he come in. But that don' matter. So I says to him, I says, 'They browse at the WalMart, and the Kmart, ain' no reason they cayn' browse here at the Garbage-Mart. You helps yo'self,' I tell him. 'There a ole black bicycle somebody jus' done throw away, perfect good condition, no rus', like new. Gots a bell go *ding* jus' sweetes' little *ding* you ever hear. I gonna take it home give it to one o' my gran'kids nobody takes it.' 'Where that at?' he all excited and wan' to know. 'I show you,' I says, 'jus' follow me.' So he follow me 'roun' the side the recyclin' shed, and there be the bike leanin' up agains' the buildin' where I puts it befo' he come up. I takes a ole hancruchief out my pocket and I starts wipin' it off, you follow? He standin' there, tall, strange-lookin' dude, very dark skin fo' a white boy. An' he starin' at that bike with them eyes, givin' it a four-o-six. I could tell he was impress'. 'Try it on,' I says. 'Go 'head, you puts youself up there an' sit on that bike; give it a ride 'roun'.' He set up there on that bike and off he go ridin', dingin' the bell so many times I gettin' sick o' the sound. He sittin' up there on that bike so big he lookin' like a circus clown his knees stickin' way out, them feets like two wings cuttin' the wrong angle from the bottom. 'Woa there,' I shouts to him as he go pas' me. 'You gots a'jus' the seat,' I tells him. 'Yeah?' he say as if he surprise'. Any foo' could see you need a'jus' the bike seat, but he prob'ly ride right on out o' there wit' the seat like it was. He get hisself down off the bike an' I takes the bike and we walks over to the garbage compression, over there where I gots my tools, you follow? He starin' at the bike the whole time. 'Where you from?' I axe him 'cause I know automatic he ain' from the area. 'Eas' Coas',' he says. 'Eas' Coas' a big place,' I say. 'Which part o' the Eas' Coas'?' He pause like he not sure fo' a secon' and then he say, 'Connec'-a-cut.' 'Connec'-a-cut?' I star's jokin' wit' him, 'you some kinda Ivy League boy, call yo' paren's Mumsy an' Popums?' 'What?' he say like he never knowed 'bout that kinda stuff, that kinda stereotype.

"So, I goes into the back room an' gets my tools and starts to work on that seat. The nut kinda stubborn, an' I gots to squeeze out some oil on that sucka befo' she done move some, follow me?

An' while I'm doin' that, he start axin' me questions 'bout my name an' my family an' the war I be in. He a real nice person I notice, the way he always so in'eres'ed in you an' polite. He don' go on 'bout hisself; I could tell he jus' in'eres'ed in my story. An' when I tells him the part o' my life which has to do with my daddy bein' a musician with the circus, played the cronet, well he jus' 'bout fall out. He was real in'eres'ed in that, oh my. My ole man was Mr. Walker T. Lewis-Clark, played with P. G. Lowery in what they cawed at the time the jig ban', played cronet, like yo' brother, travel all the way to Paris, France. He could blow that horn, my daddy. He weren' much fo' bein' 'roun' wit' my mother and us kids. Originally we from Chicago, south side, actually befo' that we was from the South, Clarksdale, but when he start playin' wit' the circus ban' he move us up here so's we closer to him. But that don' matter much 'cause he ain' 'roun' whether we in Chicago o' Bar'boo. I tells you one thing, when he come home from tourin', man it were always somethin' special. Mos' kids get Chris'mas once a year, I had it three, fo' times; sometimes mo'. He wear some fresh clothes on hisself, too, carry hisself nice, my daddy did. He like' to wear them derby hats. You don' fine them these days. In fact, you fine them and you fine a lot o' money, they valu'ble now. But that's somethin' else I could tell you 'bout 'nother time. Anyways, I could tell you stories 'bout my pappy an' that jig ban'.

"So we talk fo' a long time, yo' brother an' me, 'bout that, 'bout the ban'. He show me his little pocket trumpet. Didn' play it fo' me that time. That come later. But there a irony o' coinc'dence 'bout him and my daddy playin' the same brass. Some irony there. We talk too 'bout the circus, an' the Wil' Wes' show, he like axin' 'bout that, an' the beautiful mountains we gots 'roun' here from the glacier come through, an' 'bout the Indians and the burial groun's, he seem curious all 'bout that stuff. Oh yeah.

"Then outa nowhere he say he read sompfin' 'bout bicycle seat make you sof', you know what I'm sayin'? Impoten'. I star's to laugh, but he say he serious wit' that. Tell me the bes' seat a man could have on a bicycle be a toilet seat. Keep his boys free down there to move 'roun', followin' me here? Then I really lets go a laugh. I tells him I gots a ole toilet seat right in the shed I could put on fo' him. Use the welder, put it up there, take me five minutes. He say go ahead. He serious. He got to be the funnies' goldang man I ever seen. I goes in there and gets the seat. He were smilin' at me wit' that thang, but he serious.

"Nex' hour I rigs that toilet seat up there on that bicycle, it never gonna come off. Gots a welder tool I shows you. He jus' smilin' at me. When I gets done and I flips that top up, you know, and I says, 'Here yo' throne, yo' majes'y.' He jump up there and ride that thang 'roun', you shoulda seen him. Ooo-wee, he sompfin', that man. Rode off that way 'ventually wit' that bicycle and that toilet seat. An' jus' 'bout every time I seen him after that, he on that bicycle ridin' wit' that same happy-dog look. Yeah, he pull out o' here that firs' day ringin' that bell, I says to myself, 'Chappy, you was right from the firs', that were sompfin special.' That bike never did fit him right."

CHARLIE WAS AS taken by Chappy as Chappy was by him.

OCTOBER 16, 1997
The dump is like a pot of gold, and the dumpmeister, Chappy, its wise and wonderful guardian. His dad played in the Negro band that went with the circus years ago. Played "cronet." You love listening to him tell a story. You can hear his voice now, talking and laughing inside your head. It's singing to you. It makes you joyous. It makes you want to jump up and kick your heels. It's poetry is what it is.

... And while thinking of Chappy and riding your new bike home you saw a squirrel dancing in a tree, floating from branch to branch. Seeing the squirrel move, it struck you as inevitable that there is, pro forma, a species of squirrel that flies. There's a grace, an antigravity in the way the gray squirrel moves. It's a kind of flying; it suggests flight. Proving, perhaps, that all species, no matter their shape or size, aspire to flight, even mankind, be it through art or conversation or dream. You stopped and wrote a poem:

Flying Squirrels
[in the shape of a flying squirrel]

Flying squirrels of the forest float
Beyond the Darwinian moat.
On wing'd membrane they glide like kites
Over sylvan knolls; dappled starlight.
Flying in the face of reason
For other mammals it's treason
That a rodent be not earthbound
Let to fly, not walk, o'er the ground.
But the message they send is clear
Do not panic and do not fear
And you as well will pierce the air
And soar in flight without a care
Like the flying squirrels that float
Beyond the Darwinian moat.

WHEN THE SPRINGTIME came, Charlie began to wear the clothes given to him by Oscar Rightpath's father, Joseph Rightpath. It was an impressive outfit, like something you might see in a pictorial anthology of Native Americans in traditional dress. His lodge was finished, and the canoe he had spent all winter carving was river-worthy. So on the opening day of the circus in early May 1998, he paddled upstream to see the show.

It was a glorious day for him, one of great triumph and fulfillment. Afraid people would object to or perhaps steal his craft, he paddled it to a spot just downstream from the big top and hid it behind an ancient willow tree — in his words, "whose massive trunk and ciliary branches formed a river gateway to the museum like an ogee arch." Midway through the season he would abandon this procedure and park the canoe right below the big top for all to see, then proudly bound out of his craft and strut into the facility.

But his costume was not quite complete. Close to a month after opening day, he met Gino Crivello, the tattoo artist. They met at the Village Tavern. It was a Sunday in June.

SIXTEEN

Gino Crivello

The Vietnam War gutted Gino Crivello. Married three times, divorced three times. Washed ashore in Baraboo in the mid-1980s as the result of his second marriage, he opened a tattooing salon on Main Street and made his living that way. As a result of his war wounds — a shattered pelvis and a broken femur — he walked with a severe limp. His face, too, had deep scars from the shrapnel that exploded upward two feet in front of him. He, like Charlie, suffered from a panic disorder. He wasn't disabled by it like Charlie; in fact, he talked candidly about it. He also had a little tic that pulled at the side of his mouth as if some invisible fisherman behind him had a hook in his mouth with a microfilament attached and occasionally tested the line to see if he was still attached. He was a short, stocky, balding man with a sunflowerlike face. He wore a lush red beard to cover the scars around his cheeks and mouth. The beard literally glowed. What was left of his hair resided on the sides of his pate — red but peppered with gray, and not as thick as the hair of his beard. His pale blue eyes rarely focused, never stopping for too long at one point as they floated about like a honeybee from flower to flower. His ears were crowded with rings, as many as seven on one ear, and his short but powerful hands were heavily tattooed. Forever dressed in black leather, he was a walking advertisement for Harley Davidson & Co. He loved conversation and the company and attention of other people. We met at his shop.

"HE WAS A legendary figure, your brother, like somethin' out of a fairy tale. Ho-Chunk think he was divinity. I believe it. One thing I know, he come here lookin' for me. I was the man he was looking for to do the artwork on him. No question there. The stars was all lined up for that, man. He needed the 'toos. I seen it the minute he walked through that door with that long chest of his. ''Too me!' it said all over it, like a neon sign. Fuckin' A. Now this picture here is of me and him next to his canoe. He's probably rowing that thing right now up in the happy huntin' grounds." Gino limped across the room and pointed to an eight-by-ten-inch photo in a black frame right in the middle of the wall; there were no other photos or artwork around it. It was like a shrine. "He took me out a couple times on the 'Consin. That's the only one I've got of him and me fishin'. Chappy out at the dump made him a trailer for that canoe so he could pull it around behind him. He didn't drive, man. Wouldn't even touch a car, let alone sit in one.

"Yep. I tell you, I ain't religious or nothin', I grew up in Jersey City, New Jersey, but he really made me think that maybe there's somethin' goin' on up there, somethin' more happenin' that mere mortals like me and you don't know about. You know? Just weird how it went with him. No one knew where he lived. He walked in there that day at the tavern. It was a hot day. Hot, man. Got nothin' on but a piece of deerskin wrapped around his waist, tail hangin' down in the back and some bundle thrown over his shoulder. Look like somethin' out of *Star Trek*, you know, the one where they go to that planet and everything is back in time, like prehistoric days. He's got that crazy hair, moccasins. Sherry, she's the bartender there, real bitch, nasty to most people, it don't matter if she knows you or not, says, 'Sorry pal, no one allowed in without a shirt.' And wham, that body, that face comes up and slams heavy against my eyes. I can see it, you know? It's like he's standin' there with the 'toos already done. And he could see 'em too. I swear he could see 'em. The Ho-Chunk say he was a prophet, well, he was a prophet for me, that's for damn sure. I know just how Michelangelo must of felt standing around that piece of Carrara marble. Wham! I was drinkin' a lot that day, I do most days, but suddenly I was sober, cold sober. And I seen the whole thing there in my mind's eye and I say, 'Let me give you a 'too, man, that's all the shirt you'll need. My shop's right next door.' It was a Sunday. Well, his eyes get like this, like two half dollars. Shit! That was the moment. I don't know why exactly I got into 'tooing. I always wondered myself. I guess 'cause I could draw a little and I liked 'toos, liked talkin' to people. But it was Charlie made me realize that I was really a tattoo artist. All the shit I done in life was preparin' me for that moment on him. I swear I feel that way about it.

"We come back over here. I unlock the door real nervous, like I couldn't wait to begin. And he just naturally walked over there to the chair and sat down. Didn't say nothin'. I got everything ready and he just sat there, that goofy face, you know, the big brown eyes lookin' around, watchin' me. He was smilin', sweatin', you know, a shiny slime on his body. I got a towel, wiped him down before I started. He never asked nothin', just sat and watched me. Well, before I started, like a little kid, he asked if it was gonna hurt. I told him a little, but nothin' he couldn't deal with. I don't know, I don't know. To this day I go over it again and again in my mind wonderin' where I got the stuff I did. How did I know? I must of seen that De Bry picture somewhere and it was just in the back of my mind. I didn't follow no pattern or nothin', just started drawin' — improvisation. I was like Coltrane but playin' a 'too needle, you know? And I never done that before.

Always go with the pattern; always follow the pattern. But with him I just started 'tooin'. Started with the circles on his shoulders, then the stripes down the arms, the collar, the circles on his stomach, then around his nipples, the buttons on the wrists, then I come back up to the chest. Everything's perfect as far as I can see, but there's somethin' that's tellin' me somethin', knockin' on my head and callin' my name, tellin' me, *Hey stupid! Yo Gino! You're missin' somethin'!* And he's sittin' the whole time, not sayin' nothin', just trustin' every single move I make. Then I'm lookin' at the chest and I swear to God, he says, and I think at the exact same moment — 'Goose.' 'Goose,' he says. Shit, I think I probably started drawin' it before he finished gettin' the words out. It was small, only about three inches. But it was the colors, man. It seemed to glow. Everyone said the same thing. No matter what I done since, I can't get that same color effect. Charlie was the one who later told me it reminded him of something Botticelli would paint. I didn't know who Botticelli was at the time, I mean I heard of him a little, but I wasn't sure who he was exactly. Man, when I saw that *Allegory of Spring* and the way those ladies glowed like that, it was spooky. That was it, the same friggin' colors. It was like I had stolen somethin' from the picture and planted it on Charlie's chest. Botticelli, yeah. That's *The Birth of Venus* over there, and I got *The Allegory of Spring* in the back." He had a replica of the painting on the other wall, facing the photograph of him and Charlie. It, too, sat alone.

"When we was finished we didn't say nothin'. We were kind of quiet, like we knew we had done somethin' amazin'. You know, I don't even know how long it took to get all that done. I just remember it was dark by the time we got back to the tavern. That friggin' goose, man it was somethin'. I see it in my dreams some nights, lookin' down at me from the sky, glowin' like a spotlight in my eyes, honkin' at me, too. Like it's watchin' over me, I swear to Christ.

"I'll tell you, we laid into some beers that night. Charlie wasn't much of a drinker. Can't believe he's dead. I want to get a plot close as I can get to Charlie's grave. Figure if I'm dead and there's a heaven, Charlie'll be there, show me what to do. He'll be there waitin', too, knowin' Charlie. He'll show me the way."

JUNE 14, 1998
Boy, did Mr. Schniderwind look at you when he saw your new decorations. "Ach du lieber Gott! Vhat you doing? You making painting on yourself?" Eva didn't seem to notice.

Tattoos
[in the shape of a goose]
The body is a canvas
For an artist's needle-brush.
Not stroked,
But poked,
No oil,
Dye.
It scabs.
Then it's worn
Like a medal of honor
Even in the shower.
Bigger than a haircut
Smaller than a limb.
Not exactly fashion,
A symbol of passion.
It's a perfect fit.

SEVENTEEN

Billy C.

I'd been around musicians all my life, and I could tell you that they're just like everyone else, only more so. Billy C. was a strikingly nondescript-looking man, about forty years old, of average height, thinning dirty-blond hair, a mustache, greenish gray eyes, and a pale complexion. Easy to be around. Never at a loss for words. He was as talented a musician as they come. He could play it all — jazz, Dixieland, blues, classical, polka. He attended the prestigious Berklee School of Music in Boston as a college student, but he split that gig early on and joined a traveling big band. He toured the world and played in all kinds of venues before ending up at the Circus World Museum as the band director.

"FIRST TIME I met Charlie or actually spoke to him was the day I threw my back out, the day he took the band. It was the Fourth of July, nineteen ninety-eight, just before the Great Circus Parade. Of course, that's a famous circus date now. Yeah, I'd seen him around a lot, you know, he was this eccentric character dressed up like an Indian, came to all the afternoon shows, sometimes both shows. Everyone was aware of him. How could you not be? Like a great big kid, always walking around with an ice cream cone in his mug, that curly black hair longer every time I saw him. This was four years ago. Had those tattoos. All the circus people knew him. Just from looking at him, he looked like one of our own. The real ones are born, not made. Plus, it's a small kind of community around here; anyone different hanging around, you notice them. He was friends with Judd Barkin, Squeaky the Clown, and every once in a while I saw the two of them walking around together, coming out of Judd's trailer, sitting on the benches talking. Your brother was a real circus buff, and Judd's the guy you want to talk to. He's been in it a long time, knew a lot of the famous people. I'd also heard through the grapevine that Charlie had spent a lot of time up in the library reading musical scores, so I wasn't completely surprised when he was able to play the music. You probably want to hear all about that. Still pretty amazing to me even though I understand everything now.

"It's funny, this business is the kind of a place that plods along waiting for legends to be born. The stories and the people materialize out of thin air, and like I said, circus people are born, not made. Charlie was one of the ones born. The jury's still out on me. I've been playing this gig fourteen years now, toured both hemispheres, Tropic of Cancer and Tropic of Capricorn, played for three presidents and as many prime ministers. But you know what, they don't have a display wall in the Feld Pavilion for me, and I don't think they ever will. I'm not bitter about that. A lot of people think I'm bitter and jealous. I'm not at all. That's just the way this business is. It perpetuates itself by its own legends and stories. I'm not a superstitious guy or anything like that, but I just know, I've been around the business long enough to say with certainty that your brother was born to lead the circus band. He's what keeps them coming back year after year. And that's what this business is all about. No matter how long I stay here, my one claim to fame will always be the story about your brother. And it's not much of a story from my end. I guess now I need to start embellishing it, ha ha, you know, for my grandkids, even though

I'm not even married. Anyway, they've got that silly quote of mine up on the exhibit wall, the one where I grab Charlie's arm — which I never did — and say, 'Make the elephants dance.' Like I said, I'm not a superstitious person by a long shot, but sometimes I go over that episode in my head and it just seems so obviously fated. I don't know.

"Fourth of July that year was a big deal. I'm sure you've read something about it. The United Nations people were here that day from their conference in Chicago. I don't remember the exact reason why they had come, but if I'm not mistaken the Hungarian minister had some relatives who were performance artists for P. T. Barnum way back when, and he wanted to make that family connection. So, from my understanding, all the dignitaries decided to join him for the day and they all came up for the event. For the Fourth we always have a bigger parade, little longer show, bring in some extra clowns. We've got a lot more personnel around because we're gearing up for the Great Circus Parade in Milwaukee. Anyway, I was rushing around my trailer less than an hour before show time. This was the second show, we'd already done the ten o'clock performance. I'd overslept. I usually take a little nap between shows, and I wanted to practice the two new songs we'd added for that day, for the introduction. They were older songs that we didn't play much. I'd just gotten my uniform on and was heading out the door when the phone rang. It was the way I turned — I had one foot out the door on the top step of the landing, one hand on the doorknob, and I was a little tense about those charts and the audience, and then when the phone rang I kind of jerked backward and *snap*. Man, that was painful. I just collapsed right there on the threshold. That was bad.

"So I started trying to cry out, to get someone to help me or whatever. I've got the first trailer on the row here, and so who're the first people to come around the corner? Your brother and

Judd Barkin. Charlie's licking on a cone, dressed like an Indian as usual, and Judd's got his clown costume on. A clown and an Indian. Just my luck. They both stopped dead in their tracks and stared at me for like ten seconds, I swear. I was really in pain. 'What the hell are you doing there like that?' Judd says. 'I wrenched my back,' I groaned. Actually it was a lot worse. I'd displaced two vertebrae. 'Well, you better unwrench it in about twenty-five minutes, 'cause you're on,' he says sarcastically. I say, 'Just help me up.'

"So the two of them climb the steps and start yanking on me and I let out a scream that frightened the giraffes. Man, was I a hurtin' cowboy. Judd realized then that I was out of commission. He ran down the steps and around the corner, up to Brenda Mihulka's house on the hill behind the trailers — she's a nurse and she was home. He left me there with Charlie. I'm groaning and swearing and his face is very sympathetic. You know, he was that way. So I'm lying there and going on about how there'll be no band, and how Chico Avalos's act will have to be omitted because he didn't have a tape backup. We had tape backups for most of the acts in case of an emergency, but they were rarely used. In fact, they'd never had an incident when the band couldn't play. The jugglers, clowns, aerialists, tightrope walkers, elephants, they all go with live music. And even the acts that went with the tape backups, a lot of new stuff had been added that wasn't covered on the tapes. It was a bad situation. And all this was shooting through my mind while I lay there with Charlie looking down at me. See, our band is only four pieces, and the cornet is the melody line. We got trumpet, piano, sax, and drums, and they didn't have first parts built into those scores for the others. We also have substitute musicians, and they're on call, but most of them live in Chicago. The closest one was in Madison, but it would take him at least an hour to get there. The whole thing was really desperate. And of course with all the dignitaries in attendance, a lot more was at stake, so I felt I was letting everyone down. I thought perhaps if I could just sit up, then they could put a stool there for me to sit on and I could do the show that way. Not! I was in such pain I was starting to pass out. Well, Charlie is there with those big eyes, you know, like a kid looking down at me. And he's real calm, respectful, still holding his ice cream cone. Then he just says out of the blue, 'Don't worry Billy, I can play the music.' Of course I didn't or couldn't believe him, who would? About then Judd comes back with Mrs. Mihulka and she starts checking me out. She has them lift me up and carry me into my living room here. Talk about screaming bloody murder.

"By this time there was a little crowd gathered, Ivanoff was there and Artie T., one of the clowns, Winkleman — the ringmaster. I can hear them even through the fog of pain talking with anxious voices about the band situation. Ivanoff is cussing in Romanian, and I'm hearing my name thrown in there every once in a while. That's when I hear your brother pipe up again and say he can play it. There was all this murmuring, then silence. That's when I yell out, 'Let him play it!' I must have blacked out because the next thing I remember is the sound of 'I'm an Old Cowhand,' real tight notes, sweet tone, sure fingers, right over my head. He was playing it without music on a little pocket trumpet, the one on display down there. That little horn had good tuning; the notes had good density. Amazing. Well, he played it through once, even played the coda. Every measure was exactly the way we did the piece. Amazing. Perfect intonation he had. It was like I was listening to a tape of myself play. I asked him to play 'Gallop Go' and that, too, he played without the music. So I asked him if he could read. He said sure, but he said he knew most of the stuff by rote. Said he had it under his fingers. See, it's hard to explain, but playing circus music isn't like playing any other kind of live music, not even jazz. You're as much a part of the acts as the props. You've got to be able to anticipate, modify tempos, change melodies, adjust constantly. You're right there in the performance itself. You're using your eyes as much as any other part of yourself. We actually practice along with the acts. Yeah, we usually play the same numbers, but we have backup stuff in case somebody falls or drops all the pins or decides to omit part of an act. So you have to be intimate with the performers, the acts. It's hard to explain, but it's almost impossible for anyone, even the greatest player in the world, to just take over the circus band. You'd have to watch the show many times to understand all those nuances. Like your brother. That's why I say there's this feeling that it was all meant to be. I mean, what are the odds that there's this guy who can flat-out play; who comes every day to study and watch and listen to the music; who plays the horn; who can play by ear? That's when I asked him, 'Name the lineup!' He did it right off, no hesitation. And that's when I said, 'Okay, it's your band now, make the elephants dance.' I didn't grab his arm. How could I?

"By the time the ambulance came, he was dressed in my uniform, everything about six inches too small for him except the hat, which was about three sizes too big. Of course with those feet they just let him wear the moccasins. On stage they were hidden anyway. They had makeup on his face covering the tattoos. And out he went. The rest, of course, is circus history. He took the band till the end of the season, which was real late that year. As I recall they went all the way to Halloween. I was out of commission for six months. I'm certain, had he wanted it, he could have taken my job. But we know he had other fish to fry. Never took a penny for that gig. That was fifteen full weeks of work, too. They just gave him the honorary lifetime membership, let him do his Indian thing. That was what he wanted anyway. Hell, he was more an attraction the last two years than anything else around here. This place owes him a lot. Of course you know about all that. I heard they're talking about burying his body on the grounds, up top by the library. That's what I heard. I think he belongs here.

"Anyway, it was really something to see him paddle up along the river in the summer, with his loincloth and the tattoos, and knowing how he could play that horn, and yet he'd walk around, the same as always, like a little kid, you know, eating an ice cream cone, saying hello to everyone. Sometimes taking in both shows. It's funny, I'd always ask him to come on up and play a song or two, but he never would. The owners, the Felds, even encouraged me to ask him to play every once in a while, but nope, he just wouldn't do it. It was like he knew that the legend would be tainted, lessened, if he ever played again. A lot of people think I'm jealous of him, but I'm not at all. He belongs up on the wall and his uniform and trumpet in the display case next to Merle Evans and even the Ringling brothers themselves. And they should bury him on the grounds. If you could only have seen him paddling up the Baraboo River, coming to see the show. What a sight! That was circus, man. Charlie was circus with a capital *C*."

JULY 5, 1998
If only your Uncle Pete were alive to see you! You led the circus band! You didn't panic either. When you got up on stage with the bright lights in your face, you thought you might lose it there for a minute, the feeling was so close, but then you saw the elephants come out and you heard the note before you played it — and the next thing you know you're halfway through the song and the feeling is completely gone. It was like you were right there on top of the elephants, riding along. Yes, the elephants! The elephants were the toughest. They sway a lot, kind of like

a basketball player warming up to take a foul shot, doing all his idiosyncratic moves before he shoots the ball. But you don't know which movement is a warm-up and which is the real thing, so your trills just kind of hang there. It's hard. Man, you need to improve your wind and your tongue if you're going to make it through this. The horses were easier because they're so fluid and graceful, like swans on a lake, around and around, their heads held so proudly. Actually, the uniform was the most difficult part of it all. It was way too small and uncomfortable . . .

The owner, Mr. F., came over to you after the show and said he thought you were terrific and gave you a big hug. He really meant it. He wants you to lead the band until Billy C. gets better. They don't know how long that'll be. But they want you to lead the band. Yes, you led the band! You're the leader of the band! This, you realized, is what you've always wanted to do. Then he wanted to lay some money on you, but you wouldn't take it. He really insisted, but you were more insistent. That was perfect, telling him that he'd need the money for Billy C.'s hospital bill. That made him think. Then he said whatever you wanted at the circus, you could have. Wow, that was great. "Anything!" he said. You didn't even hesitate. You told him that if you were going to lead the band for the rest of the week then what you could really go for most of all was a uniform that fit. Right away Mr. F. had a person come over and measure you and said he'd have it all ready the next day. Boy, you felt like a movie star then. And he said he'd have one of the unused trailers out back ready for you to use if you wanted a dressing room. And then he invited you to his house for dinner! You had to decline, though, because you had a date with

Jane for that movie at the Al Ringling Theatre and then the fireworks display from her rooftop. She's really sensitive about that stuff and would have been heartbroken if you had canceled. He gave you a rain check. Then all the circus performers came over to you and patted you on the back and told you how well you had done. First it was Romanoff and his beautiful little wife, then Mrs. G. the elephant lady, Squeaky, all the girls from the ropes, Mrs. D. and Mr. D. of the horses, Chico Avalos the juggler, Mr. T. and the other clowns. Everybody. It was while you were talking to them that you had that ironic thought: *You're probably the first person in history who ran away and the circus joined you!*

EIGHTEEN

Karina

A diminutive block of chiseled marble, Karina at five foot one, 110 pounds, was 100 percent muscle. Just to see her walk you understood instantly that this was not a normal person but a phenomenon capable of one-armed handstands, back flips, double back flips, splits — almost any move invented that defied the laws of human flexibility and strength. And what a beautiful face she had, too. It glowed. A Mona Lisa face, dark hair, big brown eyes, round cheeks, angular jaw, a bold yet playful smile, a tender forehead. And her beautiful countenance sat atop a bull neck that represented the prodigious power, grace, and agility of the rest of her body. She wore a choker necklace around it as if to keep it bridled, to keep it from growing too large. To see her close up in a leotard took your breath away: a nexus of muscles, sinews, and tendons interwoven across silky, porcelain-white skin. Then the buttocks! Charlie described them in his journals as "Michelangelo buttocks — no less hard, perhaps a bit more feminine." And then, most distinctive of all, that sweet, risible accent.

"CHARLIE VAS PASSIONATE man. I loved him. He vas beautiful person for me [she began to cry]. Forgive please. Difficult for think 'bout Charlie gone. He vas my prince. He save me from beast. [She sobbed balefully for a full minute.] My poor Charlie! Vas after first time he play vith band, I talk vith Charlie 'lone. Fall vith love for Charlie. Ve ask him for come our trailer, talk vith him for change music. Charlie come in trailer, sit in couch, no clothes, just leather part for middle wear. He vas not vear circus uniform, dress alvays like Indian man. Dress circus uniform only for show. 'Ve change act,' B. say him. 'You must to change songs.' B. say he must play two new songs. Charlie smile, alvays smile Charlie, and say he vill study and play next day, no problem. He say he go to library right now, study songs, get arra'gement. B. not like Charlie, think he is crazy man with tattoos all over his body and dress like Indian man. He not trust Charlie play music for us right, but Charlie alvays play good music, not make mistake like Mr. Billy. He alvays play sveet, just right. B. make fist at Charlie, yell him play right or he get angry, hit him for not he have some crazy man make stupid him front of audience. My husband yell from everybody; shake fist from everybody. I get Charlie beer. My husband tell ugly joke for Charlie, then leave trailer vith big laugh for himself. He go for get massage from fat whore he like with big bosoms, come give massage him two for veek. He like only the bosoms, B., I don't have. He no like me for that. He has sex with her. I know. I vatch him. I know vhen he make sex after. But I don't care now for him make sex vith anybody. I'm not married him now. I vish for Charlie come back. [She cried for a long time. She had a large handkerchief and was able to stem the flow.] I'm sorry. I'm sorry. But I know not say vith Charlie sit there. Then I start cry. I no understand vhy cry, but maybe because I know Charlie is sympatic person. His eyes sympatic. I tell him my husband bad man all day — not love me; not care for me; not vant sex with me. Charlie reach me, hold me in his arms, say nice things; tell me how beautiful I am, describe my face, my hair, my legs and bottom. I tell him B. hurt me, hit me, not like me, not like my bottom, only like bosoms. Charlie start rub my bottom, say he no understand my husband who have such beautiful girl as vife not treat her right, not treat her like princess, have bottom like two giant pearls. All my life I vant man speak me like that, say like that to me. Romantic things. All Romanian girls like romantic talk. Then he start kiss me. He say he vants sex with me. He say me I have best bottom in vorld and vant kiss it. He take me vith his arms and for carry me bedroom, but fall on floor vith foots too big on carpet. On floor he kiss my body, 'specially bottom. Oh it vas for heaven. He vas passionate man. He take me there on floor. Kiss me everyvhere my body. He not miss one place, everything he kiss. Everything! He vas passionate man. I loved him. He vas beautiful person for me. [Again she cried, blowing her nose when she was done.] Forgive please. He save me from beast husband. Ve made sex again on floor. Two times ve make sex.

"Ve start vorry for B. come home. He leave from me; kiss me; say he come back next time. Say me he love me. Kiss me again. He vas secret lover three and half years. I perform with smile, I smile for Charlie. He alvays there in audience. Ve go back Romania after season, stay six months. I cry for Charlie. But come back April and he is there vait for me. Ve make sex three times, same night. Ve meet sometime late night, in big top for lovemaking. In center ring he take me, make love in center ring, late at night. Ve alvays find vay for come together for lovemaking. Then he die. [A waterfall of tears this time. It took her five minutes to recover.] It not fair. He vas my prince. I vant marry him, divorce B. Two years 'go tell B. vant divorce him, marry Charlie. He laugh me. He think I make joke. He think Charlie crazy man, dress like Indian man. Who vant marry Charlie? he think. He not believe me. That's when I follow Charlie to his home, follow in voods along river. Quietly run after boat from behind. Follow him up to his home. Long vay it vas. Charlie surprise, then angry, then happy. No one see his home, he say. Ve make sex all night. I not go to circus four days. They look everyvhere, can't find me. I stay in Charlie's house like Indian squall. I can tell you story if you vant hear, yes?

JULY 13, 1998
Boris Romanoff told you a joke in that Romanian accent of his. At first you thought it wouldn't translate. But it did. He even got the *W* right at the end:

"Feesh in lake see fly above vater, say, 'If fly go down six yinches, I yit fly.' Eagle passing over pond see fish, say, 'If fly go down six yinches, fish yit fly, I yit fish.' Beer on shore see eagle, say, 'If fly go down six yinches, fish yit fly, eagle yit fish, I yit eagle.' Hunter in voods see beer, say, 'If fly go down six yinches, fish yit fly, eagle yit fish, beer yit eagle, I shoot beer.' Mouse under log see hunter, say, 'If fly go down six yinches, fish yit fly, eagle yit fish, beer yit eagle, hunter shoot beer, drop chyz sandvich, I yit chyz.' Cat nearby see mouse, say, 'If fly go down six yinches, fish yit fly, eagle yit fish, beer yit eagle, hunter shoot beer, drop chyz sandvich, mouse yit chyz, I yit mouse.' Suddenly fly go down six yinches. So, fish yit fly, eagle yit fish, beer yit eagle, hunter shoot beer, drop chyz sandvich, mouse yit chyz, cat miss mouse and fall in lake. Vhat is moral of story? Every time fly go down six yinches, pussy get wet."

What a laugh on that Romanoff. Too bad he's such a wife beater . . . Little Karina with the most beautiful ass in the world. She threw herself at you the minute Romanoff left the house. You had sex right there on the floor. What a tigress she is, but you rode her all over the room, up and down, in and out, over and under, around and through. You knocked over a table and a chair, cut your cheek, twisted your ankle, wrenched your shoulder, stubbed your toe. What a ride! You don't like the thought of fornicating with someone's wife. However, in this case it's justifiable adultery. She desperately needs someone, the poor thing, and he obviously treats her like chattel. Never a kind word to her. He must be close to twenty years older than she is. She said she's twenty-five. He's got to be well over forty. She's got an ass as hard as a rock. I bet you can crack an egg on it . . .

You've always admired aerialists most of all. Then you got to thinking of a poem on the paddle back:

Never a Plop!
Suspended from a cottony rope
High above the center ring
Like a drop of water
Swaying, elongating,
Flouting physics
With muscle ups,
Kips and Ls,
Pointed
Poised
Yet
Never a plop!

NINETEEN

Susan Green

Susan Green was the mother of Charlie's third child. She was a
visiting professor of botany who worked for the Aldo Leopold
Foundation through the auspices of the University of
Wisconsin — Madison. I met her alone at nine o'clock on
Wednesday morning, March 13, at the Aldo Leopold shack along
the Wisconsin River. It's a beautiful place, an arboretum of sorts,
a quiet, contemplative setting in the woods. It served as the laboratory of the famed naturalist.

Ms. Susan Green, PH.D, attractive in a girl-next-door way,
was a green-eyed, red-haired Celt; a diminutive, nervous woman
packed neatly into a square yet solid frame, about five foot four,
with a bob nose, soft and expressive cheeks, a freckled face, a
determined Gaelic look. She dwelled exclusively in the world of
plants with the occasional visit to the hallowed halls of acade-
mia for her assigned round-table discussions on policy, pro-
gramming, and poppycock. After the arrival of Charlie into her
life, she had to adjust herself to a radical new perspective. At
twenty-eight, she no doubt had dreams of grandeur. Perhaps
she envisioned herself as one day becoming the *Grande Dame of
Dendrology* or even the *Fine Femme of Phytology*. But with a one-
year-old child to raise, no husband, and a mere starvation
stipend, it had been hard times for her; I could see it on her face
and read it between the lines she spoke in her lilting brogue.

She talked to me outside the Leopold shack, next to the shag-bark hickories.

"CHARLIE WAS PROOBABLY the most frequent visitor we had here at the reserve. He would arrive on his bike and spend the day wandering the land, observing. He became an arborist, totally self-taught. We normally doon't allow people to just coom to the reserve and wander aboot, that's not how the center ooperates. But Charlie, of course, was different. I doon't knew if you are familiar with Aldo Leopold's writings and work, or the Leopold Foundation. Mr. Leopold was an environmentalist, an educator and writer who wrote aboot the land and the land eethic. I would suggest reading his moost famous work, *A Sand County Almanac*. The foundation that supports and manages the reserve was originally created in nineteen forty-nine by the Leopold family to preserve Mr. Leopold's farm and shack in perpetuity. Ooriginally we were called the Aldo Leopold Sand County Trust. Then in nineteen eighty-two the trust was incorporated and later renamed the Aldo Leopold Foundation. We're a fourteen-hoondred-acre reserve involved in public education, conservation, ecological restoration, management, and scientific research — a loot of which we do right here at the reserve. Our mission is to promote care of natural resources by foostering an eethical relationship between people and land. Forgive me for smiling, but your broother had memorized the mission statement. He sang it, as a matter of fact. He'd invented a little song. I think everyone who works here knews the song noow and as a result can easily remember the mission statement. [She paused for a long time to fight back tears.] I was quite close with your broother. We were lovers. [She paused again for an even longer time.] He is the father of my soon. [She began to cry big, sorrowful tears.] Excuse me. I get very sad when I think of him gone. We talked aboot getting married this past winter. [Again she paused.] Forgive me, I have a problem with leaky tear ducts. [She sniffled indelicately, then blew her nose.] Blast! I'm sorry, I told myself before you came that I wouldna get emotional, but here I am. I can't hide myself, I guess.

"You knew, there was a period at the beginning when I wouldna tell anyone aboot my relationship with your broother. I didna want anyone to knew. I doon't knew why. The usual reasons, I guess — a professional woman hanging aroond with a will-o'-the-wisp. No one knew we were intimate. They knew we were friends. But then the father of my child? How could I hide it? Oh blast! [For a long time she gave in to the tears, sniffling and wheezing, trying to let it all out so as to be done with it.] I have a child noow who needs to know who his father is. I'm not embarrassed. I'm prood. Oh, he was fantastic, your broother. Exciting. Interesting. Looving. We had a wonderful time together. He looved this place. He was ablaze when he came here. Like a child in a toy store. He lived the life that Aldo Leopold spoke of. It was like Professor Leopold's soul had been born into Charlie's. To see him walk aroond here, looking at the trees, marveling at the river, studying the sedges, sometimes playing a song on his little troompet. He was magic, truly. He lived in nature as part of it, he did. Like Pan himself. He had the land eethic, your broother, that Professor Leopold spoke aboot. He practiced a rational restraint; he understood the earth's cycles. He was close to them. He was like a Native American. I doon't knew what his life moost have been like before he came here, but here he was blessed. Now you tell me he lived in a city. That he was sick with agoraphoobia. You couldna tell he had eever lived in the city, that he was afraid, that he was full of panic. His music spook noothing of that. I heard noothing of the fear or the anxiety. His songs were eethereal, like the soond of wind more than symphonic music. It was music for the open sky, not of the cooncert hall, certainly not of the city or a phoobia. There was such freedom in his soond. How many people can just pull out a little instrument and play, just like reading a book? He carried aroond that little troompet and he would play it, oh, he would play it. [Again the tears began, but they subsided quickly this time.]

"But you asked aboot the first time I saw Charlie. Oh yes, I remember that. It was November sixteen, nineteen ninety-eight. It was the prairie restoration project. We have a tradition here that Professor Leopold himself started, which was to replant new prairie onto formerly cultivated land. We had volunteers froom the community, maybe thirty people in all, and Charlie was one of them. Of course, how could you not remember him with his leather boockskins and tattoos, his height, his feet. Oh goodness. He came right o'er to me and was quite warm and friendly right froom the start. He was extremely curious to knew how we had coom by the seeds we were planting, which of course is the main point. To get the prairie seeds was the real work; planting the prairie took only a few hours. But to get the seeds to plant took hoondreds of hours of painstaking work collecting — getting the right mix of grasses, sedges, and wildflowers, some of which are extremely rare. He was fascinated by this. Not many people would think to ask these questions so easily. But he had that intuitive reasoning. But back to the first day we met.

"Our group of volunteers of course were outfitted with canvas sacks full of the seeds. They were shown how to disseminate, keeping in a relatively straight line as we spread the seeds o'er the field, scattering them left to right. Charlie was oot there in the middle of the pack, whistling, you know that Disney song, 'Whistle While You Work,' and he was kind of hamming it up, making soom of the high school students laugh, especially the girls. And all of the soodden those big feet get caught on a cornstalk and *plop*, down he goes, seeds flying oop in the air. The fields were very mooddy; moost of us had boots on. We had in fact instructed all of the volunteers to wear them. He had his boots on. Anyway, he hit the mood headfirst — *splat*. Everyone stoopped. Ha ha ha. He really was soomthing. He rose slowly to his feet and that face was coovered. Al Jolsen. Just two white spots when he opened his eyes. He had seedlings sprinkled all o'er his cheeks, so he looked like a chocolate-coovered coon with sprinkles. His clothes, too. Oh, you should have heard the shrieks of laughter! He took a look aroond himself, didna say anything, didna laugh at himself, found his sack of seeds, started to whistle that same song, and off he went. All day like that. Neever washed his face off. Oh, what a character he was. But he had made a statement, I think. It was very clear to me. The mood, the soil, the earth is an extension of ourselves. We try to separate ourselves froom it, we wash it off our bodies daily, wipe it froom our shoes, distance ourselves froom it as if it weren't a part of our lives. But it is. It is our lives, it sustains us, it is our final resting place.

"After the seeding, and when all the volunteers had left, only Charlie remained, sitting oonder the groove of white oaks straight oot from the shack there on the north side of the ridge coming down there to the left. You can see. He was sitting cross-legged reading from *A Sand County Almanac,* his face still coovered, only now the mood had dried and cracked and he looked more like an African shaman than a chocolate-coovered ice cream coon. I walked o'er to him and asked what he was read-ing. I'll neever forget that moment. He looked oop at me and said, 'The wind that makes music in November corn is in a hurry.' He had recited the opening line from the chapter 'November' of Professor Leopold's book. He took out his little troompet and played the most beautiful song I have ever heard, it is our song. 'My One and Only Love.' It echoed throughout the valley, swirled aroond in the freshly planted field to the north, then settled into my heart. It lies there still. I can hear it just as clearly noow as the day he played it. Our song. When he was done, he turned to me and said, 'Human music is not in a hurry; it is defiant. It hints of the eternal.' Those were his own words. I believe I fell in loove with him right then and there. We sat and talked for hours.

"Then, somehow, it was nighttime and we were in my bed, warm and close. I doon't remember driving hoom, or eating, or even what we said. I just remember being next to him in my bed, warm and close. And you won't believe it, or maybe you will because he was your broother, but he neever washed the dried mood off his face."

NOVEMBER 18, 1998

Warly Go Amang the Seeds
(a Scootish rhyme)

Poured in rows o'er the field
Wee hoopes of flowers sealed.
Whisps of scratch a pitch in air
The batch of oospore sink alair.
Will sproot a spring, sparkle, shine
Like florid grapes atwinkle vine.
Children chance to see and play
On afternoons in moonth of May.
Coolored lasses, waves of grasses;
Loord amarcy, the goldfinch passes!
So, warly go amang the seeds
Or nought will pass a fruitful deed.
The warl' of man depends on you
To fooster grooth; the earth renew.

She had a book of Robert Burns's poetry. You read a couple of poems, then you thought up your own and wrote it down. Susan inspired it. She's a beautiful woman. Smart, passionate about the earth. You will make her a present of the poem somehow. You will make her something with the poem written in the middle — a rabbit pelt or a birch stump. Then after you wrote the poem, you heard the song in your head louder than ever before. But this time the music was in the sound of bagpipes. Two new measures; the bridge. You'll have to borrow her bagpipes. She has them.

THE FIRST YEAR of Charlie's new life was over. He'd met and begun relationships with all the allies, adjusted to the sights and sounds and smells of his new world, but above all healed and thrived. As Wakdjunkaga he was, perhaps unwittingly, beginning to work his magic on the earth.

Judd Barkin, aka Squeaky the Clown, in his interview with me, described Charlie's return to the circus that next summer, 1999. It was a story that some people would like to forget, but most will never be able to.

TWENTY

Charlie Day at Circus World

(JUDD BARKIN)

"Here's a story that's perfect. This is Charlie wit' a capital *C*. After he took the band, season was over, Mr. F., the owner, came to me just before the start of the next season and he had it in his mind to employ him, employ Charlie. He knew I was probably the closest to Charlie, and he wanted me to get a feel for the guy, see if he'd sign a contract. He knew Charlie was an attraction, he wanted to make sure he was always there. Basically, what he wanted was Charlie to become a clown. Wanted us to work him into the act. He had this great idea to inaugurate Charlie as an entirely new type of clown — a fourth category. So Mr. F. thought he would introduce this new type of clown, which is your brother — a tattooed Indian, basically. It was a neat idea. It would kind of fuse the two circuses together, you know, the Wild West shows, kind of rodeo, and the big-top circus variety. It's about eighty years too late, but what the hell, better late than never. I think he said he wanted someone from the Smithsonian to come up and do this whole induction ceremony. Anyways, I tell Charlie about it and he says no way. But when I told the boss it was a no go, Mr. F. wouldn't take no for an answer. He had me relaying messages back and fort' to your brother, but Charlie wouldn't have it. No was no wit' Charlie. But Mr. F. was goddamn insistent on getting him under contract and getting him in the act, even if we had to do it wit' Charlie sitting in the audience like he always did — that was fine wit' him. He was right, Charlie would have made a fantastic clown, I'd even told him so myself. But I knew the guy, I knew your brother, he didn't want no employment. I told Mr. F. that Charlie was Charlie, and the circus was everything to the guy. In fact, he was better than an employee, because he didn't have to pay him nothing. But I also knew he wouldn't sign no contract. Owners are like that — they don't feel secure unless they've got a contract wit' your name signed on the dotted line. So he comes up with an alternative idea: If he won't sign no contract, then he's going to have a new event — Charlie Day at Circus World. They're going to do a tribute to Charlie, bring him out in the ring, shine the spotlight on him, have us clowns jerk around wit' him, present him wit' the award for bein' a fourth kinda clown. Get the press to cover it. Get him up there wit' the band in his Indian getup and play a couple of songs. Charlie won't want that, I told Mr. F. In fact, I told Mr. F., in my opinion, I wouldn't look a gift horse in the mout'. But Mr. F. wanted to examine every molar and bicuspid.

"So the season starts, and there's Charlie the first day, just like he was before he took the band, in his skins, paddling the canoe, eating ice cream, looking at Mrs. G. washing the elephants. Anyways, after the first show, ten o'clock show, I ask Charlie back to my trailer. We sit down, I make him some lemonade — he likes that. I ask him how the winter was and all. He said it was cold. I told him it'd be a lot less cold if he put some clothes on — *Honk! Honk!* Couldn't resist. But I knew Charlie well enough then just to put it to him straight. I tell him about Charlie Day, 'Mr. F.'s way of just saying thank you for taking the band last year, you know, he felt bad you wouldn't take no money.' 'No Charlie Day,' your brother says wit' no hesitation. Fine, you know the poor guy just wants to do what he does, he don't want nobody

messing up his one great love in life. I take the info back to Feld,
tell him no go all the way around. Charlie just don't want it. Well,
the Felds go way back wit' the circus, and they go way back
because they're used to getting what they want. Charlie might
not want to be honored, but it's his circus, goddamn it, and if he
wants to have a Charlie Day, then he's gonna have one. This is the
way Mr. F. was thinking.

"A week goes by. There's Charlie every day now with the
canoe, the Indian suit, the whole nine yards, kids are loving him.
I even put a little thing in the act where I go up to the edge of the
ring and bounce a ball off his head. The first time I did it, he
didn't even respond. I swear, I t'rew the ball, it bounced off his
head, and nothing. I did it a couple more times, but there was
nothing happening, so I stopped it. Anyways, week goes by, two
weeks, then Mr. F. calls me into his office. 'Judd,' he says, 'I've
decided we're going wit' the Charlie Day idea.' I tried to interrupt
him, but he continued anyways. 'Judd, I know exactly what you're
gonna say, but legally there's nothing the man can do. If I want to
honor him, give him an award, and he don't want that or like that,
well then that's the way the cookie crumbles. It'll be June
eleventh, Friday the eleventh. The only thing I'm gonna tell you
and everyone is to keep it a secret from him. I don't want him to
know. It's to be a complete surprise.' I didn't like the sound of that
at all. 'Mr. Feld,' I said, 'what if he don't like it?' 'It don't matter,'
he says stubbornly. 'But what if he gets so angry he don't come
back to the show? Is it worth taking that risk?' 'In my mind, yes,'
he says. I had a bad conscience for a long time wit' that. I wanted
to tell Charlie in the worst way, but if I did Mr. Feld, oh hell, I
don't know. I had kind of figured out in my mind that we'd just
present the goddamn award, take the pictures, he'd not like it, but
it wouldn't turn out so bad. Boy, was I wrong.

"A week before the show, Mr. F. calls me in again. He's got a new brainstorm. 'A dock.' 'A what?' I cough. 'A dock wit' his name on it, wit' a welcome sign. He pulls up in the morning, and there's the dock for his canoe.' Now, this here's really starting to smell bad. 'He don't even have a rope inside that thing to tie it to a dock,' I tell him. 'Good point,' he says. 'We'll make sure we have them leave a rope there. They'll build it the night before.'

"Day comes, and we're all instructed to be out by the dock, which is right out in front of the big top. There's the dock wit' the banners saying, WELCOME CHARLIE. Banners all around saying, FIRST ANNUAL CHARLIE DAY. So there we are all waiting around the dock, about one, one fifteen. They've got the elephants and camels and giraffes all out there; video crew, cameramen, aerial ballerinas ready to give him a big smooch. And as if cued exactly when to arrive, there he comes paddling along. It's upriver, you know. He has no idea what the hell's going on. He's so dumbfounded by the sight of everyone out there, the elephants, the girls, the band, all of it, he don't even see the dock, the sign, none of it. He paddles right past us as if he thinks there's something coming along behind him that he better make room for. Quickly Billy pipes up the band with a round of 'For He's a Jolly Good Fellow.' He slows down and stops in the middle of the river; the boat starts drifting back the way it came. Paddles some more, stops, drifts back, paddles again. Classic stuff. Then you can tell it hits him. It's all for him. That sinks in. Your brother didn't like being the center of attention, I can tell you that.

"Slowly he paddles in toward us, his face just terrified — it wasn't red, it was green. You could tell even then he was getting all trembly, shaky. 'Charlie, go to the dock, paddle to the dock!' I yell at him. He hears me, kind of looks up like he's relieved to hear a familiar voice. He steers over to the dock, which is much too high for its purpose. He pulls up alongside it and puts his hand up on the dock, looking around very self-consciously, shaking visibly.

Now the video crew jumps into action wit' the cameramen right in his face, barking orders at him. 'Tie the canoe down wit' the rope and jump out on the dock,' they're instructing him, the cameras two inches from his nose. He's about as comfortable as a blind date at a drive-in. Someone hands him the rope, and he starts to look around. There's nowhere to tie it. He's got that dugout kind; there ain't no hole or nothing for him to tie it to. He stands there holding the rope, looking around, the canoe starting to drift back out again. Then he starts to panic. Everyone's starting to laugh now because he's looking exactly like a clown, I swear, the way he's overreacting it looked staged. And the more he cries and distresses, the more everyone laughs, you know that act? Jesus Christ. But I got this bad conscience, and people are laughing and the cameramen aren't telling him to forget it, so I come over and tell him forget about it, lose the rope, and just get out. He's got those feet. He tries to get out of the canoe and onto the dock, but wit'out the canoe being tied down and the dock being way too high, he puts one foot on the deck and the boat starts to slide out from under him. He does a split, then *splash*, in the drink he goes. Everyone's laughing now. The whole place is in an uproar. He's all embarrassed, humiliated. Looks like a drowned rat coming up out of that water. Retrieves the boat, pulls it up to the dock, and actually picks it up over his head and puts in on top of the dock. He had some muscle, that guy.

"He come sloshing out of the river, soaking wet. Cameramen are in his face, people are laughing. Billy C. pipes up the band for another round of 'For He's a Jolly Good Fellow.' He staggers out of the water and everyone kinda crowds around him. Then, uh oh, Charlie's not looking too good. Halfway t'rough the song he blows his breakfast. That was a bad moment. He's throwing up while the cameramen are filming, and in between heaves he's waving the cameramen off; women are screaming, little kids crying for their mommies. That was bad. He disappears into the men's room and the crowd breaks up, everyone goes back to the big top to get ready for the show. They mop up the puke. I go in to check on Charlie. He's lying there in the stall, all panicky. 'You all right, Charlie?' I ask him. 'Yeah,' he says. 'Well, when you're done, you come on into the big top, they've got a little award they want to present to you,' I tell him. Someone said they saw him about five minutes later come sprinting outa that bathroom, took a hop, skip, and a jump into his canoe and off he went, paddling like the devil himself was after him. That was the first and last annual Charlie Day at Circus World.

"And you know what he done? That night he come back and tore that dock out of there. It was gone the next day. Nothing left. Not even a nail. Took all the wood wit' him. The good thing was, old Charlie was back in his usual ringside seat the next day. No one said nothing to him about it. What a washout that was. Mr. F. never said a word about it to me after. Not a great circus moment. That one won't get up on the wall in the pavilion."

JUNE 11, 1999

They threw you a party and you threw up on it! They stood there singing your name and you gagged up goose meat in front of the kids. Squeaky was trying hard to calm you down, but you lost control. Completely lost control! Total panic! Your worst nightmare! And yet . . . if they just hadn't built that dock, it wouldn't have been so bad. That ridiculous dock! Who in their right mind would think to build a dock for a canoe? Riverbanks *are* docks for canoes. That's what they're there for. They go together like peanut butter and jelly. A canoe dock? Seagulls shit on docks. Even rocks are better than docks. *Fuck docks! Docks suck rocks!*

TWENTY-ONE

The Min'ster's Cat

(KARINA ROMANOFF)

"I tell you story for time I run 'vay to Charlie in boat, follow him his home on small hill in voods. B. hit me, hurt me, call me fat calf, ugly bitch, not like my food, not like my performance, not like my bosoms. I hate him. I run 'vay, follow Charlie vhen he leave from end second show. No one can see me, I run from tree for tree. I follow Charlie. He love me, I know. I follow follow through voods, far back from Charlie he not see me follow him. I crying running, follow him. Vhen he put boat on land, then boat on head valk through voods, I valk close him, up hill, not make noise on floor of voods, break sticks, no. He valk up hill, go to home, put down boat. Vhen he do I stand front him crying, but smile him vith big teeth. He big surprise find me there suddenly. He first angry, 'No one come here!' he say. I cry harder, smile fast gone. He put his arms 'round me and valk me inside home. Vhat place vas that! All vood, he make, pictures, fireplace, furs of animals black and brown of floor and vall. Place for man before mechanic time. He put me on bed of blankets, put fingers through my hair, kiss mouth, ask questions vhy for B. not nice vith beautiful vife. Say special vords me vhen I stop talk. He roll me over, massage my bottom, kiss it, say it most beautiful part of body in vorld. Take egg and break it on my bottom, rub it on my chest. Ve make sex together for long time. He very gentle man, very passionate.

"It get dark for night. He leave me, ask me if hungry. But before I say, he valk out home and gone. In ten minutes is back, no clothes, but carry long rabbit from ears. Say vith happy smile, 'Look for Mr. Johnson find.' I not know who is Mr. Johnson, but maybe he take rabbit from farmer Mr. Johnson. He go to big pot, cut skin from rabbit, make rabbit ready, put rabbit on stick and to fire, turn it 'round, vant me next him. He have vater in kettle in fire, make cup full tea. Together ve drink, next fire, he turn rabbit stick, smell like flowers of meat. I very hungry. He have carrots, too. He throw them in kettle for cooking, then corn in kettle too for cooking. He make joke with rabbit on stick, play games with it, make it dance and talk, I laughing. 'Ouch, is hot here,' say rabbit. 'Yes and is hot even I have no fur.' I laugh long time for that. No more sad, but happy. Vhen is ready, he prepare beautiful table vith candle. He play music on radio and ve eat rabbit, carrot, corn, bread, and vine. Ve drink Romanian vine, Premiat, vhich is famous vine my country, not best vine, but he has there for me. Turn teeth color of grape. Very romantic night ve have. The rabbit is so good eating. Tender. He know how add spices for cooking. Garlic, salt, lemon. Oh, I love Charlie lot. He vas — [she began sobbing]. Oh Charlie! Vhy he has die?

"I stay Charlie house four days. He not say I must go back circus. Keep me safe, take care me. He still go for circus every day not vant them think Charlie help me run 'vay. These best four days my life. Svim in river no clothes. Make sex three, four, times day vith Charlie. That time and place my little Carlo made. He sleeping now. You must see. He look same as your brother Charlie. But vhat food Charlie can cooking. How you say gooz? He cook gooz. Drink vine, run through voods no clothes, like salvages. Freedom.

"One day out in field corn, all mud after rain, ve play game. Frog jump. No clothes. Every time you say 'Min'ster Cat' like something, you jump frog over back of Charlie. You have only time from jump to time come back on ground vith feet think vord and say vord. It funny because I not know English and can't think for vord say. Just famous people I know how say. Make Charlie laugh so he can't jump and alvays fall on top me from laughing hard and ve get all in mud. Min'ster Cat, you never play? It easy. You say, 'Min'ster Cat is *big* cat.' See? Each time jump, it next vord in alphabet. But I not know lots vords for English. Some time I say vord, I think of famous person. 'Min'ster Cat is Barry Man'low cat.' That vas one make Charlie laugh and fall on me and can't get up laugh so long. Ve make sex in field of mud.

"Charlie have tree with branch run straight, strong, vant me show him do routine. Vhat funny happening. One morning I vake from sleep, go outside. On branch Charlie make trapeze, hanging from tree. He make for I use for training some time. He come home from circus I show him back lever. I show him, then he try. He take clothes down. He hang from bar no clothes. He try back lever, but no too good. He not have strong enough stomach. He try many times, he cannot do it. I tell him keep legs straight vith point toe. He try again, but not point toe, not keep legs straight. Just penis. Ha ha ha. Then he do 'nother move. He hang upside down for ground. He sving back and forward. Then funny, he does something hands in mouth and teeth. 'Vhat doing?' I am asking him. 'Flushing,' he say. He is flushing teeth, svinging back and forward with vhite string in mouth, flushing. He say me put flushing teeth in routine, send good message for audience, he say.

"He finally say me one day they can get new act soon. He say circus ready fire us from show, use 'nother act, hear from friend Mr. Barkin vhite-face clown. They get new act ve must go back Romania and I never see Charlie 'gain. I go back circus. B. know I hate him, but he not treat me so bad like before. He not say anything, let me sleep in other bed 'lone. Then I am pregnant, have Charlie's baby. [She sobbed long and hard.] He vill never remember his father. I no vant talk 'round Charlie now."

<u>JULY 19, 2000</u>

You made her rabbit. She loved it. Followed you home like a stray dog. You turned around and there she was crying, all out of breath, in her leotard. She'd run all the way. What a heroine she is. What a coward that Romanoff. He beats her like a dog. Look at her asleep there. She's adorable. You'll have to tea-bag her. You'd love to keep her. There's a new power in your home with a woman in it. You sleep better. Even the food tastes better. She really liked the rabbit. You'll make her a hat from the pelt with that little poem you thought of written on the inside:

Thanks Rabbit

Your hair fits on my head;
Insulates me instead.
Warming with no less zeal,
Not to mention the meal.

But she's got to go back. She can't stay. You were right, you *can* crack an egg on her ass.

TWENTY-TWO

Turtle Menu

(CHAPPY)

"Ev'y day a story wit' that man. He jus' a livin', breavin' story. I hear all 'bout him an' the circus. My brother-law deliver the feeds fo' the animules over there once a week. They tells him all 'bout the Chaz man, comin' ev'y day; playin' in the band, playin' trumpet jus' like my daddy; dress' hisself in them buckskins. Only time I been there was when they open the museum firs' year, give a tribute to the Lowery Ban'. I awready tole you 'bout my daddy, he one of the trumpet players in the ban' with P. G. Lowery. Soun' crazy to you, I bet. I been livin' here fi'ty years, I ain' been down there but one time, and that when they have a tribute to my daddy's ban'. He long dead when they have that. Don' 'member the date. Fi'ty-nine maybe. I gots to go over there one o' these days, when I gets me some time together. But the Chaz man, he love that place. He paddle that canoe up the 'Boo to the circus ev'y day they gots the show, May to October.

"Yeah, he use' carry that canoe on his back sometimes when he need to portage. I seen him one day walkin' wit' that boat on his head. I jus' comin' to work early in the mo'nin' in my pickup truck. I pulls over side o' the road and tells him he crazy son-abitch. Tells him I gonna make him a pull-trailer fo' his bike. 'Bout a week after I seen him on the road with that canoe on his head, we starts makin' the pull-trailer together. Didn' need no extra supplies — couple tires off a old kid's bike, alumynum frame from the handles on a couple lawn mowers, I think they was. I gots that welder back there an' we fires that thang up together one night. Come out real nice. Somebody say they gots that on display down at the Circus Worl'. Say they gots the bike an' pull-trailer there on display together. Gots to get down there one day and see that. Never did see Chaz's place neither. He pretty secret 'bout it, I s'pose. Built it from the stuff he 'cumulate from here, tell you that. Don' know when that was we fires up the pull-trailer, maybe three o' fo' years back, my memory ain' no good fo' years. But ever since then he have a easier time wit' hisself 'cause he always here, always pullin' somethin' back home to his house from here.

"Sometime he jus' sit an' watch me, say nothin', just relax and keep me comp'ny. Lots o' time he help me out a little, liftin', packin', stuff I does end o' the day. The Chaz man that way. He gots time. Rich wit' time that man. I tol' him one day, I says, 'Chaz, they gots the billionaires wit' they money and big houses on the beach, but they ain' got the mos' important thang they is, an' tha's time, free-wheelin' time like whachu got. Anybody gots free-wheelin' time, they the riches', money ain' the thang, it's the time.' He ogree wit' that. He were the riches' man I knew wit' time. Never had no plans. He smart that way.

"But speakin' 'bout comin' through that gate, yeah, here's a story fo' you if you lookin' fo' a story 'bout yo' brother. He come in through them gates on the bike, wit' the pull-trailer. It after closin' time. He hop down off that bike an' say real casual, no dif-f'ren' tone, 'You 'member what you tol' me 'bout eatin' turtle, 'bout turtle jus' like po'k chop? Well looky what I got here.' He walk me back to the pull-trailer an' there he got the bigges' meanes' snap-paturta you ever seen. 'Ouch, that one bad turtle,' I say. Musta be three foot long, fi'ty, si'ty poun' at leas'. Ah never see a turta like that. He chuckle a little. 'My present to you, Chappy,' he say. 'I jus' wanna keep the shell. Gonna make me a mirra wit' that,' he say. 'A mirra,' I says, 'you that kinda vanity?' I teasin' him. He shake his head and say it fo' one o' his janes. He always talkin' 'bout his janes. Musta been a half dozen he talk about. He never say a bad word agains' a one o' them, neither, which was mos' su'prisin' to me. Mos' mens have that many janes, they disrespec' 'em, talk behin' they back. Not him. Don' know how he done it, runnin' roun' wit' that many all at once at the same time. But he done it, 'parently. No offense, but he got them tattoos all over an' always stink with them skins on his body. I tells him that, too, one day, right to his face I says, 'You stanky!' an' 'What jane gonna wan' spen' time wit' you?' An' he say the janes love give him the bat', bave his ass. He say to me he stank pretty awful sometimes wit' lotions and perfumes they put on his body. I axe him why I never did catch no whiff o' him smellin' like roses. Hee hee hee, he was sompfin', yo' brother.

"But the gaydacuda, the snappaturta. That good eatin'. White folk don' eat that. They missin' out. He got that big ole snappaturta tied back o' his pull-trailer an' we lookin' down on that ole gian'. 'Tha's a present,' he say. 'That a lot o' meat,' I tells him. 'More meat than we can eat. I gonna caw my brother-law, have him bring over his kids, my sister, we have a party righ' here.' He ogree wit' that. I go caw, comes back an' he got that gaydacuda on the groun' pushin' a stick upside its head. 'They snap yo' finger righ' off they catch hol' it,' I tells him. 'I hears that, but he ain' but doin' it now,' he say. 'Tha's 'cause you ain' makin' him mad 'nough wit' that,' I tells him. 'You lif' that 'cuda up an' you shake him 'roun', then you watch him bust up that stick.' He squat hisself down, pick that ole 'cuda up over his head, not a easy lif', and he run 'roun' screamin' wit' that gaydacuda up there like a green halo. Hee hee hee, oh he a cutup, yo' brother. He come back, put that ole 'cuda down, and push that stick back upside his head. *Wham!* You hear that stick snap in half like lightnin' hittin' a tree. *Crack!* He jump back and say, 'That work.' He real curious, yo' brother. He get real quiet he see sompfin' new, almost like he got a person talkin' upside his head, tellin' him what it about. I seen him that way lots o' times. He never see no snappaturta break a big stick like that, and there he jus' seen it an' he take a moment let that voice upside his head tell hisself what he done jus' seen.

"Then we stops gets us sompfin to drink, think 'bout it. I mix sompfin' up quick. We sittin' right here where we sittin' now, lookin' at that ole 'cuda, drink in our han', nice an' peaceful out, birds singin' they sweet song. This maybe late September, beautiful faw day, blue sky, trees all diff'ren' colors. Warm as toas' outside. Chaz say, 'How we gonna kill that turta, Chappy? I ain' never kilt no turta befo',' he say. 'You know what they say?' I tells him. 'No, what they say?' he axe. 'You can't kill no snappaturta.' 'That a fac',' he say. Then I axe him, 'How you think you kill that turta?' 'Never thought 'bout that,' he say. 'I s'pose chop off his head,' he think to hisself out loud. 'That one way you can kill it,' I says. 'We can shoot it, too, I s'pose,' he say out loud to hisself again. 'That'd work,' I says. 'Course we couldn' drown him,' he shake his head out loud. 'That'd take too long,' I says. 'We could climb him up top the roof there and drop him off, but that bus' up the shell. You ever kilt a turta?' he axe. 'Sure I done, but that yo' turta, you the one should kill him now,' I says. 'You right there, Chappy,' he say. 'S'pose choppin' his head off the way bes' go 'bout that,' he say in that kinda sophisticate' way he talk. 'Good luck get his head out that shell now,' I says. That ole 'cuda jus' lie there, all hunkered up inside, nice an' secure. He throwed his drink down, get up, and walk around that snappaturta. 'He real big,' he say out loud to hisself. 'Yeah he is,' I ogrees. 'I gonna chop his head off,' he finally decide. 'That a good choice,' I tells him. 'Gots a ole machete in back the office, nice an' sharp,' I tells him. He fetch that, come back wit' that piece ready to go. He go over to that ole 'cuda an' give it a kick; it jus' sit there inside it shell. He push it 'roun' a little, jab the blade up in there, but that head don' wanna come out in the air. 'I gonna have to get him mad again,' he say. 'That'd work,' I tells him. See, I know aw you gots to do is put a little fire up by his hole there an' he come outa that hole fas' as you can snap yo' finger. But I didn' want to spoil my fun watchin' him. He ben' down and hef' that animule over his head again and run 'roun' screamin'. Hee hee hee. He sompfin' else. He gettin' aw red in the face, stagger back, throw that ole gaydacuda down, push 'nother stick upside his head, and *wham,* that turta crack that stick in half, but he not fas' enough wit' that blade and befo' he can chop off his head, that turta shoot his head back in there save hisself. So, again he pick it up, run 'roun'. He not so lively anymore, he kinda wobbly carryin' that shell top his head — too many drinks we done drank. Throw him down, 'nother stick. *Wham* come the head, down come the blade, but again that too slow. He don' swear much, yo' brother, but he swearin' like a sailor now. He determine'. He barely able to lif' that 'cuda over his head thir' time, carry him 'roun', then he step on a rock, trip over hisself, the 'cuda go flyin' out, rollin' like a broken tire 'roun' the dirt. I starts to laugh, hee hee hee, he lyin' there aw red in the face, got hisself a cut on the chin.

"He come back to me, look at me like he angry at me. He go pour hisself another drink and sit down. He don' say nothin' fo' a long time and I don' say nothin', waitin' out respect fo' him. 'Don' wan' ruin that shell,' he finally say. 'He too smart get his head chop off,' he say nex'. I was goin' tell him 'bout lightin' a fire outside his shell, but I was havin' too much fun to stop now. Then he start lookin' at that tree up nex' the shed house over there. That ole maple. 'Where that rope you has?' he axe. I tells him back o' the office, up on the wall. He walk back there, get that ole rope, an' tie it 'roun' the 'cuda. What a smile he give me. Then he carry it over to the tree, throw one end o' the rope over that low branch there, and pull that ole 'cuda up like he raisin' the flag. Gots that turta danglin' there, head down. Sompfin' wit' hangin' a turta upside down, gets they head out o' they shell I guess. That head and neck jus' hangin' there now. 'You blinefol' yo'self, make it a challenge,' I says to him. He look over an' nod, realize that fair game. He come back over to me an' tell me put a blinefol' over his eyes. I gots a ole cloth right there an' I blinefol' him. 'Give me a drink firs',' he say. I gives him a drink an' he throw tha' down fas'. Like a piñata that ole 'cuda danglin' there, an' he start swingin' wit' the blade. Missin' hittin' the shell, *clang*, missin'. 'Wait a minute,' he say, 'I don' wanna hurt that shell.' He take off the blinefol'. 'I gots a pair o' hedge clippers,' I says. 'That's the ticket,' he respon'. I go fine them clippers, brings them out, blinefol' him again. Then he go 'bout his bus'ness, chop choppin'. He missin' fo' a good while, then swish, he cut that turta head off clean. Fac' he don' even knowed he done it an' I gots to stop him, yell to him he done chop its head off.

"We cook that ole 'cuda up on the grill an' it jus' as tasty as can be. He like it a lot, yo' brother, and brought me another one nex' year. Not so big as that one. Nowhere near so big. But we had quite a time that night. He had brung his little horn in his bag. He play that all night, jus' as sweet an' comf'table as you please. Oh he jus' kep' playin', even when I pull out fo' the night, he still playin' that little horn, jus' as sweet and comf'table as you please, sittin' right where you sittin' now. Play a song I ain' never heard befo', beautiful. 'I Remember Charlie' I think it cawed. He was sompfin'. Ain' the same wit'out him 'roun' here. But that time, Chaz an' that ole snappaturta. Hee hee hee. That a livin' sight. That a sight for these sore eyes."

SEPTEMBER 26, 2000

Of all the animals in the kingdom, only the turtle surpasses mankind in longevity. And they ain't afraid of nothin'. Least of all a toe, which they would and could bite off in a blur. No doubt that very thought — of an unsuspecting wader inopportunely placing his fleshy big toe in front of a turtle's nose — has given many lake and river enthusiasts cause to walk gingerly across the muddy bottom, or to simply dive in and swim. But then the concatenate thought of the same creature coming up from the murky depths to snap off a flaccid penis, which for all intents and purposes could be misinterpreted as an intruder, a challenger, has likewise given many an intrepid male skinny-dipper cause to abandon the water altogether. Fortunately, on land, even with a shell, a turtle is no match for a man with hedge clippers, especially when *Chelydra serpentina* is suspended upside down from a tree.

. . . And after you'd eaten it you were surprised that someone hasn't come along and opened up a chain of turtle fast-food restaurants — like the catfish craze. Your own father would probably jump at the chance. You pictured teenagers wearing turtle-shell uniforms behind the counter.

"Can I help you, sir?"

"I'd like the Double Snapper Menu."

"Fried penises or toes?"

"Toes."

"Seasoned, sour cream, or plain?"

"Plain. No, wait, seasoned."

TWENTY-THREE

Mr. Johnson Comes A-Callin'

(Jane Reardon, mls, Head Librarian)

"Though every moment we spent together is emblazoned not only in my memory, but in my heart as well, there were times of greater, more intense joy and passion; their images are stronger, more visual, sensual. He loved the ART, the Al Ringling Theatre. It is one of the world's great theaters. Our town's little secret. It was designed to replicate the Grand Opera House of the palace of Versailles and is on the National Register of Historic Places. It is a touch of the Italian Renaissance, a cavern of many-colored jewels, where iridescent lights and luxurious fittings heighten the expectations of pleasure. That is how it is best described. We would often go to watch a film or sit in the box seats courtesy of the ART Friends Association. I am a member, of course. We would listen to the chamber orchestras and jazz bands or watch the local productions. It is a world-class establishment. It was our favorite venue. But the venue in which we spent the lion's share of our amorous nights alone together was right here in my apartment. And one of those nights that I recall in partic-ular detail is the night he came to call with his Thanksgiving present — the turtle-shell mirror, which is now a footstool there by the window. I was offered a great sum of money for it by a col-lector recently, but of course I declined. It was meant for only me and so it will always be only mine. It is the symbol of his singular love for me. When I rest my feet upon it I feel him and see him as well. I see his shining smile. He is here with me always.

"When he came that Thanksgiving Day at dusk, playing his little trumpet outside my window, it was just before nightfall. The sweet melody wafted up to my apartment from below — the theme from *Romeo and Juliet*. There was a dusting of snow falling, the air was dry, the sky was a blush of crimson to the west, stars to the east just visible in the freckled gloaming. I was preparing dinner, a walleyed pike fillet in garlic butter and white wine with green beans, baked potato, a Salade Niçoise. His favorite. I had a bright-patterned sarong wrapped around my waist, with a light blue argyle pullover, no bra. He liked me best that way. I held back a moment, listening to the song. Through the dry night air it came as if amplified, through the closed window into my soul. I gasped at the sound, how pure, how beautiful. I held back until I could hold back no longer and flew to the window. He was there below, Argus-eyed in his leather skins with his backpack stuffed full of the turtle-shell mirror. He played as if hypnotized, watching me, moving his torso ever so gently in time with the music — such profound melody it contained. I bit my lip to keep from calling out. Oh, how I wanted him then. I could not contain myself any longer and uttered a sigh, to which he suddenly stopped playing and looked up, saying — 'She speaks: O, speak again, bright angel! For thou art as glorious to this night, being o'er my head, as is a winged messenger of heaven.' How could I not then reply, 'O Romeo, Romeo, wherefore art thou Romeo? Deny thy father and refuse thy name; or, if thou wilt not, be but sworn my love and I'll no longer be a Capulet.' His response: 'Shall I hear more, or shall I just take out Mr. Johnson?' He had a wonderful sense of humor that way. Sophisticated and yet quite libidinous. He often referred to his penis as Mr. Johnson.

"There is an impoverished but quite sturdy hackberry tree outside my window there, you can see it [she pointed], and before I knew it he was shimmying his way up to me with fire in his eyes. There were no branches, no toeholds, and the exercise was an arduous one. He was like a great ape. He carried on his back the masterpiece, held securely inside his leather pouch. He managed to ascend to a few feet above the level of my window; however, the distance from tree to window was farther than he had anticipated, and it was quite evident that he could not simply reach out and pull himself across. He would have to jump. And in jumping from tree to window ledge, he precipitated headlong with ample kinetic force through my living room window. His trajectory was perfect; however, he failed to take into consideration . . . Mr. Johnson, who was at that moment stretched to his full magnificent extent, but unfortunately perpendicular rather than parallel to his skyborne frame — forced downward by gravity and his heavy leather britches. As a result, his flight was arrested as Mr. Johnson caught onto the windowsill, and he was catapulted backward out the window and down to the ground about fifteen feet below. It was the turtle shell that saved him from any serious injury, but the mirror was of course smashed to pieces.

"I flew from the apartment and gathered him up in my arms and brought him up to my bed, where we weltered about in the sinful delights of sensuous pleasure for hours. Oh it isn't polite to speak of such bliss around others, especially in front of one's relations, but we took part in Belshazzar's feast that night. I remember marveling at the exquisite craftsmanship of the turtle-shell mirror, ruing the fact that I would have to wait for him to fix it before I could mount it on my wall and display it along with all of the other artifacts I covet so. Of course it wasn't meant to be. He couldn't or wouldn't chance another breaking of a mirror, and instead he made it into a footstool with deer hooves as the legs."

DECEMBER 1, 2000

Give a woman a present made from nature with your own two hands, and then present it to her along with your very best erection — adamantine — and she'll worship you for the rest of her life! Mirrors and erections, however, don't go well together, you found out. You thought about mirrors subsequently. Perhaps a mirror is not a good invention. It forces the eye to see the self too clearly, too plainly, and nothing in nature should be that fully exposed. Nothing. You began to think that most of life, most of existence, is hidden from view. All organisms naturally shy away from exposure. Perhaps that has been part of your problem all along — too well exposed. Better to look at yourself in the turbid and rippled image of water. The river's reflection is best, it presents a more accurate representation of the self, as both the mysterious and ridiculous creature that you are, Narcissus be damned.

. . . And on your way back to your riparian retreat you walked by the river just as the creeping, hairy orange presented its muted warmth to the needy day. You were struck by the difference in the river's sound, its shape, its smell from just a few weeks ago. You wrote:

Ba'boo River's Many Faces
[in the shape of a meandering river]

Ba'boo River has many faces
That change according to the seasons and the places.
He meanders along when the sun is high,
Then rushes headlong once the rains go by.
He wends his way by moonlight under the nictitating owl,

On balmy summer nights he gurgles lullabies for a nidificating fowl.
His color can go from silver to rust,
Like coal that burns from briquette to dust.
He's on a mission to renew the land —
Like the function of a marching band —
To glorify the day;
To foster somehow a way:
For all
To live,
To flow,
To change.

TWENTY-FOUR

Bad Constipation

(OSCAR RIGHTPATH)

"My grandfather, before he passed from this world, gave me explicit instructions to look after, to succor Wakdjunkaga at appointed times. Because he was brought new again into this world, he would need assistance from time to time, especially in performing the ancient rites. He instructed me to listen with my heart, to feel with my mind, to watch with my serenity, then I would know when Wakdjunkaga would need me.

"Again, because this story is *waikan*, I must ask my ancestors' permission to tell it. [He chanted loudly for a minute or more.]

"It was just six months ago. There was a breach inside that I felt, and I went to find him. My grandfather told me that I would find him by the stinking waters, where the remains of the ancient ancestors sat in council on the high ridge above the river, beside two ancient bur oaks. I knew the place; I had visited the spot when I was a boy, and so set off. I arrived in midafternoon to find Wakdjunkaga alone, frantic with constipation. He seemed very surprised to see me, yet at the same time there was a knowing response to my presence, an attitude that communicated, *Yes, now that I think of it, I was expecting you.* He welcomed me into his lodge and offered me drink. I accepted and we sat in silence in these two chairs you and I sit in now, the flames from his thin little fire dancing in his eyes. The room was no different than it looks now. Only the headdress from the war bundle is missing. I have secured that back at my house. Anyway, he pointed to it, then at the bow and the quiver filled with the ancient arrows. He chuckled and said he could not use it, he could not shoot straight, but with guile and patience, he explained, he had become an adept hunter of the night and was never without meat. Which led him to talk of his predicament. He was gravely constipated. I understood immediately, removed the ceremonial ingredients, and prepared the tobacco offering and the *man-ka* balls with many questions from Wakdjunkaga about the origin of the sacred ritual. We smoked and chewed the *man-ka* sitting in silence.

"Much of what occurred subsequently is lost to me in the smoky depths of the dream world; however, the major events that illuminate the cycle remain clear and large in my heart, and I will attempt to recall them as they happened. Wakdjunkaga, once the power of the *man-ka* had taken effect, went racing from the lodge out into the coal-gray day, running at full speed. I tried to follow, but my feet were much heavier, and my stamina no match for his. He ran south and west, toward the sun, and I could see the prints of his footsteps sparkling like fluorescent moss on the floor of the forest. For miles and miles I followed the prints, stopping occasionally to catch my breath.

"For hours I followed the path, over streams, up cliffs and down, through fields of mud. I neared the point of exhaustion and was almost broken, when, coming around the bend of a riverbed along which I was running, I heard shouting. Up ahead I saw Wadkjunkaga standing motionless, pointing across the river yelling, 'Stop it! If you stop, I'll stop! The better man will stop first!' I looked across the river and there stood an old tree stump, black as pitch, with a branch like a man's arm pointing across the water at Wadkjunkaga. As I approached he finally gave up, saying, 'This is stupid. I'm just imitating what he's doing.' He pulled his arm down. Together we walked away. I asked him what he had been doing, and he explained that he was pointing in imitation of the man across the way, but when I told him that what he thought was a man was in fact a tree, he turned and nodded with a chuckle, seeing the stump for what it was.

"We walked on together, Wakdjunkaga with his long loping strides, I with my short heavy gait. I asked him if he had had any action from his bowels, and he sighed longingly, saying that he had not. I remembered at that moment the bud known to cure constipation. No sooner had I thought of this than there came to my ears the sound of a voice saying, 'He who eats me will defecate.' Wadkjunkaga heard the voice, too, and together we searched for its source. It took some time, but finally we located it — a small white bulb on a bush close to the river. He immediately grabbed the bulb and ingested it without hesitation. 'Well?' he began to ask the bulb, now inside his stomach. 'Why am I not defecating?' But as he spoke these words he began to pass wind. 'That is not defecating!' he responded and passed even greater billows of wind. Again he spoke to his stomach, claiming that breaking wind was not what he had in mind. And as the words left his mouth, he registered such an explosion of gas that it made him wince with pain — the pressure too much for his rectum. And what a stench! 'So,' he said, 'it can sting my sphincter and smell like the very devil, but it can't make me defecate.' Once again, as the words left his mouth, there emitted from his rectum a powerful explosion of gas so strong that he was impelled forward and then thrown down harshly, coming to rest on his hands and knees. The very next time he broke wind he was holding on to a tree, but the tree was too small and it was pulled up by its roots and together, like a rocket, tree and Trickster were shot up into the air, coming down with a crash not far from where they had departed the earth. He scrambled to his feet, his eyes wide with fright, and raced to find a bigger tree, which he did, an old red oak, and he wrapped his arms around it. He passed wind again, a short, extremely noxious explosion, and because his legs were not tightly secured, he was flipped up in the air so that his heels smashed up over his head against the tree. But he held on.

"He was wild with fear and raced on through the woods, coming out near the truck route off the interstate and heading into the parking lot of a rest area. I followed. When I broke the tree line, I saw him standing in the middle of the parking area breaking wind with huge leaps into the air, being borne forward like the astronauts hopping on the moon. Horrified by the noise and smell and sight of him, those in their cars or trucks sped away in fright. He stood there laughing. 'Well,' I heard him say, 'this flower has made a lot of noise, but it couldn't make me defecate.' But as he spoke these words, the feeling came over him and he began to run again, this time with great joy, jumping past the rest area and back into the woods. I followed after him and found him hanging from the branch of a tree, ten feet from the ground, defecating and laughing at the same time. There was below him a huge pile of excrement, and he was mad with laughter. Then he fell into his own pile of excrement and lay there as if dead. Suddenly he revived, stood up, and ran at full speed through the woods. I gave chase but it was futile; he was much too fast. The rest of the story is lost in the dreams."

AUGUST 31, 2001
Ahhhhhhhh! At long last! Your magnum opus. Later you wrote a poem:

The Outhouse
[in the shape of an outhouse]

The outhouse is where you go
To deposit your fertilizing dough.

Upon the redolent, noxious heap
A pound at least to stink and steep.
In the cold and in the dark,
Seated upon your throne of bark.
It sure is quiet in there,
And you're safe from the bear.
That's about all you can say . . .
Oh yeah — there's a foldout of Miss May.

HIS LIGHTHEARTEDNESS would not last long. The forces of evil that had stalked him ever since his reification confronted him for the first time soon afterward. The war had finally begun. There was no turning back.

TWENTY-FIVE

Fistfight at the Okey Dokey

(SUSAN GREEN)

" Aye, I'll tell you a story. We went oop to the Wisconsin Dells one day. Rode our bikes. I lived a wee bit north of Baraboo at the time, and it was my day off. Charlie was o'er and he insisted on riding oop to the Dells. He wanted to find a meeting-place, he said, where the Indians long agoo used to gather. He didna know where it was, but he was determined to find it. Oh, he was very impulsive at times, and once he'd set his mind on soomthing, he wouldna stop until he had investigated it. You must knew that aboot him. It's aboot twelve miles, which was a wee bit of a bike ride, but it was a beautiful day. I doon't knew if you are familiar with the Wisconsin Dells? They have water-slides, miniature golf, river rafts. It's a great amusement park, a bit like Disneyland, but built on top of a natural woonder. Of course it's a bootanist's nightmare. Anyway, we rode up there; this was late last August, in fact it was August twenty-second. I knew I was pregnant then.

"When we arrived in town, Charlie was thoonderstruck. He had no idea what it was like there, or perhaps he had, but he hadna expected it to be as . . . as it was. He'd neever been before. We didna stay long, I can assure you. He came into town on his bike, riding right in the middle of the road, his mouth oopen in shock, looking at all the rides and things. Cars were beeping. He was creating quite a stir — just his appearance, you knew, with his tattoos and no shirt and his hair. People were stoopping to look at him; cars were passing and beeping, teenagers and soome adults saying things out the window at him. This was aboot lunchtime. He was like an anachronism. Like soomething froom a film where a man froom the past cooms back to life into the present. That was exactly what it was like. And what that man finds is an aboomination. The Dells — aye, the beautiful environment raped and smoored by man and his amusements. He rode along not saying a word, his expression changing from disbelief and incredulity to horror and finally to rage.

"I told him befoore we left my home that I was going to buy him an ice cream coon. There's a place with the best soft-serve ice cream in the world. Your broother was very particular aboot his food. He normally wouldna eat food made at a restaurant unless he knew the place well, so if you wanted to go oot to lunch or dinner, you had to ask him beforehand if it would be okay. He knew I was pregnant, and he knew I was craving the ice cream, so he agreed to go there.

"We parked our bikes at the Ookey Dookey, that's the name of the place, and went inside. It's an ice cream stand fashioned in the style of an old western saloon. Unfortunately, it was filled with loots of people havin' the same idea as us. There was a long queue in froont of us. I knew right away that this was proobably not a good idea — the combination of the people in the place and the idea of your broother awaitin' in line. Right away, the wee children came up to your broother and started tooching him and talking to him. He looved children. But then the parents wanted Charlie to pose for pictures with them. They thought he was part of the whole production, you see. He refused, of course. He hated to have pictures taken of himself, and he told them to leave him aloon and grew angry. The parents got indignant, cussed him out.

It was awful. Then soome man, I doon't knew who he was, with a great big head, snapped a picture of Charlie. Well, he went quite mad. He grabbed the man's camera and began to smash it on the groond, jumping on it with his big feet. Soodenly, from oot of noowhere, a monstrously large, bloond-haired man dressed in boockskins himself grabbed your broother and started to shoove him. Well, they had at it right there.

"They wrastled from side to side, tables and chairs being oopended while the people who were eating loonch began to roon from the room screaming. It was quite a sight, I tell you. One in boockskins and fringe with long bloond hair and a goatee, the oother in a breechcloth and dark skinned, having at it acroos the tables, fists a-flying. And of course the place looked like an old stoore oot of the past with the log beams all aroond. I'm telling you it was like a fight oot of the pages of a Wild West novel. At one point the brute took your broother by the neck and hurled him across the room. Charlie was gangly, doon't you knew, but he was wiry and very agile, and he spoon aroond and hit the wall right oonder this mounted booffalo's head without losing his balance. When Charlie hit the wall, the head swoong on its mooring and it looked for an instant like it was a-going to coom crashing doon. That's when soomething uncanny happened. I'll never forget. Everyone paused. Everyone heard the same thing. It's crazy, but I knew what I heard — the head of that booffalo gave a great snort. Withoot a doot in my mind I heard it. It didna coom froom Charlie, it came froom the beast's head. I'm certain the rest of the people in the room heard it as well, because there were many who gasped. Even the thoog who was assaulting him had stoopped for a moment.

"But then he came toward Charlie again. In an instant he had Charlie by the throat and was beating his head against the wall, quite violently. And then the booffalo head came crashing doon.

It was an awfully large head, and when it fell, it fell on toop of the man assaulting Charlie, knocking him to the groond, unconscious. Charlie was mad with rage and . . . and wild. He held his large hands oot in claws as if he were a-going to strangle the next thing that moved, I tell you. His face was red, and his eyes wide and wild. His expression was frightening. He stood there looking aroond as if he didna knew where he was. People were screaming. And there stood Charlie, the booffalo head at his feet lying on toop of the man who had been knocked unconscious by the beast's fall. Enraged, wild, and with superhuman strength, he grabbed that man's long bloond hair, twisted it aroond his fist, and pulled it. The man's head jerked up horribly, and it looked for an instant like Charlie was intending to break his neck, but instead he put his big foot o'er the man's face and pulled again. This time you could hear a ghastly ripping soond. A piece of the man's scalp came loose, it did. The same that the sheriff's department has on file, I knew aboot that. It was nauseating to see.

"Then your broother started to shout. It wasn't a human shout, or maybe it was, but it seemed it was anoother language or soomething, and deafening. Screaming, really, not words. He held the tooft of hair up aboove him for everyone to see. The people in the room all got quiet. Then as if he had droopped his hat, with superhuman strength, he picked oop that booffalo head and placed it o'er his head. I doon't knew how he could see, but he stood there for a moment and the head swiveled aroond on toop of Charlie's shoulders as if he were looking at the world aroond him. And suddenly, just a moment befoore he stampeded froom the room, there eroopted from that beastly moont once again the sound of a loud snort. I doon't knew how it was possible. Till this day I question my own ears and eyes of what actually happened. But it was like he was half man, half beast. He was no longer Charlie, but a . . . a minotaur monster!

"When I went to look for him ootside, I was told by doozens of onlookers that a man had coom charging out of the restaurant with a booffalo boost on his head and run off down the street. But no one knew who Charlie was, and they neever foond the buffalo head. Not until after his death. I've been told it's moonted on the wall of his home still. Aye, I will always think of it as the very last time the booffalo stampeded through the Dells. And it will be my favorite story to tell our soon when he is old enough to appreciate it.

"We never talked aboot that incident afterward. He never said a word aboot that incident, and I never pushed him to talk aboot it. But he did sneak back and get his bicycle, apparently, because one week later he was riding it when he came to my house. He grew a bit strange froom then on. He'd coom oover and play my bagpipes, play the same song o'er and o'er. The song he wrote. But he grew more distant, brooding. I doon't knew what it was. I almost think it had soomething to do with that fight. Soomething was preoccupying him. Perhaps it was my pregnancy. I doon't knew why, but from then on he grew a bit more serious and sad."

SEPTEMBER 29, 2001
Okay, it's come down to this — *mano a mano.* You should have broken his neck when you had the chance. Too many kids in the place. He's been stalking you all along. You realized that today. You've been aware of his presence for a long time, he just hadn't had a chance to ambush you until today. He's a great big fraud! He knows you know that. He knows the Wild West shows have got to go. If it's a fight he wants, you'll give him a fight all right. And you'll be sure to carry a knife so that next time you'll take away a real scalp, not just a fistful of hair. But at least you got a little something for Yellow Hand!

I WAS CURIOUS about the allusion Charlie made to what sounded like an Indian chief — Yellow Hand — and did some research with a little help from Jane Reardon, MLS, head librarian. It turns out that in 1876 when Buffalo Bill heard about the Little Big Horn, he quite literally jumped off a Broadway stage in the middle of a scene where he was (fittingly) playing himself and headed out West to avenge his friend Custer's death. In his first engagement against the Cheyenne, Buffalo Bill shot and killed a subchief named Yellow Hand, then scalped him and held the hair up for the men in his company to see, declaring, "The first scalp for Custer!" I deduced from what Susan Green had told me about Charlie holding the fistful of hair up over his head and yelling something unintelligible that he might have yelled in French or even Ho-Chunk something like, "This scalp's for Yellow Hand."

TWENTY-SIX

Wakdjunkaga's Final Appearance

(BILLY C.)

"Ialready told you the most famous Charlie story of them all — him taking the band. But there is one other story that's always kind of in the back of my mind, that kind of haunts me. Actually, it kind of freaks me out, to tell you the truth. It's a weird story. It was the last time I saw him, too. It was Halloween, just last year. Man, that seems like yesterday. Hard to believe. Wendel and me, he's the sax player in the band, went over to the Ho-Chunk Casino out on Route Twelve toward the Dells. We'd go out there once a month. I like playing the two-dollar blackjack. Wendel's a slot man. Anyway, we're in the parking lot walking up to the place and there's Charlie, skulking around outside by the dumpsters. Now, this was the last day of the year at Circus World, so me and Wendel were gonna let loose a little bit. I was, anyway; Wendel's a teetotaler. It was a crisp night, I remember, below freezing definitely. There's Charlie, like I said, skulking around, and with a big raccoon coat on. I'd seen him in some bizarre getups before, but I never saw him in that. He looked like Cruella Deville with that thing on. 'Charlie! What's going on?' I call to him. He was a strange guy, your brother. He's there by the dumpsters talking to himself, pacing around like a tomcat. 'Nothing,' he mutters, kind of confused looking, seeing me there. 'Got ants in your pants?' I ask him. He just shakes his head. 'Come on in. I'm buying you a drink and a hundred dollars' worth of chips.' So I grab him by the arm with both hands and drag him inside the place.

"So I was dragging him in and he was protesting and putting up a good fight, but I wouldn't take no for an answer. I just wouldn't let go. So we go inside. It was perfect. It's Halloween, people are dressed up in costumes, and I'm there with Charlie with his tattoos, his raccoon coat, that hair of his. There were lots of people in costumes. He fit right in. He's blinking to beat the band because it's brightly lit inside there. I'd never noticed it before, but Jesus it's bright in that place. Loud, too. Lots of people; lots of colors. I take him over to the two-dollar table. Wendel disappears into the silvery slot-machine jungle. Charlie tells me he doesn't know how to play blackjack, but he ends up winning every hand. I never saw anything like it. A dozen times in a row. But he doesn't like playing, he says, even though he's winning.

"So I take him over to the bar and buy him a beer. He seems real distracted, looking all around nervously. They have a big bingo hall out there beside the casino. The Ho-Chunk Nation was having some kind of celebration back in there. Lots of Indians in the place that night. Funny thing was, not to sound prejudiced or anything, but here it was Halloween and you'd think they'd take the opportunity to dress up in their costumes, you know, like Charlie. But they were just wearing their regular clothes — flannel shirts and jeans. He was the only one dressed like an Indian. He sees some guys, some Indians, come out of the bingo hall and he excuses himself from my company — he was always very polite that way — and disappears into that room with the Ho-Chunks. I always thought that that's where he really belonged anyway.

"So I went back to the two-dollar table and sat right where Charlie had sat and damn if I didn't win just about every hand myself. I've never had a streak like that in my life. I won over seven hundred bucks. Charlie was good luck for me.

"About three, four hours later, Wendel and I are leaving. Then I remember your brother. I was a little on the sloppy side, you know. Wendel was driving. I tell Wendel about Charlie disappearing in the back there where the Ho-Chunks were partying, and we go over to the glass doors and take a peek inside. We look in there, and Christ, there's this big brouhaha going on, a large circle of people, at least a couple hundred of 'em, with an opening just so Wendel and I could see, and who's in the middle of the circle? Charlie. Charlie, and he's face to face with this character, with Buffalo Bill or General Custer — some guy all dressed up like that. This big tall white guy, same height as your brother, blond hair, goatee, buckskins, white gloves. Guy really went all out on the costume that night. The thing that got me was that their faces were real tight and mean, you know, they were really snarling at one another. I couldn't believe it. I just couldn't ever picture your brother mad at anyone.

"I open the door and Wendel and I sneak in and stand there listening. I couldn't hear too well because we were under a fan or something and kind of far away. That hall is a big place. I remember the Buffalo Bill guy yelling at him, telling your brother that 'he had better just leave the damn dead alone, leave things be,' something like that. But Charlie was back in his face telling him he wasn't gonna do that, he wasn't gonna leave it all be. Something along that vein. Then the Buffalo Bill guy took a swing at Charlie. Charlie was quick as a cat. He ducked right under that first punch and came up at that man and had him by the throat. The two of them were going at it, man alive, it was a good old-fashioned tussle, rolling around on the floor just like, just exactly like the Wild West, you know, Indian against scout; hand-to-hand combat. The Indians all around weren't doing anything, just letting 'em fight, whooping it up.

"Then the weird thing happened. Jesus Christ, I get goose

bumps just thinking about it. Buffalo Bill's on top choking Charlie, then Charlie manages to roll him over so now Charlie's on top. Only now Charlie's got this huge buffalo head on him and he's snorting loud, sounded exactly like a buffalo. What the fuck? I look at Wendel and he looks at me. And Wendel doesn't drink, remember. Someone must have stuck that buffalo head on him or something. But how? I don't know! And it looks like it's really attached to him. Then I start looking for the cameras, thinking this is all some kind of staged performance or something. But there are no cameras. I didn't feel too well at that point. The whole night was too weird for me. I'd just won about every hand of blackjack I'd played. Winning like that never feels comfortable. I had maybe eight hundred bucks in my wallet. And seeing that whole thing happening, Jesus, I felt like that guy Ernie in *It's a Wonderful Life,* you know, the taxi driver, when George Bailey is romping around his old house after his past life had been taken away from him and he's looking for his wife and kids and calling Ernie by his name as if he knows him. You know what I mean? I just wanted to clear out of there and get home.

"I remember we drove home in silence. What could you say? Ask Wendel about it. He saw it, too. I had a gig in Chicago the next day. I wasn't right in my head for weeks after that. The buffalo head? That was really screwy, man. And that was the last time I ever saw your brother. Fighting Buffalo Bill, and getting the better of the man, too."

OCTOBER 31, 2001

You thought you were at the feast, eating, dancing. Then Buffalo Bill showed up. You fought him again. He bites, the bastard. You pulled back your arm to punch him and nothing, it all disappeared. You were all alone, out in Schniderwind's field. It was only the wind. The wind was blowing through the cornstalks, whistling. Whistling a name — Wakdjunkaga . . .

. . . I want to know you, Wakdjunkaga, you who are reaching deep into my soul and ravaging my life, a savage gale . . .

. . . Beyond the north ice, and death — our life; our happiness . . .

. . . With more daring than is prudent, perhaps, we "little brothers" have suffered much and often enough, but we are, to repeat it, healthier than one likes to permit us, dangerously healthy, ever again healthy. The life I want is a life I could not endure in eternity. *Hey Hey!*

THIS WAS THE one and only journal entry in which Charlie referred to himself in the first person, and the first time he referred to the Trickster, Wakdjunkaga.

Intrigued by the two episodes of the buffalo head, I did a little more research and found an explanation in the creation myths of the Ho-Chunk. It was believed that in the beginning one of the firstborn sons of Earthmaker could transform himself into a buffalo. He would do so whenever he was angered, and it was he who always bore the brunt of the fighting for his people.

And fight he did. Until the bitter cold end.

TWENTY-SEVEN

Goose Music

(JASPER MILES)

"It was January, just a few months ago, and he came to the library lookin' for the Colonel. Oh yeah, he was madder than a hatter. He was rantin' and ravin' about how the Colonel was out after him, tryin' to kill him, he said. Even said he saw him and Buntline come runnin' into the library. Crazy Charlie was really crazy; either that or he must have gotten hold of some bad liquor or something. Said he knew I was hidin' them somewhere in back. Wanted to jump over the counter and look around. 'No sir,' I told him. 'He ain't here.' 'Course maybe now we know he was lookin' for those two drunks out there we just seen. But I didn't know about that then. Yep, he swore the Colonel was out after him and he wanted me to know he was ready for him. Said he had a knife, had been practicin' with it. I liked to play with him a little, you know. Nothin' mean and malicious, now, just havin' some fun. So I told him the Colonel was aces with a knife, could strip a buffalo hide in five minutes, stem to stern. Yep, told him he best be careful if it was gonna come down to man against man. That made him madder. 'Well, I got a few tricks up my sleeve myself,' he said. 'Oh yeah, and which sleeve that be?' I asked him. 'The leather one you got there, or the one tattooed to your arm?' Hya hya hya. Started in on me then, said he'd buy up the memorabilia and burn it all, erase forever the Wild West *shows* and I kept correctin' him, tellin' him they was called *exhibits*. Oh that got him all-fired mad. He skeddadled after that. Real cold day as I recall, too. Wasn't wearin' more than his buckskins and a couple of old rat-eaten sweaters. He was a crazy man, no question. That was the last I ever saw of him."

JANUARY 12, 2002

There is no shame in following the music; the end result is best for everyone. You can attest to that . . .

You had that dream again. In it you were the goose man, flying with the flock above the treetops. Then the trees turned to roofs and the flock was gone. You were alone. You had to blow extra hard on your trumpet. Your notes were very clear. It was your song — Goose Music. You heard the entire piece, every note, all the different instrumentation, the harmonies. People below, on the streets, looked up and pointed. You could see their faces. Odd faces. Old faces. Native faces. Most were disbelieving; many were aghast; some were curious. But there were just a few who heard and believed and understood. You moved higher into the sky. You filled up more of the world with the song. And down below the streets turned into rivers and the cars into buffalo and the fields into forests, and all seemed to flow in time with the music . . .

. . . You went outside and looked at the thermometer. It read eighteen below. You laughed. You boiled water and thought about the cold and the animals and how weak and pitiful man is next to the entire lineup of warm-blooded beasts. The cold! It, as much as any disease or gene, has controlled the populations of species since the beginning. You wrote a poem:

The Cold

The cold,
In days of old,
Would winnow
The mollycoddles
From the tribe,
And force the men out,
With pendulous doubt,
To uphold the sacred rite
Of enduring the long winter night.
With fire, fur, and sacred gear
They took out after the deer.
Always with the best in the lead,
The rest supporting the deed.
With bow
And arrow
And spear,
They followed
The tracks
And sounds.
The moon
Would light
The way.
Miles away
They'd stop
And eat
And rest,
And look
For signs
Under the pines.

. . . There is an owl hooting outside. The haunting sound made your thoughts drift to Buffalo Bill. His image filled your mind with dread. You could feel him all around you. You could smell him. The drunkard, too. You became nauseous with the thought of them. You began to prepare. You boiled more water. You practiced with your knife. You gathered the ingredients for your war bundle. You knew they were waiting out there, waiting to ambush you, to outnumber you, somewhere in the cold.

CHARLIE'S FROZEN BODY was found on top of the Man Mound, in Greenfield Township just east of Baraboo, his head scalped and facing east, on January 14, 2002. He was smiling.

Three months later, on April 17, 2002, Charlie, Wakdjunkaga, was buried where he had died, in the crotch of the singular effigy mound. The funeral ritual lasted four days, and his passing was mourned by the entire Ho-Chunk Nation. As they lowered his body into the bosom of the earth, a great formation of geese, stretching as far as the eye could see, flew overhead, just above the treetops, singing his song.

Gallagher read the document through, every word of it, in two days. As he read, he explained it all to his wife, who was too distracted with her two new baby daughters to read it herself, although occasionally she would take time out from caring for the babies to read a journal entry or one of the interviews. At night, in bed, Gallagher read her passages. During the day he called her from work during his lunch hour and read her some of the poems or interviews over the phone. And when he was done, he was a believer. Who wouldn't be?

Gallagher had taken a course in anthropology at the University of Chicago during his college days. He remembered an old professor of his who had lectured about the Winnebago. This same professor had even spent some time living with and studying that tribe. He recalled the professor talking about the conical mounds at Aztalan and Lake Koshkonong, which he had helped excavate. He even vaguely recalled the name Wakdjunkaga being mentioned. Gallagher got in touch with the professor and told him about the document. The professor, retired now, was curious and asked him to send a copy, which he did. The man read the document and was intrigued. In a subsequent conversation with Gallagher he explained that many of the stories in the document, especially those told by the allies, were near-replicas of some of the mythologies of the Winnebago people — now called Ho-Chunk. The professor explained to Gallagher that the Ho-Chunk were very protective and secretive about their culture, especially the mythologies, and a document of that sort written by a non-Native was "strange" — that was how he put it. He wanted to meet the person who had written it. They agreed that Gallagher would arrange for a meeting between his former professor and his brother-in-law.

The next morning the Sauk County Sheriff's Department contacted the Gallagher home again, this time to inform them that they had found the body of Leslie Siconski on top of an effigy mound outside the town of Baraboo, Wisconsin, in Greenfield Township, dead. The body had been beaten up pretty badly and scalped. The official cause of death was listed as massive internal bleeding. There was a hole dug in the mound next to the body, as if someone was planning to bury it right there. They had only one clue — a tuft of blond hair that was found in the grip of the deceased.

"Is this some kind of joke?" Gallagher responded.

"What do you mean by that?" the detective answered him.

"Leslie?"

There was a pause. "I'm sorry sir, I don't understand."

"First Charlie, now Leslie? How can that be?"

"Charlie?"

"Yes, goddamn it, you know what I'm talking about! Charlie!"

There was a long silence on the other end of the line. Then a clearing of the throat — "Sir, I'm not sure exactly what or who you're referring to. I don't know who Charlie is, but I'm calling to inform you that we have a dead body here, found last night by a park ranger. The car recovered near the scene was registered to a Jacob Siconski, now deceased. I've done a lot of checking, sir. A lot of checking. The man had about a dozen false identification cards on him. Only one card, an old military academy student ID, seemed to be authentic. And that was twenty years old."

Gallagher's mind clouded over. It didn't make sense. Was this a joke or a trick of some kind? Leslie dead? They'd just heard from him a couple of days before. The document! And on the top of the Man Mound with a fistful of blond hair. He was describing Charlie, not Leslie. He shook his head, asked for the detective's name and number, hastily wrote it down on a yellow Post-it, and told him he would call him right back. He wandered through the house as if in a trance, finally ending up in the kitchen, where his wife was sitting, holding the twins, cooing and rocking them, one in each arm. He stopped and stared at his family for a long time, but not seeing them. Then their image came into view — his black-haired beauties. Mary looked like the Madonna. He smiled at her and turned away, not wanting to disturb her bliss.

"Who was that, dear?" she asked warmly just as he was leaving the room.

He hesitated, then turned. "Sauk County Sheriff's Deparment," he said, trying to hide the confusion in his voice.

"Oh good God, what is it now?"

With an apologetic expression, he sighed and said, "They found Leslie on top of an effigy mound. Dead."

"What!" She stopped rocking the twins.

"Yes, and clutching a tuft of blond hair."

IT TOOK THE Gallaghers some time to gather their thoughts. The dead had them beleaguered, it seemed. Mary's eyes soon ran dry of tears. Gallagher fought against the frustration caused by his confusion. Husband and wife sat and talked for a long time, trying to sort it all out. After an hour they had come up with nothing. The only item they kept coming back to was the fact that Leslie had always been an "unknown commodity," as

Gallagher put it. But now that he was dead, there was no arguing the point. In fact, Gallagher had asked the sheriff more than once just to be sure. Yes, it was Leslie who was dead, the description fit Leslie; the sheriff knew nothing about Charlie.

Gallagher had read the document. He believed Leslie's story. But how did this fit into the mythic cycles? Perhaps Washchinggeka, Leslie, was playing a trick on them? No, not now, how could he now? Their present situation precluded any joking. Secretly, in the back of Gallagher's mind, he couldn't help but think that perhaps those two men found drowned in the Wisconsin weren't Buffalo Bill and Ned Buntline as assumed. Maybe it had all been a decoy, a setup to get Leslie, too. Oscar Rightpath had warned him to be on his guard against the evil forces. They had gotten Charlie, and they could just as easily get Leslie. But the sheriff said he knew nothing about Charlie . . . Perhaps it was being kept secret to help find the murderers. All this Gallagher reasoned. The document was still very much on his mind.

Then Gallagher decided to go up to Baraboo and, like Leslie before him, identify the body and figure out this situation. That was the only way. He'd leave immediately. He regretted having to leave his wife and two beautiful baby girls, but perhaps he could sort it all out and be back by mealtime. He stood up to call the Sauk County Sheriff's Department.

"Now, what did I do with that number?" Gallagher felt inside his pockets for the name and numbers he'd scratched down a few minutes before.

"I've got it right there, on the refrigerator, dear," Mary said, pointing with her chin, still holding the babies.

"Sauk County Sheriff's Department?"

"Yes. That's the one Leslie gave me before he left. It's right there."

Gallagher picked up the phone, read the number aloud, and dialed. There was no answer. He put the receiver back in place. "What the hell?" Then he became aware of something stuck to the bottom of his shoe. He reached down. Sure enough, there was the little yellow Post-it with the name and number of the Sauk County Sheriff's Department that he'd misplaced. It was not the number he'd just dialed. "That's funny." He dialed the Post-it number; right away a woman answered. He asked for Detective Luciano and was immediately connected.

"This is all quite confusing for us. I think before we talk further, I should just come up there. You'll need someone to identify the body anyway," Gallagher reasoned.

"Yes, that's true. I'm not going anywhere. I'll be here all day."

"Okay, I'm leaving soon. I should be there after lunch."

"Not a problem."

"Now, you're in the county courthouse right in the center of town, is that right?"

"Exactly."

"And which phone number is the one to reach you at just in case there's a change of plans? I have two numbers here." Gallagher read the detective both numbers. The one he'd just called was the correct one; the second one, the one he read from the paper on the fridge, the one Leslie had given to his sister, was not one of their department numbers. "Maybe that's Detective McNutt's home phone," Gallagher offered. The man on the other end of the line did not respond.

"We'll expect you, then, after lunch."

"Yes," responded Gallagher distractedly, and he hung up.

GALLAGHER DROVE NORTH into Wisconsin on Interstate 94. He was thinking of the whole cast of characters from the document — Chappy Lewis-Clark; Karina; Squeaky; Jane

Reardon, MLS, head librarian; Professor Miles; McNutt; Oscar Rightpath. He felt a bit of excitement about the prospect of meeting them all. He reasoned that if he could just find Oscar Rightpath he, more than anyone else, would be able to explain to him what was going on. Then he remembered something — Rightpath would be in his pickup truck parked outside the morgue, standing guard over Leslie's body. He would have the answers. Gallagher eased his speed up to seventy-five.

Gallagher was now moving in the flow of the mythic cycles himself, being carried along by the current. He could feel it. Leslie was right. But why no Charlie? Why did the sheriff or detective or whatever he called himself deny any knowledge of Charlie's body? He kept coming back to this question. Was this being held secret in order to flush out the murderers? Did the Ho-Chunk, maybe, have something to do with that? And Leslie's death . . . Why? How? Gallagher's mind played these thoughts back and forth as his car moved north.

He traveled past the city of Milwaukee, then west through more places with Indian names — Pewaukee, Oconomowoc, and Waunakee.

And then there he stood, just as his two brothers-in-law had stood, on the bow of the square little ferry, cutting through the muddy waters of the Wisconsin River, staring off at the great green hills in the soft distance. The sun was powerful, pouring down its handsome rays on the newly greening earth. Gallagher took a deep breath of watery air and scanned the sky for geese. Sure enough, to the west about a quarter of a mile downriver an uneven arrow of geese cut through the air toward the hills. What did it all mean?

And there he was, driving up through the Baraboo Hills, just as Leslie had described it. Past the entrance to Devil's Lake, up and over the wooded hills and down into the plain. And there was the serpentine Baraboo River to his left. Then around a couple of turns and Circus World popped into view, almost an imitation of itself. He slowed to a crawl. The big top with its blue and red canvas puffed up to its full extent stood like a cartoon monument. And there was the river wiggling in through the middle of the grounds exactly as he'd pictured it. Yes, a medieval moat. He could see the row of trailers to the right of the giant tent where the people Charlie had known lived, the same ones who had taken Leslie in and revealed to him the stories of Charlie's life. He drove past the brick edifice — the Feld Pavilion — where Charlie's display wall was. He suddenly grew excited. He felt that centeredness that Leslie described. Gallagher was indeed among the myth makers.

And there was the Sauk County Courthouse, precisely as described. A gray-sandstone building with a gothic facade right smack-dab in the center of town. The Civil War statue was there, and around the corner was the Al Ringling Theatre. He parked in front of it. Yes, this was right. This was how it should be, he thought. His heart was pounding. He locked the car door, looked left, then right, and walked hurriedly across the street. He knew the way. He saw it all before it happened.

Inside the entrance was the door to the left with a sign above it that read SHERIFF'S DEPARTMENT ADMINISTRATION DIVISION. He opened the door and walked in. But the interior was not at all like he'd pictured it. There was no dispatch window, no waiting area, no windows looking out at the ART. There was an entrance area, but instead of one door as Leslie had described, a hallway led to a host of doors and offices. A tall, gangly man in shirt-sleeves and a loosened tie carrying a handful of papers came walking by.

"Can I help you?"

"Yes, I'm looking for Detective Luciano."

"He's down the hall in the Detective Division. Just go out the door and take a left. Last door on the right."

Gallagher was confused. He didn't understand. Without thinking, he followed the instructions — out the door, to the left, down the hall, last door on the right. Inside there was a dispatch clerk, but not behind a window — she was seated behind a desk facing the door, while behind her a labyrinth of cubicles filled the bright room.

"I'm looking for Detective Luciano," Gallagher said to the woman as if in a daze.

"Yo!" A man's head popped up in the back. A tall, broad, bull-necked man walked toward Gallagher with a jaunty stride. The light glistened off his balding pate. "You Mr. Gallagher?"

"Yes."

"Right on time. Just finished lunch." In fact, he was wiping the crumbs from the corners of his mouth with a napkin.

If Gallagher, a sandy-haired, well-balanced six-footer, were the quarterback of the team, then Detective John Luciano, a much bigger, less well-balanced man, would have been the defensive tackle. The two men shook hands.

"I gotta tell you, Mr. Gallagher," Luciano began, "we got a résumé on your dead brother-in-law a mile long, and I've just started." Luciano clearly did not mince words. "Come on back to my desk."

Gallagher, feeling the myths beginning to sputter, followed the big detective back through the line of cubicles to a disastrously cluttered desk with a glowing computer screen rising up out of the mayhem.

"You know much about your brother-in-law?" Luciano asked him.

"Not really," responded Gallagher as the two men came to the big detective's desk. "He's always been an unknown commodity in the family." "Ran away from home when he was a teenager." Gallagher noticed the size of the man's forearms: like the trunk of a beech tree, smooth and muscular, swollen in a thick arc from elbow to wrist.

"You want some coffee or a soda or something?"

"No thanks."

Luciano sat. Next to his computer and on top of all the other papers was a yellow notepad with its top page full of scribbling. He grabbed it and held it up so that Gallagher could see. Gallagher scanned the names of countries, cities, dollar amounts. "You speak French?" Luciano asked.

"No."

"Damn it, got to find someone who can speak French. Here, sit down."

He jumped out of his seat, pulled a chair away from an empty table behind his desk, and patted it twice, loudly. Like a boy in trouble with his elders, Gallagher sat. Indeed, Luciano had stumbled onto quite a trickster. His investigation had revealed a web of malfeasance a mile long *and* deep. In fact, his head was swimming in a fast current from all the information.

"What do you have?" Gallagher asked him uneasily.

"Confidence man," was what Luciano said first. "Checked the IDs he had on him. He was a con man from Montreal to Guam, and a crapload of places in between. He's got arrest warrants out all over the world."

The myths were winding down now with an audible creaking and grinding. Gallagher said the first thing that came to mind — "There a detective around here named McNutt?"

"You said something like that on the phone this morning. No, no one by that name in this department. Hey Becky, anyone named McNutt on the Baraboo police force?" Luciano called out to the woman who sat at the receiving desk. Luciano had a deep, unignorable voice. He turned to Gallagher, saying, "Sometimes people get us mixed up. Baraboo Police are just down the street."

"Who?" shot back a peeved voice.

"McNutt? Anyone by that name on the Baraboo force?"

"Uh uh, not that I know of. McNaughton. But he's retired. He's got gout, too."

"And you didn't find another body two months ago out on the same burial mound, dead from hypothermia, clutching a tuft of blond hair?" Gallagher asked in a monotone.

"No. One's enough."

The myths came to a hissing halt. "Con man, huh?"

"Yep, a real operator. Worked the five-star hotels. Preyed on rich older ladies, mostly widowed or divorced. Montreal police have practically a whole book on the guy. Worked a lot in Paris, and lots of places in Europe. I got to find someone who can translate for me. It's all here on the computer, but it's in French." He turned the computer screen to show Gallagher. "Can't read it. Spoke on the phone to a guy in Montreal who knew a lot about him. Been trying to find him for ten years. Said he spoke a half dozen languages, conned all over Europe. Lots of aliases. Real professional operator. Played trumpet or saxophone, I forget, for a circus band up in Montreal for a long time before he left Canada. Was a nightclub singer, played in a bunch of cabarets in Paris and Amsterdam. Stole sixty-eight thousand dollars' worth of jewelry from one lady. She's dead now. That was in Milan."

Gallagher suddenly felt exhausted. All that excitement he'd had simmering within had been flushed out of his system, leaving only fatigue. How could it be? Why? Then it hit him — Charlie's inheritance. That was it! "That goddamn stupid . . . !" Gallagher stood up, his heart racing with anger. How dare Leslie play a trick on him and his wife at a time like this? "He was after the inheritance," he said aloud. How stupid he felt. "We would have given it to him, too. All he had to do was ask."

"Excuse me?" asked the amiable detective, surprised by Gallagher's sudden outburst.

"He got left out of the will, so this is what he did. Son of a bitch! My father-in-law recently died, and he wrote him out of the will. Leslie pretended like he didn't care. Like he was glad. The crazy thing is, my wife and I would have given him part of our inheritance. But we thought he was too proud to take it. Hah. No, he didn't want it given to him, he wanted to take it from us. He wanted to fool us out of the money. Charlie's dead body . . ." It was all cascading into place. All the subtle proposals in the book flooded his mind. The children — the unresolved issue there. Buying and burning the Buffalo Bill exhibit. The subtle suggestion of the millions needed to "finish Charlie's work." All a trick. A con. But something had backfired. Now he was dead. Someone murdered him. Something went wrong . . . Gallagher's thoughts were racing.

"Well, with people like this, that's all they know how to do. That's all they want to do. It's the art of deception. They lust after excitement. It's a sickness," Luciano explained.

"Did he work alone?"

"Not always. Had some help, I would suspect. They all do."

"But no clues as to who might have killed him?"

"Not yet. We got just that hair sample I told you about. I've got someone spreading the guy's picture out all over town to see if they recognize him."

"Detective . . . uh, Luciano?"

"You can just call me John."

"John, I think I can help you find some of the people who knew him and maybe even those who killed him. I'm not sure."

"Oh yeah? How's that?"

Gallagher accepted the second offer of a soda and explained the document to him. Explained the whole nine yards — the inheritance, the family, Charlie's disappearance. It took him no longer than it takes to drink a can of soda, which he crushed in his fist upon finishing his summation. It was an appropriate final punctuation mark. And all the while, Detective Luciano sat shaking his head, whistling softly at some of the details.

When he was through, Gallagher's face was red. He was angry — three and a half hours to come up there, and of course the time spent reading the document. He saw himself lying in his bed at home reading passages to Mary, his head replaced by the head of a giant ass — buffalo head be damned! He wanted to go home. Maybe he could do that; just give the detective the document and let *him* sort through it all . . . Why shouldn't he just get in the car and go home? But there was an itch inside poor Gallagher. He had read that entire document. He'd been completely duped. But the answers were out there, all around him — just down the street at the circus, over off County W, at the Man Mound, in town, all around. He knew it. He felt it. There were scattered puzzle pieces just outside. He could scratch the itch if he wanted to . . .

BOTH MEN WOULD soon learn that Leslie Walter Siconski had other names — Jean Decora, aka Guy d'Oltremont, aka Jorge Espinoza Maria Serrano, aka Walter Armando Guttierez, aka Walter Heinz Mende. He was well-known throughout France as L'Oie — the Goose. He turned tricks from the great city of Paris to the sunny seascape of Nice. He posed as a young gallant, a poet, a musician, and he preyed on women, especially older women who had lost their husbands but were well heeled and often well endowed — physically speaking. He tricked them into believing he cared for them, then he took all of their precious stones, drained their bank accounts, even stole their purses. In

Madrid he was known as El Bascon — the Swindler. Pretending to be a rich American who loved to sing and play the piano, he conned for a living there as well. In Munich he was Der Hahn — the Cock. In Monte Video he was El Picaro — the Trickster. And the career of this infamous trickster had begun long ago.

Leslie became a grifter under the tutelage of his own uncle. Peter Decora was a circus musician but an illustrious con man as well. The little circus he owned and ran, and for which he led the band, was not the kind of circus most people think of when they hear the word *circus*, or *cirque* in his native land's tongue. Actually, Le Cirque du Québec was a small outfit of weak-of-arm-and-leg acrobats, off-the-mark knife throwers, fumbling jugglers, dipso-maniacal clowns, out-of-tune musicians. It was a throwback to the time early in the history of circuses when small wandering bands would travel from village to village, playing to small crowds while stealing the wallets from the back pockets of their unsus-pecting audience. Under the wing of his Uncle Pete, young Leslie learned the tricks of the trade. He learned to play the trumpet, the clarinet, the saxophone, the drums, and the piano. He learned to sing and dance, do card tricks, play the clown, short-change customers, and pick a pocket. And from the time he was sixteen until his death at age thirty-five, Leslie Walter Siconski had never earned an honest dollar or lira or franc or mark or peseta. This and more Gallagher and Luciano would understand when all was said and done.

THE DETECTIVE WANTED to take Gallagher over to the temporary morgue, west of town in the parking lot next to WalMart, to identify his brother-in-law's body. Gallagher knew the details.

"You know, I don't need to do that," was Gallagher's response. "We got pictures. You can do it that way."

"That's fine." Luciano was back in a minute with an envelope. He pulled out a big square sheet on which Leslie's battered face and scalped head had been photographed. "That's him," Gallagher declared loudly, without hesitation. "Man, that's ugly, where they took the scalp. Was he dead before that happened?"

"We don't know."

Gallagher felt a twinge of remorse for his brother-in-law. After all, he knew about the dolorous conditions under which Leslie had been raised. The father was a brutal man. And no mother. But as quickly as the feelings of compassion came over him, they were spent as he thought of his own wife and adopted daughters. No, he had no time to waste on sympathy. In fact, he was still determined to get back home that night, albeit not in time for dinner. Luciano showed him another photograph of Leslie, this time from the side. It looked as if someone had taken a bite out of his ear. "Looks like he was in the ring with Mike Tyson," Gallagher commented.

"What did I tell ya?" a voice crowed from the receptionist's desk.

"She said the same thing," Luciano said, smiling respectfully. Gallagher chuckled.

"Let me ask you this, John — is there an old German man who lives out on County W east of town named Schniderwind?" Gallagher wanted to pick up the pace a bit.

"I don't know. But let me check." He pulled out a phone book, his thick forearms suggesting he could rip it in half. The muscles tightened as he thumbed through. "Yeah, there's a Rolf Schniderwind, County W."

"That's the guy. I might suggest that we take a look out there first."

"Let's go."

"I've got this document here. Maybe you guys should have someone make a copy of it for your records," coached Gallagher.

"Yeah, we'll do that."

"Better yet, I'll just give it to you. I don't want it." Gallagher liked that idea a lot better. He picked up the swollen manila envelope he'd carried in with him and slapped it down hard on top of Luciano's nearly toppling pile of papers.

From that point on, Gallagher took control of the case.

THERE IT WAS, the blue farmhouse, exactly as described, and the old barn right next to it. It was at the crest of the rise, looking south toward the wall of hills. Once it was all in full view, Gallagher saw behind it the wooded ridge, which indeed rose up from the earth "like the raised backbone of a giant beast." Gallagher was amazed at how similar it looked to what he had envisioned. It made him sad to think it was all just make-believe.

LUCIANO KNOCKED WITH his fist on the front door. He had a great knock. The whole world echoed with the sound of that knock. A dog barked. A little dog. Another knock. The dog barked more frantically. There was a shade on the front door, and it was moved slightly to reveal an eyeball.

"Go around to the back," a man called angrily through the glass.

It was just exactly as Leslie had described it. They went around the house. Only this time there was no dog outside waiting, wagging his tail. In back was an old, rickety porch, with the squares of glass on the door ready to fall out — most of the putty in the frames was crumbling or gone. Three rotted wooden steps led up to the porch. The men opted to stand on the grass and wait. The old man appeared suddenly, bent, cadaverous, gray complected, wrinkled. The dog was barking manically and he was telling it to shut up, grumbling, cursing. He closed the inner door and turned to face the two men. Then he opened the porch door just a few inches, using it more as a shield and something to lean on than as an obstacle to be moved out of the way.

"What do you want?" he asked, scowling at the big detective.

Luciano flashed his badge. The old man didn't flinch. "We'd like to talk to you for a minute."

"Well go ahead, talk." This was not the man described by Leslie. First of all, he had no accent. Second, there was no love of life in this crusty old codger. He glowered hatefully at the two younger men.

"Did you have contact with a man recently, a Leslie Siconski, here at your home, sir? This man . . ." Luciano pulled out one of the eight-by-tens of the dead man, walked a step closer, and showed it to him. "Did you have any contact with him?"

The old man squinted. "The photographer?" he barked.

"He came by and talked to you?"

"Yeah."

"What did he want? What did he do?" Luciano had to pull hard for every response.

"Wanted to take pictures. Up back there on top of the ridge."

"How long did he stay?"

"Came a couple of times. Couple different days."

"Where did he park?" Gallagher piped in.

"Where did he park? Hell, I don't know. Out on the street. Jesus Christ!"

"Are you aware that mail was sent to that man at your address here?"

There was a pause. The old man repositioned his grip on the door. "Yeah," he said, with a slightly weaker-sounding voice.

"Why is that, sir?" asked Luciano.

"Said he had film coming from Chicago. He needed to do it right." He stopped and licked at his dry old lips. "He paid me a hundred dollars."

"That's actually against the law, sir, for a person to receive mail at an address he doesn't reside at."

"Oh yeah?" He had a *What-are-you-going-to-do-about-it?* tone.

"Why did he pay you?"

"For the land. For taking pictures. Any other questions?"

Luciano looked at Gallagher, who shook his head.

"I guess not, sir. Thank you."

Without even a nod or a grunt, the old man let go of his grip on the porch door and shuffled toward the inside of the house. "Oh, may we have a look up there on the ridge?" Luciano called after the man as Gallagher touched his arm and nodded up toward the wooded ridge.

"What?" It took a long time for the man to turn and face them again.

"May we have a look up there, where he took the pictures?"

"You're the goddamn police, do whatever you goddamn want." He started to turn.

"Do you have a cow out in that barn?" asked Gallagher, aware that this question would probably really ruffle the old man's feathers.

He froze in his spot as if someone had dumped ice water on him, turned once more, and unfurled his head from his neck. His eyes were wide and on fire. "Cow?" He pronounced the word as if it were foreign. "You a dairy inspector?"

"No, just curious."

He shook his head once, more a movement to communicate that he felt the two men were complete fools than an answer to the question, and shuffled back inside the house.

IT WAS NOTHING like the document. Not even close. Undergrowth tugged at their pant legs; burrs and prickers stuck to them as they wound their way up the hill. It was much steeper than described. And at the top there were no big, expansive, picturesque bur oaks to welcome them. But there was something up there. At the top, under the thick but scrubby canopy, was a large pile of rocks that someone had neatly stacked. And next to it, scattered on the ground, were long tree branches recently cut down. Nine in all. And beside them, all wet and covered in dirt, were some camouflage and army-green tarpaulins.

Gallagher looked around. There was an old wooden canoe, charred from front to back. It looked like someone had poured gasoline on it, then let it burn. There was no view of the river, although it looked like someone had cut a couple of trees down, which did give a little glimpse of the horizon to the west. There was no swath down to the riverbank. Instead, there was a rocky precipice. Gallagher walked over to the edge and looked down. Below was a cornfield.

"Where's the river?"

"What river?"

"The Baraboo."

"That's a mile or so back down the road. We drove over it coming up here."

"How did he think he'd fool us?" Gallagher stood on the edge of the precipice, shaking his head. Beyond the cornfield, about a hundred yards from the base of the hill, was a line of trees that bisected the field all the way to the county road. Maybe he could have convinced people that the ancient river was there, but still there was no bank to see, no swath, no clear forest floor, no dugout — not much of one anyway — and no lodge, just a pile of rocks and branches. Gallagher turned to survey again the entire scene, trying to remain objective, looking at it as if he had not known it was all a hoax. True, he saw a hint of similarity between what the document had described and what he was now looking at. Apparently, Leslie believed it would be enough to do the trick.

"What was he doing up here?" asked Luciano, who was examining the long logs.

"This was where he said his brother Charlie had lived for four and a half years. And this is where he said he was living when he wrote the document. He obviously wasn't sure what he was doing. But one thing is obvious — he was going to use it to try to fool us."

IN THE SQUAD car driving back into town, Gallagher asked, "Is there a general store in Baraboo by the name of Stetson's?"

"Stetson's? No."

"There a shop or something that two old twin sisters run and own?"

"Uh uh, not that I know of." Luciano picked up his radio, pushed a button, and asked the same question to the dispatch woman on the other end.

There was a ten-second pause, then a muted voice came in loud and clear: "No, that doesn't ring a bell."

"Hmm. I think maybe we should just go to the circus," Gallagher suggested.

"All right. You got me my first lead in town, I'm following you," winked Luciano. Gallagher noticed that the detective's big round Italian nose was covered with blackheads.

BOTH MEN ENTERED the Feld Pavilion of the Circus World Museum. Gallagher was a bit excited by the sight of it. In front of them was a small gift shop with brightly colored books, clown posters, small stuffed animals, glass trinkets, a circus train in miniature. To their right was a long hallway lined on both sides with giant eight-by-thirty-foot black-and-white photographs of the original Ringling Brothers and Barnum and Bailey Circus. Mammoth gray elephants, horses and wagons, clowns, and acrobats looked down at them from above.

Gallagher felt dwarfed. At the entrance to the corridor a woman sat on a tall stool next to a wooden box, dressed like a clown, ready to sell entrance tickets. Just to the left of where the men stood, to the right of the little gift shop, was a glass door with CIRCUS WORLD ADMINISTRATIVE OFFICES stenciled on it. They went inside.

A woman behind a long countertop was sitting at a desk, typing on a computer.

"May I help you gentlemen?" she asked, stopping and looking up.

Luciano deferred to Gallagher. Poor Gallagher didn't know what to say. He was certain any question he would ask today would be followed by a frown.

"Is there any way we can talk to some of the circus performers from the museum?"

"Now?"

"Yes."

"Not now, sir, I'm sorry, but no one is back yet. The circus doesn't start up until May thirty-first this year."

"So there's no one even here? No clowns, no musicians, no acrobats?"

"That's right."

"How . . ." Gallagher caught himself thinking aloud. What he'd been about to say was, *How did Leslie hope to fool them if the circus wasn't even in town?*

"What sort of information are you gentlemen looking for?"

Gallagher now deferred to Luciano, who took the opportunity to show his badge and delicately explain the situation. Luciano, Gallagher realized, was a master of understatement — making a homicide sound more like a fender bender. ". . . And the circus, we know, had a certain attraction for the victim. We think, maybe, he had some contacts here," the detective ended.

The woman had immediately gotten out of her seat when she heard the word *homicide*. Now she walked over to the counter and introduced herself as the assistant to the director of operations.

"We do have circus performers using the facility at this time," she suddenly admitted in a lower voice.

"You do?" responded Gallagher, the words bringing him hope.

"Yes, there's a small troupe in from Canada that's renting the facility from us. You could talk to some of them, perhaps. Maybe they knew the man."

"How long have they been here?" Luciano questioned.

"They've been here only four days. They're training in the big top. We don't usually allow this sort of thing, but the weather has been so mild, you know, and they were desperate for a place. Our director knows one of the performers. But they're leaving tomorrow. Originally they were going to be here until the first of May. Apparently a show had been scheduled that they'd forgotten about and they have to leave right away. They just informed us of this change of plans about ten minutes before you walked in."

"Yes, we'd like to talk to them," Luciano said.

"They're probably all packing up. I'll get one of the maintenance people to take you back there."

"So they have clowns and aerial artists and musicians?" Gallagher wanted to know.

"Oh yes, it's a regular circus. They need to practice just like any other professional team."

IN LESS THAN five minutes a teenage boy appeared dressed in a red uniform. The clothes hung loosely on his bony frame, and his red hair looked as if it had been applied with spray paint. He rushed into the room, glanced at the assistant director of operations as if to say *I'm here*, then looked at the men disinterestedly and motioned with his head back out the way he'd entered. By the time Gallagher and Luciano were out in the Feld Pavilion again, the teen was halfway down the bright poster-lined hallway.

They went into and then through the Picture Gallery of the Feld Pavilion. Gallagher's eyes boggled. Unconsciously he was looking for the display of Charlie that the document had mentioned more than a few times. He marveled at the three-story-high ceiling and the maze of old black-and-white photographs dramatically displayed on the walls with written descriptions and dates mounted alongside. They wound around, passing many different collages of circus history. He wanted to slow the pace a little, to stop and examine a few photographs, but it was hopeless. Too fast. It was like watching MTV. They were outside and headed toward the big top in a handful of breaths.

They crossed a gently arcing bridge over the Baraboo River. There it was, Gallagher said aloud, "the beloved Ba'boo," gurgling along at a rapid pace. Gallagher slowed in order to let the image he held of Charlie in his dugout paddling against the fast current wash over him. But the image didn't hold. It foundered in fact. The current was much too strong, and the absurdity shocked him. "Ridiculous!" he shouted. Luciano turned to look at him. "No way, José! He couldn't have paddled against that." Charlie, the eerie, creepy brother who lived reclusively in the old Frank Lloyd Wright home, always pale as a ghost, hopelessly unathletic, with his huge feet and big vulturish nose and no chin. A ghostly human specimen. Couldn't look you in the eye. Always so shaky and anxious. Hardly ever spoke. No way could he paddle upstream. How could he have been so naive to think of him as the heroic god Leslie had painted? And all those glib, humorous poems; the self-reflective journal entries — "negate the disorder antistrophically." Bagh! The man was mentally ill. Totally out of touch with reality. Women? Yeah, a real Casanova. Gallagher felt humiliated for having been fooled so easily, for not seeing the gaping holes in the document from the start.

Before he knew it, they were there. The big top loomed above them like a cloud of blue canvas. For this sight, not even the legerdemain of Leslie's words had prepared him. They stopped at the entrance to the small avenue of trailers — eight of them in all, four to a side.

"You guys want to talk to anyone in particular?" the orangehead asked impatiently.

"No," Luciano coolly responded. He walked up to the youth, towering over him. "We're fine right here, thanks." The gesture communicated — *Go!*

Before Luciano had uttered the word *thanks* the boy was in retreat.

The two men stood side by side, looking down the alley of mobile homes to their right, and occasionally glancing up at the imposing round blue giant in front of them. Both were under the spell of the big top. Gallagher turned to his left and was about to say something to Luciano, but stopped in midbreath as a tall, dark, bosomy woman appeared from the first mobile home, not ten yards from them, holding the hand of a young boy just barely able to walk. She slowed and looked at them, then hurried on her way down the row, picking up the child and disappearing into the last trailer on the left with flight in her footsteps. There was something familiar about her.

Again Gallagher opened his mouth to say something, but again he was interrupted, this time by two men emerging from the second trailer on the left. They were midgets. One had dark hair slicked back and was quite portly; he leaned way back on his heels. The other was equally roly-poly. Gallagher thought *clowns* right away. The dark-haired man was talking, but he suddenly stopped when he realized he was being observed.

"Excuse me!" called out Luciano.

They stopped, and the dark-haired man leaned his head toward them as a sign to speak.

"We're looking for the owner. Where can we find him?" Luciano asked.

"Big top," the man said.

"Thanks."

The two men turned left and waddled down the row to the last mobile home on the right, across from the one the bosomy woman and child had entered. Luciano and Gallagher watched them disappear behind the door, then walked straight ahead into the big top.

THE FIRST FIFTY yards under the canvas was the animal menagerie. On either side there were corrals, six in all, but only the last one on the right, just before the main arena, held any animals. White horses. Beautiful. Regal. They glistened, even though there was very little light to reflect. A short, attractive young woman with red hair, dressed in a leotard, was brushing one of the horse's tails. She stopped and looked at the two men as they came abreast of her.

"Hello," said Luciano.

The woman stood up straight and turned to face them directly. She did not reply. Her painted eyebrows were bent down, and the rest of her face echoed the scornful superciliousness. She looked to be quite physically fit, with biceps bulging under the skintight leotard.

Luciano, always upbeat, never intimidated, said, "We're looking for the owner. Is he inside?"

"I doon't knew." She had a brogue. And at that, one of the three horses, the one with its backside to the men, lifted its tail and defecated, dropping two stinking, greenish turds to the hay as if to punctuate her statement. The smell of manure engulfed the trio. She smiled ghoulishly.

"Well, we'll just check anyway, thank you."

Again she said nothing. She held the brush in her hand and slowly dropped it down so that it rested at her side, along the hard curve of her hip and leg. It was this movement and her voice that made a connection for Gallagher. His heart began to pound. These people were *them* — the enemies and allies! The two midgets, the tall bosomy one carrying the boy, this little Celt . . . He had a hunch he knew exactly who they were. Had this woman read the document? She was staring back at him now, defiantly, as if she were reading his thoughts.

Luciano, before he took a step toward the ring, asked, "The owner? What's his name, again?"

"Peter."

"Peter, that's it. Thanks."

She didn't move a wink, just stood and watched them as they walked away.

TEN FEET FROM the entrance they could see movement and hear people inside talking loudly. There was also the unmistakable sound of a metal winch being worked. They crossed the threshold from animal corrals to arena, and it was like walking from water onto land. The echoing voices stopped immediately, as did the ringing steel sound of the winch. All eyes were focused on the two men entering the arena.

The main ring was a perfect circle set up below a half moon of old wooden bleachers. It was a tight venue, perhaps smaller than it seemed from the outside. The circular ring was made of red clay and defined by a shin-high wooden border. Where the two men entered, there was a break in the rows of bleachers and the wooden border. They went straight into the center ring.

It was apparent that the people in the room were in the process of breaking down the apparatuses. There was one man high up on a little platform that held the tightrope line, now sagging; he bent down to work at a toggle joint. An older black man was below with the winch, helping him in some way. There was a web of ropes, some loose, some taut, running downward at sharp angles attached to the ground. One man was stacking three two-foot-high, star-studded round pedestals. Half a dozen people, men and women, watched Gallagher and Luciano silently.

"Anybody here the owner?" The words seemed to fall on deaf ears. They looked dumbly at the two men, like cows in a pasture watching a porcupine pass through. "Peter, I'm looking for Peter," Luciano bellowed. He had a deep stentorian voice that startled Gallagher and, of course, went a long way toward impressing those he addressed.

"He in his trailer," the black man said. No one moved.

"We just came from there. They said he was in here."

Their eyes now began to dart around in confusion among themselves. In this awkward moment, minds clearly working frantically to manipulate the truth, Gallagher was struck again by a bolt of understanding. All these people here were the characters in the document! The man who had answered Luciano, the old black man working the winch, was Chappy Lewis-Clark. The man stacking the elephant stools, the short and stocky redhead, tattoos running up his shirtsleeved arms, that was Gino Crivello. There was a comely young woman dressed in gymnastic clothes packing long, cottony ropes into large duffel bags. She had a neck like a wrestler. That was Karina Romanoff. He went through the list of characters in his mind. Who was missing? The trumpet player, the man with the long name. A very common-looking man. That was the guy helping Chappy with the cables up there on the little platform. And Squeaky the Clown — Judd Barkin? What about him? Or the twins? Or Oscar Rightpath himself?

And as if on cue, in walked a group of six. "You gentlemen

looking for me?" Dressed in a cowboy hat, long salt-and-pepper hair falling down to his shoulders, leather boots, black jeans, a poncho, dark sunglasses, one arm. Gallagher gasped. Rightpath! Filing in behind and around him was most of the rest of the gang.

"You the owner?" Luciano asked, turning to face the group, most of whom just stood looking at the two men.

"Guilty as charged," the man said. He was dark, indeed Oriental looking, in his late fifties, early sixties. Gallagher went right down the list in two seconds: The two short men they had seen before — Miles and McNutt — stood to the right of the owner with another midget, Squeaky the Clown. To the owner's left were two elderly ladies who looked exactly alike — the twins. They all came walking out into the arena. And the woman with the horses, that must have been the little Celt, Susan Green. And the one with the kid? It had to be!

Gallagher grabbed Luciano's right arm and whispered into his ear, "It's them, no question. All of them here. I'm sure of it."

Luciano took the information without as much as a blink, reached out his right arm, and introduced himself to the man.

"John Luciano, Sauk County Sheriff's Department."

And the one arm came out from his side. "Peter Decora. And you must be Colin Gallagher," he said, turning his head to Gallagher before the words had a chance to sink in. He held out the one arm, but Gallagher was too shocked to take it.

"Decora? Peter Decora? Uncle Pete? You're . . . you're — "

"Dead?"

"Yeah."

"No. But your brother-in-law is. That's why you fellas have come, isn't it?"

"Yes," said Gallagher and Luciano in unison.

"Why don't you guys come back to my trailer, and we can talk there in private."

GALLAGHER WAS CONFUSED again. A few moments before he thought he understood it all. But Peter Decora? Uncle Pete? He'd never met him in person, but he'd seen pictures of him. Certainly heard a lot about him. But he was dead. Killed in a car accident four and a half years ago, just before Charlie had disappeared. It was his death, Gallagher had always believed, that formed part of the reason for Charlie's flight. Charlie had loved that man. How was it possible? Did this mean Charlie was in on the con? Could it be? But he wouldn't need to be; it was his inheritance.

They arrived at the last trailer on the left, the same one they'd seen the woman and child enter. There, parked next to it, was a large white Cadillac El Dorado, and on its front was an ornament — a bucking bronco. It had been hidden from view by the trailer in front of it. Gallagher shook his head. They climbed the little steps and entered.

There were lots of pictures of the circus on the cheap paneling inside the little home. With the three of them in there, especially Luciano, it was a tight fit. Rightpath/Uncle Pete motioned to the right, indicating they should go into the little living room and sit. The room looked out on the row and back west toward the Feld Pavilion. Watching closely where they stepped, the two men managed to sit down. It was very close.

"Can I get you gentlemen anything to drink?"

"Nothing."

"No thanks."

"We'd just like to ask you a few questions and get on our way," said Luciano.

"I hear you."

Gallagher realized that Uncle Pete had a slight French accent. It reminded him of Leslie. He watched the man walk into the kitchen and pour himself a healthy glass of Scotch from a half-gallon bottle, splash some water on top of it, and come back out to the front area where the two men sat uncomfortably.

"Are you sure you gentlemen don't want a refreshment?" he asked again unctuously, his gnarled countenance frozen in a taunting, sardonic smirk.

"How did you find out about the deceased, sir?" Luciano put it right to him, ignoring the question.

"When he didn't show up yesterday, we assumed something was wrong. Jane, that was Leslie's girl, was up in town buying supplies, and she overheard a lady in the grocery store talking about a dead man who had been found in the park on the effigy mound. She knew right away it was him."

"Did you know about the document he wrote?" Gallagher asked.

"Oh yeah. I helped him."

"And you were going to try and trick us with that? To get Charlie's inheritance?" Gallagher was angry.

"Now, that is a difficult question to answer," Rightpath/Uncle Pete smiled knavishly. "What do you mean, 'trick'?"

"Trick. As in, informing your family that you're dead when you're not," Gallagher answered mockingly. He was repulsed by the thought of this man, his wife's dead mother's brother, pulling a fast one on his own family.

"Ha ha. Yes. Look, I'm sorry about that. I almost did die, as you can see." He held up the one arm, turning it over to reveal how mangled it actually was, and then inclining his head toward the missing one. "The circus wasn't doing well at the time, and I wasn't sure I'd even be able to walk or work again. We just thought you folks there in Chicago with all your big dollars would take pity on me and my enterprise and send a generous donation just as we asked, in my name, to the circus. And you did. You sent money, and we're grateful for that. But you didn't even come to the funeral, and we had quite a setup waiting, too."

Gallagher looked at Luciano as if to ask, *Isn't that an admission of guilt?* Luciano didn't respond. "We couldn't come. Charlie had disappeared and we were involved in that," Gallagher retorted defensively, then regretted it; he didn't need to dignify the crime with an excuse.

"Well, you missed a good one." Uncle Pete reached over and felt the empty sleeve of his shirt to make his point clear. Gallagher was not convinced. He wanted to get up and reach behind the con man's back just to make sure he didn't have an arm hidden there. "But you, sir, are here to investigate the death of Leslie Siconski, am I right?" he turned now to Luciano.

"Yes," the detective nodded.

"Well, I can vouch for all of us, we had nothing to do with it. We did not murder him. We have no idea who did. Jane, come on out here," Rightpath/Uncle Pete called out.

The woman Gallagher and Luciano had seen before appeared like a shadow from the back room, holding a little boy, perhaps two years old, in her arms. He was dark, with huge round eyes that looked back and forth at the two strangers quizzically. The woman, in her late thirties, tall as Gallagher, with wide hips that held the boy like a saddle, had been crying. Her eyes were red and swollen, and her jet-black hair was tangled and wet with tears.

"This is Jane Deerrun, Leslie's girl. She's originally from this area — her grandfather was an Indian in the Wild West shows with Buffalo Bill way back when. She arranged for our using the facility. That's their little boy, Charlie. Jane, come on in here and tell these men what you know about Leslie's, uh . . . disappearance. It's okay. They're not going to arrest you." Rightpath's words were reassuring, paternal, controlling.

She came into the room uncertainly, holding the child like a shield in front of her care-worn face. She sat next to Gallagher. Her features struck him as much more Indian than he had pictured Jane

Reardon, MLS, head librarian. But it was her — everything but the snow-white complexion. He nodded slowly without uttering a word. She did the same. So did Luciano.

"Do you know how he died, ma'am?" Luciano asked.

"No, I don't. I haven't a clue. I don't know what happened." She began to weep, pressing her face into her little boy's side. The boy continued to stare at the two strangers suspiciously, as if he blamed them for his mother's grief.

"When we found out this morning we were as shocked as anyone," Uncle Pete/Rightpath continued for her. "We put our heads together, but we couldn't figure out a thing. We've known him a long time. He's my nephew. We go way back, as Mr. Gallagher can tell you. We figured it must have been an old grudge — someone from his past following him here and when the time was right, doing him in."

"Do you know anyone who could have wanted to murder him?" Luciano pressed.

"Not in this area. Not in this country. Certainly not us. We had a lot to gain by Leslie's life. I just don't understand. How did he die anyway?"

"We can't say. But I'll tell you this: Someone didn't like him because . . ." Luciano began coolly, but when he realized his mistake in revealing this in front of the woman, he bit down on the end of the sentence.

"Any clues?"

"Not much."

Suddenly the weeping woman broke in, pulling her head away from her child, her eyes frightened. "I told him not to go fooling around out there on the effigy mound. I told him, but he wouldn't listen. I taught him all about the mythologies of my people, about the importance of the Decora name to the Ho-Chunk. I taught him about Wakdjunkaga and Waschinggeka and the mythic cycles for his story, but I told him never to upset the mounds. Never dig up the sacred burial grounds. I told him, but he wouldn't listen. 'Yes, you can write all you want about the myths and legends. That's okay,' I said. 'But don't fool with the dead. Never disturb the dead. Bad things will happen if you do.' But he wouldn't listen. He went out there and dug into that mound anyway." She began to weep with great gasps and hiccups. "He dug into the mounds. He angered them. He awakened their wrath. They taught him all right. They taught him . . ."

"Who, ma'am?" asked Luciano.

"Choke 'aywira."

"Who's that?"

"The Grandfathers."

GALLAGHER DID MAKE it home for dinner that night, albeit a little tardy.

TWO MONTHS LATER, after extensive DNA testing of the hair samples found on Leslie Siconski's body, the laboratory failed to link any of the Circus World people with the crime. In fact, the yellow tuft of hair found in the dead man's grip could not have come from a living person. Carbon testing proved that it had belonged to the scalp of a human who had been dead for nearly a hundred years. There were never any other clues or leads in the homicide of Leslie Siconski. The case remains unsolved.

Charles Siconski has never been found.

But the Ho-Chunk believe they know the story of the two brothers.